THE BOAT SHED

Robyn Cotton

The Boat Shed is dedicated to all children who have been taken
from their families and commercially exploited.

Acknowledgements

Writing a novel is not unlike achieving an endurance activity such as running a marathon. It would be difficult to complete the task without support and encouragement from family and friends. But more than other endurance feats, it benefits from their trusted feedback and critique. To this end I want to single out a few special people.

I want to start by thanking my Nepalese friend for sharing her story and to all the dedicated staff at International Needs Nepal for introducing me to the Lydia programme that helps educate and upskill young women from all around Nepal. Also to our friends at Sano Diyo, for inspiring me through their work rescuing and raising at-risk girls. These experiences motivated me to write this story.

Thanks to the Maritime Police Unit for hosting me and taking me out on *Deodar III.* This visit enriched my imagination and contributed to the descriptive writing in this book. A special thanks to Murray who was kind enough to give my manuscript a credibility check.

I am also especially grateful to Lesley, Mike, Alanah, Matt, Jay and Robert who read my manuscript and provided their critique and encouragement. Special thanks to Glenys for her attention to detail with the final proof reading. And to Betty, my talented niece, for the cover design—I love it!

And last but by no means least, I owe much to my husband and best friend Geoff. Not only did he critique each chapter as I wrote my first draft, but he encouraged me and gave me the space to write.

Please note I have included a glossary of maritime and New Zealand centric terms at the end of the book.

"There is no trust more sacred than the one the world holds with children. There is no duty more important than ensuring that their rights are respected, that their welfare is protected, that their lives are free from fear and want and that they can grow up in peace." ~~Kofi Annan

I

Jeff Watts followed his long-time friend and fellow photography enthusiast, Rochelle Ioane, along the path that was littered with scoria. Her lithe body moved with a rhythm that matched her carefree personality. A camera hung across her shoulder and swung in time with her gait, gently bouncing against her as she picked her way over the rocks.

Ahead of them was an old wooden boat shed with a concrete ramp leading down to the water, nestled under a backdrop of pōhutukawa trees. Once used by the weekenders who frequented the island for respite from the growing metropolis of Auckland city, it was a testament to times gone by. Rangitoto Island, a dormant volcano in the Hauraki Gulf, was one of the many treasures in this part of the world and a photographer's dream.

"This one's worth getting the tripod out for." Rochelle stopped, stretched her arms out in front of her and formed a square with her fingers, before closing one eye and peering through them to size up the composition. Her face was transfixed with a look comparable to that of a child receiving a special treat.

"You're right, the lighting angle's perfect." Although she'd done this numerous times today, he watched with quiet fascination. That she meant more to him than just a fellow photography student from Unitec, a technical institute in Auckland, had begun to creep into his consciousness to the point where he'd agonised about how to move their relationship up a gear. But what with his shyness and her conservative Pasifika upbringing, he hadn't been able to pluck up the courage.

Rochelle slipped the green backpack from her back and unhooked the tripod in a single practised motion. She extended its legs then took a moment to stand with hands on hips soaking in the scene. "I love the texture the peeling paint adds. And the way the black scoria helps to highlight the colour of the water and the colours in the paint. See how the paint's peeled back to reveal earlier coats of green and pink and cream. And look how the patterns of rust on its corrugated iron roof add some punch to the image to cap it off perfectly." She giggled at her pun.

He loved how she enthusiastically viewed the world, focusing on its beauty and noting things others might miss. "The warped and rotting weatherboards are great. They help tell the story of the island's past."

"Did you read the sign back there?" Without waiting for an answer, she continued. "The baches on the island were built on land leased from the Crown in the 1920s and '30s. Three of them have been renovated and are available to rent—it'd be a special experience to overnight here, don't you think?"

Was she suggesting what he thought she was? Was it possible she felt the same way? He tried to keep his voice level as he replied, "We could come back for an overnighter."

She seemed to ignore his veiled offer. "Once there were 140 baches, but they were on dodgy legal ground and eventually most were removed, leaving only around 30."

He'd often found himself listening in awe as she parroted off interesting facts about the places they visited. "You could include that in the panel—as back story to the photos. It'd increase the overall interest."

"Mm-hmm." She gently locked her camera into the tripod and pulled her cap off her head, releasing the thick braid that had anchored it in place, and replaced it so the peak was to her back and out of the way. A dark-brown curl had escaped and she twisted it around her finger and popped it behind her ear as she put her eye to the viewfinder. Fiddling with the settings, she said, "The brief as I read it is just to present a themed panel that demonstrates our creative and technical skills."

"I guess it's up to us to interpret the brief however we like. You could be creative with how you weave in the back story."

Jeff didn't bother with a tripod, confident in his ability to hold his camera steady. Peering through the eyepiece, he placed the shed in the top left third of the composition with the rocks and curve of the deeply turquoise-coloured water providing a pleasing foreground. Breathing out to steady himself, he pressed the shutter release to take the photograph. Satisfied, he turned his camera off. Composition had always come naturally to him, like a sixth sense.

Rochelle moved her tripod a few paces to get a better angle. Adjusting the legs to level it, she said, "There're so many subjects here that it's going to be hard to pick just twelve for the panel."

"Yep, your idea to choose Rangitoto for our theme was nothing short of inspired."

The island was like no other place he'd ever seen. It'd last erupted just 600 years ago and the lava flows had left fields of scoria, some of which remained barren of any vegetation. He bent down and scooped up a piece of the scoria for closer inspection. The little black rock appeared to be porous. Rubbing its hard rough surface while rotating it in his hands, he imagined the red-hot foaming lava flowing down the slopes from the summit covering everything in its path, leaving air pockets that as it cooled became caves, the likes of which they'd explored earlier that day.

The satisfying sound of her shutter releasing told him she'd finished. "Done?" he asked, tossing the scoria into the bay.

Already packing up her tripod, she nodded her head enthusiastically. "All done. It's nearly time we headed back to the ferry terminal."

"Soon, but let's just check this out first. This old ramshackle shed might provide some good close-ups highlighting its neglect." He clambered over the rocky terrain towards the boat shed, picking his way carefully over the uneven surface. On the other side of the shed was a door that was slightly ajar. The hinges screeched in protest as he pulled it slowly open before entering. The interior was dim apart from where the odd shaft of light made its way through rusted out roofing iron and gaps in the planking. As his eyes adjusted to the light, he could make out the shed was empty except for a small shape lying on the ground.

"Anything in there?" Rochelle called from behind him.

"There's something here—but I'm not sure what." He stepped closer. As unlikely as it seemed, the shape looked like that of a child. Not wanting to believe it, he grabbed his mobile from his pocket and turned on the torch. A small figure lay apparently lifeless on the ground. "Holy crap!!"

Quickly kneeling beside the body, he could see she was a young girl, and he placed the back of his hand in front of her face in an attempt to feel breath. Nothing. He brushed her skin. Cold. Dead cold.

"What is it?" Coming to crouch beside him, Rochelle gasped. "Oh my gosh! Is that a body? Is she dead?"

It took a moment to take hold of his emotions. In a quiet voice he said, "She's gone."

His light swept over the form lying before them. The body was definitely that of a young girl, perhaps ten or eleven years old. She was thin—very thin. Her hair was long, straight and black. Bent in a foetal position with arms hugging herself and eyes closed she could have been in a peaceful sleep. The clothes she wore were ripped and grubby and could have passed for pyjamas except they were silk and lacked the colourful childlike pictures that are normally associated with a child's nightwear.

Rochelle put her hand on the little girl's forehead. "I think she's been gone some time, poor wee thing."

Jeff stood up slowly, the enormity of the find sinking in. "I'd better go outside and call the police. Will you be okay?"

Rochelle didn't answer.

With heavy footsteps he moved out into the light and dialled the emergency number.

*

Frank Smythe of the Maritime Police Unit was the skipper on duty at the helm of the police boat, *Deodar III*. Today he had a full complement of crew on board, the result of some intensive recruiting. Stephen Blackett was his leading hand and had proven himself to be a competent crew member over the last few years that they'd worked together. Although still in his early thirties, he was hard working and responsible, and tough when he needed to be. Dick Jones was navigator. A true seaman, he was an old-timer with the unit now counting down to his retirement, having been around forever. Then there was Ben Cohen, or Jammie as they called him—not only because his name was Benjamin, but because he'd won some money on a team lotto ticket that he'd purchased during his first week on the job. A recent recruit who'd come across from Auckland Central, he was an enthusiastic member of the team.

Frank himself was the most senior in rank on board. Once a detective in the Criminal Investigation Branch, he'd transferred over to the Maritime Police Unit. After achieving his Master's ticket, he did the time to qualify as Police Coastal Master. He loved having the Hauraki Gulf as his office. It'd cured him of the pent-up stress and panic attacks that'd plagued him during his last land-based year.

Frank surveyed the water from his seat in the wheelhouse. Skippering *Deodar III* was more of a privilege than a job. Every day was different. Not only was the sea forever changing, but the nature of their callouts could be anything from rescues to education to safety checks to good old-fashioned policing. Saving lives was what he liked most. Out here he rarely encountered youth offending, domestic abuse or criminals associated with the gangs, all of which had caused him endless grief when based at Central.

They were returning to base following a callout to Moturekareka Island, a small uninhabited island in the Kawau Bay area. The aqua-blue crystal-clear water of its northern bay was a favourite anchorage with leisure craft, providing shelter from the southerly winds. A partially exposed shipwreck lay in the bay providing a popular attraction for divers and snorkellers.

A concerned boatie had radioed in to report someone vandalising the shipwreck. The offender was long gone by the time they got there, but the whistleblower was able to pass on the boat's name and gave a statement meaning they should be able to track down the boat's owner through the national EPIRB register. Allegedly the offender had taken a piece of the hull as a souvenir. Not that it would be missed as the wreck was slowly rusting away and in another twenty years it could well be gone altogether.

Jammie entered the wheelhouse, interrupting his thoughts. Removing his sunnies and police cap to reveal short spikey hair, he asked, "What's the story with the wreck?"

"Now there's a story," Dick responded from his navigation station, his weathered face creasing into a grin. "Back in World War One, the home guard had long-range artillery hidden at various strategic points around the Gulf. One day they were practising their shooting, just in case the Japanese warships and subs arrived to take us over, and they misfired, hitting this coastal trader vessel and putting a hole in its hull. The boat was slowly sinking. As luck would have it, there was another barge on hand that could tow it in and beach it."

Jammie's eyes were wide as he listened. "Really?"

Raucous laughter filled the wheelhouse.

"There's one born every minute." Holding his belly as if to prevent it from spilling its contents, Dick roared with laughter.

"What's so funny?" Jammie asked, looking from one to another.

"Okay Dick, you've had your fun. Now put him out of his misery," Frank said.

"Well then," Dick said wiping tears from his eyes. "They say an old hermit, Charles Hansen was his name, lived there and he thought it a good idea to have a breakwater in the bay. Taking the matter into his own hands, he bought an old coastal trader, which he duly scuttled. The thing is, he didn't get it quite right and she settled too close to shore making her as useless as an inflatable dartboard." Dick laughed loudly.

"I heard his intention was to bring her to rest on a sand bar and set up a luxurious gambling and drinking establishment aboard her, thereby circumventing the strict licencing and gambling laws," Frank added. "True or not, she listed heavily to port and there she lay. A monument to his folly."

"When was this?" Stephen asked.

"Some time around 1930."

"Was it legal?" Jammie asked, slightly warily.

"Was it legal?" Dick repeated, laughing heartily with his generous belly heaving under his black regulation lifejacket. "I doubt he got a permit if that's what you're asking, but then I don't imagine he cared about that."

Deodar III moved at a steady 34 knots through the calm waters of the inner Gulf. The islands that made up Kawau Bay faded into the background as they neared Whangaparaoa Peninsula. It was a perfect day to be out on the briny with the sunlight sparkling on the deep blue water. A large work-up of fish was off the port side and gannets were hurtling downwards into the water like arrows falling from the sky. How they didn't do themselves an injury was beyond him, but they always seemed to defy gravity and pop back up again.

"Wish I'd brought my rod," Stephen called out over the engines.

"I wouldn't waste my time for a kahawai," Frank retorted with a grin.

Stephen returned the grin. "They're okay if you smoke them. My mum makes a mean fish pie from smoked kahawai. Next time I'll bring you some leftovers."

"Better bring enough for all the crew. I love a good fish pie!" Dick piped up.

"I'm game to give it a try," Frank added.

They were interrupted by a call on the police radio. Despatch advised them that day visitors to Rangitoto Island had just found a body in one of the historic boat sheds in Islington Bay. The relayed details were sketchy. Frank changed their heading for Rangitoto Island.

While the person who'd discovered the body had been told to wait for the Maritime Police and not to touch anything, Frank was eager to take charge of the situation. It was important that the immediate area wasn't compromised if it turned out to be more than an accident. He increased *Deodar III*'s speed to 40 knots and listened to her twin engines as she responded immediately.

Deodar III was a faithful girl and the pride of the unit, having been designed specifically as a patrol boat and launched in 2007 to much fanfare. She took her name from her predecessors, who in turn were named after a minesweeper in the Royal Navy on which many brave Kiwis had served. Each time they took her out, Frank liked to think they were paying a tribute to those who'd served and died aboard the minesweepers. Proud to be her skipper, there could be no better policing job.

Transiting the shipping lane which ran close to Rangitoto, they veered to starboard to pass a container ship leaving Auckland with a pilot boat providing an escort. *Kolkata 2* was emblazoned on its stern. Its hull sat high in the water having unloaded the bulk of its cargo at the Port of

Auckland. Dark smoke billowed from its twin funnels placing a dirty smudge in the sky. Its bridge, streaked with rust, stood at the stern overlooking a long deck carrying a low stack of multi-coloured containers.

Ahead of them loomed Rangitoto Island with its red and white lighthouse standing guard on its western approach. The island was a volcano with a near perfect cone, its skirt of green gently rising up to its crater. The pōhutukawa trees had colonised much of the rocky scoria where other vegetation had struggled to take root without a layer of topsoil to sink their roots into. Slowly the ferns and native bush were being established under the trees with more native species emerging. And with the bush came the native birds.

"Dick, what do you make our ETA?" Frank spoke loudly over the noise.

"I make it 1300 near enough."

"Can you radio that through to Despatch?"

"Copy that, Skipper," Dick said picking up the handpiece.

Frank manoeuvred *Deodar III* around the channel markers then made their way around the southern coastline of the island and into Islington Bay. Roughly fifteen boats, yachts and launches, lay at anchor in the popular and well-sheltered anchorage. In the middle of the bay was the ex-fishing boat, a relatively substantial craft for a bay of this size, that was once someone's dream project. She had been stationed here for the last five years or more and was slowly rusting away.

"Owning that boat would be a headache. Might've seemed like a good idea at the time, but it's rapidly turning into a white elephant. I wouldn't want to be the one to maintain it—she's going to take a tonne of work." Frank pulled the throttle to slow down to the obligatory five knots.

Stephen groomed his ginger moustache with his fingers, a habit he'd formed since growing it into what was starting to look like a handlebar. "Bet they regret making that investment."

"I think calling it an investment is a bit generous. More like a liability." Dick chuckled.

Pointing to a boat shed off their port bow, Frank said, "From the description, that could be the shed there. And those two sitting outside must be the two that found the body. We'll bring *Deodar* into the wharf."

"I'll get the mooring lines ready," Stephen said, putting on his sunnies before leaving the wheelhouse with Jammie in tow.

Frank, now on the flybridge, navigated their way around the moored boats towards the wharf.

*

Having ended the call to the emergency services, Jeff went back into the little boat shed to find Rochelle still sitting where he'd left her and sobbing quietly.

"The Maritime Police are sending a unit out. They should be here in around 20 minutes."

"That long?" Her voice broke as another sob escaped. "I don't suppose it matters—it won't make a difference to her."

"They've asked us to wait here until they arrive."

The dingy interior reeked of death. Kneeling down he placed his hand on Rochelle's arm and said quietly, "Come outside into the sunlight. We don't need to wait in here."

"I don't want to leave her here alone in this awful place." Her voice trembled with emotion. Quietly she added, "She's just a child, Jeff."

"C'mon. There's really nothing we can do until the police get here. And they've asked us not to touch anything. We can stand vigil outside the door." He got to his feet and helped her up. She seemed so deflated that he walked her into the sunshine with his arm around her shoulder.

They sat on the edge of the concrete ramp where they remained without speaking for what seemed like a long time. No words could account for the shock of their find. Words could not reflect the turmoil of emotions. Words were simply not adequate. Water washed over the rocks below their feet—its movement mesmerising.

"What do you think happened to her?" Rochelle's now bloodshot eyes were wide as they searched his face.

"I have no idea. Perhaps somebody dumped the body here."

"That's awful. She's so young." With the back of her hand, she wiped away the tears and pulled her cap that held her sunnies lower over her face, the peak now partially hiding her tearful eyes. "I've never seen a child's dead body before."

She seemed so fragile and vulnerable that he put his arm around her shoulders and pulled her closer in a brotherly fashion. "Whatever happened to her, she's at peace now."

"Kids don't just die for no reason." Her tone was sharp.

"Maybe she drowned."

"Then how did she get into the shed?"

Having no answer, they lapsed into a silence that stretched into minutes as each was once more lost in thought.

"And how could she have been on the island all alone at that age?" Rochelle spoke into the quiet, her tone sounding indignant and a little more demanding. "Where do you suppose her parents are?"

"I guess that job's for the police to figure out." His hand gently caressed her arm as if soothing a child.

She picked up her camera, which had been resting in her lap, and toyed with the dials. Eventually she said, "It all seems so meaningless."

"What do you mean?"

"Well, we've been cruising about the island taking photos for the faculty exhibition, full of our plans and our dreams, while inside a child lay dead, her life snuffed out barely before it began. Childhood should be a time for playing with your friends, a time of innocence, a time for dreaming about the future, when young girls should be protected from harm. But now she has no future, no hopes, no dreams. Dead! It's so incredibly final. It's just all so very wrong." She took a deep breath and said what appeared to be for her own benefit, "We're so privileged to have a future."

"Children die and the world isn't fair—never was and never will be." As soon as the words were out of his mouth he regretted them, cursing himself for being so blunt.

Rochelle moved a little further from his side and he took his arm from her shoulder. Her fingers traced the little molluscs that had made their home on the side of the boat ramp. She sniffed and wiped fresh tears from her eyes. "That doesn't make it right. If a child dies, they should have the comfort of their family around them. Not alone like this girl."

He couldn't argue with that and again they surrendered to silence. Boats floated contentedly at anchor in the bay and life went on. People lounged on decks, played with their water toys, rowed dinghies and paddled on boards, dived off boats and swam in the turquoise water. All blissfully unaware of the secret that had been hidden inside the little boat shed. Or were they? Could one of these people in the bay be responsible for the little girl being in the shed?

The mocking call of a tieke bird, commonly called a saddleback for its patch of copper-coloured feathers on its back, broke the silence.

If there was a guilty party in the bay, then they would've worked out that he and Rochelle had found the body and would likely be watching them. His eyes surveyed the boats more carefully, but as far as he could tell no one was showing any interest in them.

"Do you think she's in heaven?" Rochelle's voice was barely more than a whisper.

"I really don't know."

"I'd like to think so. How else can you deal with a child's premature death?"

The question was rhetorical, and they let the tranquillity of the bay wash over them. Heaven was a concept Jeff had never given much thought to, and he wondered if it was indeed a place or whether it was simply a concept to help the grieving. One thing was certain—if it was real, he hoped the poor child had gone there.

A short time later the roar of a high-speed motor ruptured the peace as a large aluminium craft with a whitewash of wake came into sight. The boat dropped off its foils as it slowed when entering the bay. Even from a distance, he could clearly make out the blue and navy pattern and logo of the New Zealand Police painted along its side. It weaved its way through the maze of anchored boats towards the wharf.

2

Frank skilfully docked *Deodar III* alongside the wharf and watched as Stephen and Jammie secured the mooring lines. As the only detective present, it was up to Frank to take control of the situation. Stephen and Jammie would assist him at the boat shed while Dick stayed with *Deodar III*. Their priority would be the safety of all people in the vicinity before establishing exactly what had taken place.

Assuming there was a body, the area where it was located would need to be protected allowing Forensics to undertake a full examination of the crime scene, ensuring any evidence wasn't, and hadn't been, tampered with. Only then would they take the witness accounts, in this case from the couple who'd discovered the body and called it in. All other witnesses would need to be identified and that meant talking to those aboard the boats anchored in the bay. Not only would it be necessary to conduct a thorough search of the immediate area but of the whole island.

Despite a bad knee that constantly reminded him of his younger rugby playing days, he quickly climbed down the flybridge steps eager to get into some real detective work, something he'd not had much call for since leaving Central. Stephen and Jammie were already in the gear room stowing their lifejackets and changing their footwear. The friendly banter had been replaced by a quiet exchange about the callout, which stopped soon after Frank entered the room, reminding him this could turn out to be a big deal for them, especially for Jammie who'd not yet experienced a major case.

"Boss, do we need to don our Sabre?" Jammie asked, pointing to their police issue tactical vests.

"Yep, at least until we know what we're dealing with." Frank put his own protective vest on before checking the contents of the gear bag to make certain it contained all they'd require at the scene, including their PPE gear. "Ready lads?"

Stephen stuffed his bag back into his locker, closed it and drew himself up to his full height, looking official despite his unruly moustache. "Ready."

"Sure am." Jammie looked every bit the part in his blue maritime uniform complete with cap and sabre vest. He added a little over-enthusiastically, "Let's do this!"

Stephen strode out of the room, ducking his head so as not to hit the bulkhead, with Jammie in tow. Frank picked up the gear bag and followed.

Finding Dick in the wheelhouse, they exchanged last minute instructions and Dick was able to relay the exact locality of the boathouse as gleaned from Despatch. Frank, Stephen and Jammie then disembarked and walked the length of the wharf to the track which they followed towards the crater. At the first junction they veered left to follow the bay around the rocky shore to a boathouse that matched the description provided.

A clean-cut young man in an All Blacks cap and glasses sat on the ramp next to an attractive Polynesian woman. Beside them lay small backpacks, two cameras and a tripod, backing up the intel that they were visiting the island on a day excursion. They stood up as the three men clad in blue overalls and vests, with police insignia on their shoulders and chests, approached them.

"Kia ora. I'm Frank Smythe, Police Coastal Master with the Maritime Police Unit." Gesturing to Stephen and Jammie, he added, "With me are Sergeant Stephen Blackett and Constable Ben Cohen."

The man, who was of above average height and lanky, dressed in a Nike tee and shorts, stepped forward and offered Frank his hand. "I'm

Jeff Watts—I made the emergency call. And this is my friend Rochelle Ioane."

Rochelle moved forward beside Jeff. Her sporty shorts and crop top revealed an athletic figure, and tortoiseshell sunnies straddled a cap which sat low over her face. Large brown eyes peered up at Frank from under the peak of her cap, with the telltale signs that she'd been crying. "Rochelle," she said simply, extending her hand.

Frank shook her hand and turned back to Jeff.

"We found a body in the boat shed." Jeff, his speech rapid while gesturing towards the building. "It's a young girl."

"Okay, we'll check it out. I'd like you to wait here as we'll need to get your statements."

The couple looked at each other before nodding in agreement.

Frank looked at his men. "Stephen, you're with me. Jammie, I need you to establish a perimeter around the boat shed and the immediate vicinity. Then stand by to limit access to the area. You'll find what you need in the bag—you know the drill." He reached into the gear bag and tossed both Stephen and Jammie a set of PPE overalls and took out a third set for himself. "We'll need these."

Once in their protective gear, Frank led Stephen to the boat shed door and paused, steeling himself for what might lie inside. Unhooking the torch from his belt, they entered the shed taking care not to leave fingerprints. Frank flashed the beam of light around and let it rest on a body lying in the middle of the floor that looked to be that of a young girl. Kneeling on the cold concrete, he felt for a pulse. The skin was cold and the body rigid with rigor mortis, suggesting she'd been dead for less than a day. Her clothes clung to her slight body, and his touch confirmed they were damp.

"She looks to be little more than a child, perhaps around ten years of age. What do you think?" he asked Stephen.

"She's very thin, possibly undernourished—could be she's older than she looks. See how scrawny her arms are, just skin-and-bone." Stephen was crouched on his haunches beside him.

Her hair was black and long, straight and tangled. Her skin pale. Her face like that of a China doll albeit hollow-cheeked. "By the look of her hair, skin and facial features, I'd hazard a guess her ethnicity is Asian."

"Looks that way to me."

"These clothes are an odd choice for someone who might have been visiting the island. They could be pyjamas, but they've seen better times. Look at these rips on the pants and sleeves. And the patches of dried blood around the knees."

"She could have got bloody on the scoria. And I agree, they are a bit strange."

"Mm-hmm." Frank moved the beam of light around the shed again, noting it was empty except for the body lying in the centre of the floor. Bent in a foetal position with her thin arms hugging herself, her head was furthest from the door and her feet pointed towards it. Poor, poor child. Aloud Frank said, "Child, whatever happened to you?" He looked at her for a long moment, silently willing her to give up her secrets.

Frank had witnessed death many times—it goes with the territory when you're a cop, but he never quite got used to it. Never mastered being able to separate the body from the person they'd been. When on the beat, he'd attended some horrific crime scenes and motor accidents where the bodies had been so badly mutilated and bloody that it'd churned his stomach. Suicides were equally difficult to endure—and he'd seen his share of them. Occasionally the Maritime Unit would be tasked with retrieving bodies from the water. But dealing with the body of a child was for him the most difficult of all, especially if foul play was involved. There was something about the life of a child that was particularly sacred, and each case broke his heart—something he'd never been able to overcome.

Stephen broke the silence. "There're no obvious injuries or signs of a struggle."

"No, not obvious, but we'll have to wait for Forensics to do their examination."

"Why would a young girl be in a boat shed on Rangitoto Island?"

"That's the million-dollar question. The ferry crew will know if she was on the ferry with someone."

"Or on her own," added Stephen.

"If she was dumped here then they would have to have come by boat." Frank rubbed his head. "It would be hard to do so without arousing the interest of the boaties moored in the bay. We'll need to question them and see whether anyone saw anything."

The child was so young, so small, so vulnerable. If only he'd been able to protect her. When his own children, Brian and Jenny, had been this age there was nothing he wouldn't do to keep them safe. They had been his and Margie's everything. He recalled going into their rooms after a long shift and just watching them sleep, their breathing soft and peaceful. Peaceful. This child looked at peace, but her breath had left her. Hers was an eternal sleep. His own breath increased with his heart rate, and he clenched his teeth to suppress the rising tide of emotion. She was somebody's daughter, sister, niece, granddaughter. Where was her father? Her protector? Where were the adults in her life? A child was not born alone into this world. Somebody somewhere must know something. Somebody had let this child down. Badly so.

Frank slowly got to his feet and sighed deeply. There was nothing he could do for her but determine how she'd died—and if there was foul play involved, then he would do everything he could to see that the offender got their day in court.

Taking the radio from his belt, he called Despatch to advise they were on location and confirm there was a body. He requested a search squad and Forensics team to be despatched and for provisions to be made to remove the deceased.

Stephen was once again standing, his tall frame silhouetted against the light coming through the door. "How do you want to play this?"

"I'll get Jammie to finish securing the immediate scene and stand guard while you and I take the statements from the couple who found her. We'll split up—you take the woman's statement, and I'll take his. I don't expect there'll be a problem as they appear to be genuine day-trippers, but we'll need to check their stories align." His words were measured and without any hint of emotion.

Back outside in the light it took a moment for Frank's eyes to adjust. He smiled at the couple, attempting to put them at ease, and asked, "How did you come to the island today?"

"We came over on the ferry." Jeff glanced at Rochelle and added, "But we've just missed our two-twenty ferry back to Auckland."

"You may still make the four o'clock. We'll take your statements, and you should be good to go." Not wanting to disturb the immediate area any more than had already been done, he looked from Jeff to Rochelle to Stephen and back to Jeff. "How about we use the police launch—it'll be more comfortable there."

"I assume you want me to stay here, Boss?" Jammie asked.

"Yes, make sure nothing is disturbed. And definitely no onlookers. Forensics should be over shortly to process the scene."

After removing the PPE gear, he turned to the couple and said, "Let's get going."

Stephen led them along the short track to the wharf in silence while Frank brought up the rear. Reaching *Deodar III*, they found Dick leaning on the rail and Frank introduced him to Jeff and Rochelle.

"I've just had word a Forensics team is preparing to come out to the island," Dick said. "They're also sending us six more constables to assist with the search."

"Is that all?" Frank ran his hand over his balding head. "Dick, you'd better advise Despatch that you'll return to base to pick them up. But first we'll take the statements so these guys can make the next ferry."

"If it helps, we could drop them off at the base."

Frank looked at Jeff who was nodding enthusiastically. "That'd be real cool—what do you say Rochelle?"

"I'm in." She was smiling for the first time.

"Then that's settled."

"Come with me Rochelle and I'll take your statement so you can get going. There're some comfy chairs in the saloon we can use." Stephen led her down the gangway towards the saloon.

Frank took Jeff into the wheelhouse and gestured to the seat behind the helm seat. "This shouldn't take long—take a seat."

Sitting in his own seat, Frank swivelled around to face Jeff while removing his notebook and pen from his pocket. "So sorry you've had to witness this. We need your statement—it's just police procedure. Now, if you're ready, let's start from the beginning with your full name and contact details."

Jeff obliged and Frank jotted them down, checking on the spelling.

"What brought you to Rangitoto today?"

Jeff removed his cap and sunglasses, unmasking his boyish looks. "Rochelle and I study photography at Auckland Polytech, and we came to the island to take photos for an assignment. It's for a paper on landscape photography and we each need to pick a subject and present a panel of twelve photographs. We thought Rangitoto would make interesting subject matter."

"It's an interesting place alright—quite unique. When did you come over?"

"We came across this morning on the nine o'clock ferry."

"And where on the island have you been today?"

"We hiked from the ferry terminal up through the bush to the crater and lookout, stopping at the lava caves on route. Then we detoured out to the shipwreck bay before exploring the row of old baches over there." He gestured with his hand.

"That's quite a full schedule."

Jeff grinned awkwardly. "I admit we don't muck about. We need to get all the raw images today—we don't want to have to come back."

"Did you pass anyone on the tracks?"

"Yeah, there were a few people on the island today—the ferry was quite full this morning."

"How did you come to be in the boat shed?"

"We stopped to photograph it and when I saw the door was slightly open, I was curious and couldn't resist looking inside. I thought there might be another photo opportunity. And that's when I found her. I called the emergency number right away."

"Did you touch anything or try to move her?"

"I may have touched the door." Jeff frowned. "When I couldn't feel her breath on my hand, I think I touched her face to check if she was alive, but she was cold."

"Did you touch anything else?"

"No," he said emphatically while shaking his head.

"Did Rochelle?"

He hesitated. "No, at least not while I was inside the shed. I went outside to make the call, then we both waited for you outside where you saw us. What you found in there is just as it was when we found it."

"Good, thanks. And where were you going next?"

"We were going to take the track around the coastal route back to the ferry."

"Is your camera digital? Can you show me your photos from today?"

"Sure." Jeff got his camera and fiddled with the dials. "You're welcome to look through these. Just press the left arrow to go back through them."

Frank took the camera. The photo on the screen was of the boat shed. It was good and he could see why they'd stopped there. The photos provided a clear record of their day's excursion and supported his story. "These are good—very good. You've got a gift for photography that's for sure." He handed the camera back to Jeff.

At that moment, Stephen and Rochelle came up the steps from the saloon.

"All done, Frank," Stephen said.

Arrangements were made for Dick and Stephen to take *Deodar III* back to base with the two passengers on board. They would pick up the Forensics team and extra police and ferry them back across to the island. Meanwhile Frank would wait with Jammie at the boat shed. Something deep within drew him to stay and maintain a vigil over the young girl who had lost her life on an unpopulated island in the Hauraki Gulf.

*

Rochelle sat on the grey padded seat at the back of the wheelhouse on board *Deodar III*. The two maritime police officers were busy navigating their trip back and seemed oblivious to their passengers. She tucked up her legs and hugged them, while staring out the rear window at the foam that formed in their wake as they sped across the gap between Rangitoto and Devonport Heads. Her mind was in turmoil. Beside her Jeff looked vacantly ahead, his face set with a grim expression giving no clue as to how he might be feeling.

The picture of that poor little girl was disturbing—she couldn't shake it from her mind, like waking from a bad dream that lingers in your consciousness casting its shadow over everything.

The day had begun with so much promise. The photo-hunt, as she liked to call it, was one of her favourite pastimes. Her father and brothers liked to hunt wild deer and pigs in the bush, but that only made her squeamish and they'd tease her mercilessly for being a 'girl'. After discovering photography as a teenager, she found photos made much better prey. While she was never good at painting or drawing, through the camera lens she could make pleasing compositions, and she was acing her photography assignments.

Spending the day in the sunshine with Jeff, and in such an interesting and inspiring place, had lifted her spirits. They had so much in common and he was fun to be around. It had been nothing short of perfect, that is until the boat shed.

Although the sun continued to shine brightly, it was as if the lights had dimmed when that dark cloud of melancholy settled over them. Their earlier buoyant mood was gone. She cast her eyes down, not wanting to engage in conversation. Her fingers picked at her nails, barely noticing when loose bits dropped onto the floor. Worst of all was the feeling of futility and hopelessness, of not being able to do something for the child, not being able to fix it and make it right. Something was very wrong and deep down she knew that the young girl had been the victim of someone, some adult somewhere, who must have abused her trust. How else could she have been lying there abandoned in a disused boat shed on an uninhabited island?

A single tear escaped to run down her cheek. Not wanting to appear weak in front of the policemen, she quickly wiped it away with the back of her hand.

Death was so final. There was no way back. No way to undo its grasp. If only she had her mother's faith—to believe that you simply passed from this world to the next which was better, even perfect. Where children couldn't be hurt. Was that where the little girl in the boat shed had gone? It was a nice thought—she wanted to believe it but couldn't be sure.

The porcelain-like face in the gloomy shed appeared before her and this time a steady stream of tears ran down her cheeks until she could taste their salt on her lips.

"Here." Jeff passed her a clean tissue from his pocket.

Turning to him, she forced a smile before taking the tissue and wiping her eyes and cheeks.

"Are you okay?" His eyebrows pulled into a deep frown.

"Yeah—just processing. It's been a bit of a shock." Her voice was flat as her gaze returned to the sea. The water swirled and splashed behind them as *Deodar III*'s jets churned it up leaving a trail of foam in their wake. She remained staring blankly until they docked at the Maritime Police base in Mechanics Bay.

3

Deodar III was already out of the bay and out of sight by the time Frank returned to Jammie at the boat shed. Police tape now formed the perimeter, with the little boat shed, along with its precious secret, standing in the centre. The tide was low, and the ramp that led from the water's edge up to the shed exposed the sea life that clung to it along with slime that had formed from years of being regularly submerged.

Jammie, still in his PPE suit, was pacing on the track beside the perimeter. "I took a look in the shed. She's just a child. Any clue to what might've happened to her?"

"Not as yet. Forensics will be here soon."

"Do you think it's murder?"

"Too soon to say, although it's looking suspicious." Frank began kitting up in his protective gear. "We'll carry out a preliminary examination of the area. The tide will be starting to come in, so I want to check for evidence before it's washed away. Also, I don't want to lose any time in case whoever brought her here is still in the bay."

"Do you really think the culprit might still be here?"

"It's a possibility." Once more in protective overalls, Frank paused to study the boats anchored peacefully not a hundred metres from where they stood. "If there's a clue as to how she came to be in the shed, or where she came from, then we need to find it. You can help me with a grid search, but we'll need to take extra care not to disturb anything before the photographer gets here."

They began to slowly pace an imaginary grid, looking right and left for anything that didn't fit. The rough scoria made the work especially slow—a spot of blood or thread of cotton could easily be missed. The shed was nestled into a bank of scoria with a tree on one side and shrubs dispersed among the rocks.

"Frank, over here." Jammie was crouched down looking at something on the ground just above the high tide mark.

Frank came across and crouched down beside him. Fallen leaves from the pōhutukawa tree above lay in the cleft of some scoria and they were coated with a blood-red substance. "I'm guessing that's blood alright. See any more?"

"Not as yet. The tide would have washed it away if there was any lower than this point." Jammie stood up, removed his cap and raked his hand through his spikey hair while surveying the area. "I reckon she could've been dragged up here."

"That would explain her bloodied knees. Being dragged across the scoria and oyster shells would make a mess of the skin and clothing." Frank remained crouched, staring at the blood.

"Or crawled," Jammie corrected him. "What I don't get is if she was dragged, why here? If she came to the island by ferry, then it's unlikely she'd come this way. If she came via a boat in the bay, wouldn't they go to the wharf or straight to the boat ramp? Why beach it when there's a boat ramp?"

Frank rubbed his forehead. "Perhaps she was brought across in a small vessel or dinghy at night and they had their bearings slightly off. After all, if there was a crime they wouldn't want to be spotted by the other boats in the bay."

Jammie looked across at the ramp. "Or maybe the ramp was too slippery. If that were the case it would mean she was brought here close to low tide, when the lowest part of the ramp is exposed."

"Good thinking." Frank sighed—sometimes the answer was just too obvious. Assuming she'd been brought here, it suggested the boat shed was a deliberate destination, further convincing him that something sinister had occurred. "Put a marker next to the blood and take a photograph then let's finish off the grid."

They left markers and took photos along the trail of blood-red spots they found leading from the first spot directly up to the boat shed door.

"It's a fairly safe assumption those are bloodstains," Jammie's voice betrayed his excitement.

"We'll have to wait for Forensics to be sure, but I think you're right. The young girl has somehow moved from the high tide marker where we found the first one to the boat shed. By the state of her knees, I'd put money on the fact she's been dragged across the scoria. That means someone dragged her in there and left her there."

"Assuming someone else was involved then it almost certainly indicates a crime took place," Jammie cut in, speaking quickly. "Possibly after dark so as to be away from prying eyes."

"Quite possibly. It's a full moon so there's some night-time visibility. We'll know soon enough when Forensics do their examination."

"But why? Why bring her here and leave her in there?" Jammie gestured towards the boat shed.

Before Frank had a chance to answer, they were interrupted by the familiar sound of *Deodar III*'s engines as she came into the bay. Her twin hulls sliced through the water effortlessly before slowing down and cruising through the moored boats to the wharf. Frank noticed her arrival aroused more interest from several of the moored boats than he wanted. Heads bobbed up, boaties came out of their cabins to stand in their cockpits or on their decks as curiosity got the better of them. It wasn't every day they witnessed police activity on the island.

"As soon as the Forensics team are here, I'll take Stephen and go around the boats to see if anyone has seen anything of interest or is acting suspiciously," Frank said, carefully picking his way back to the track on the outside of the perimeter to wait for the new arrivals. "You'll need to stay guard. And keep an eye out for any craft leaving the bay."

*

Frank watched Stephen lead Glenda Downey, a Forensic Investigator with ESR, Joe Tamaki, a police forensic photographer, and half a dozen young men and women he presumed were with Forensic services as well as six young constables in police uniform along the track towards him. Joe was as tall as Stephen but of a heavy build that would have added value in a rolling maul on the rugby field. Over his shoulder was slung a bulky camera bag. Next to the two men, Glenda looked petite, her bulky gear bag making her seem even smaller.

"Joe, good to see you." Frank shook the man's hand. "Trust it was a pleasant trip out."

Joe grinned. "We don't get too many chances to take a scenic trip out on the Gulf. You've got a cushy number, that's the truth. No wonder you left Central to take up with the Maritime Unit."

Glenda put down her bulky gear bag and shook Frank's hand. "And meet Delia Lee, my assistant today."

Delia was petite with skin that was pasty giving the impression she'd spent too much time in the Forensics' lab. Frank was careful not to crush her tiny hand when introduced.

"And Simon Smart from SOCO, our finger printing expert." A young man who looked like he should still be in school put down the lighting equipment he was carrying to shake Frank's hand.

"The others will assist processing the scene." Glenda waved vaguely at the small group who were already getting into their protective gear.

She beamed, revealing a row of prominent teeth. "It's been a while, Frank."

"Last time would have been when I was at Central." Frank scratched his head. "We normally don't have a lot of cause to bring ESR out on our watch. This one's a bit unusual."

"How so?" Her expression became serious as her sharp eyes, the colour of emeralds, searched his face.

"The Jane Doe is a mere child. Found in the boat shed here by a couple of day visitors to the island. I'm reasonably confident they didn't have anything to hide. We've yet to determine if a crime took place. And how she got here is anybody's guess. We've marked a few spots on the scoria that look suspiciously like blood."

"Give us a minute to kit up and we can get started." She bent down to unzip her bag. Delia and Simon followed suit.

Frank turned to Stephen. "How did it go with Jeff and Rochelle? Get them back okay?"

"Yeah, we left them at the dock to catch an uber ride. They were a bit subdued as you'd expect, but they said nothing more of consequence."

"It would've been a shock for them. Nobody likes finding a corpse, but seeing a child is ten times worse."

Glenda was pulling on a disposable white jumpsuit over her conservatively cut white top and black trousers. "What's the tide doing?"

"It's just past low water now."

"We'll aim to finish working the scene before dark, so Jane Doe doesn't have to spend the night out here." She covered her stylishly short black hair with a disposable bonnet and pulled on a pair of disposable booties. "Ready Delia? Joe? Simon?"

Delia nodded.

Simon, now dressed in white disposables, nodded enthusiastically, appearing eager to begin processing the scene.

"As ready as I ever am." Joe, also now kitted up in Police PPE, was fiddling with the settings on a camera.

"Frank, I'm sure I don't need to ask if anything has been touched or moved?" Glenda studied Frank, her tone clipped and businesslike.

Annoyed that he'd been asked, Frank answered a little too sharply, "Of course not." Then to break the tension, he laughed and added, "We may be the Maritime Division but we're still good coppers."

Glenda's face relaxed into a generous smile. "I didn't mean any offense Frank, just doing my job."

"No offense taken. Now, those blood-looking blotches are marked and there's a trail of them over there." Frank pointed. His voice had taken on a professional tone as if addressing a class of recruits. "You may want to start there, although if the tide hasn't washed them away by now it shouldn't be cause for concern. The couple who found the body went into the shed through the side door and sat waiting for us on the ramp. They are photography students and were photographing the shed before noticing the door was partially open and they went in to take a look. I'll take Stephen out to interview the boaties in the bay. We may be lucky and find someone who saw something. Jammie can stay here and guard the perimeter—he'll keep any nosy-parkers out of your way. And I'll get a search of the island underway."

"Thanks Frank." Glenda stepped over the perimeter with Delia and Joe following one step behind.

The six young constables were chatting among themselves as Frank approached. Introductions were made before Frank said, "I need you to make a thorough search of the island. Split up and prioritise the area within ten metres of the tracks. Check all buildings."

"What are we looking for?" A young fresh-faced woman who'd introduced herself as Cindy asked.

"Anything that doesn't fit such as things that have been discarded: a bag, items of clothing, phone, child's toy, could be anything. And question any visitors to the island that are still here. The last ferry leaves at four." He surveyed the group. "You'll need to work fast to complete it before dark."

Frank left them downloading maps and discussing how they would pair up to cover the island.

*

Back on *Deodar III*, Frank helped Stephen unload the inflatable RHIB from the hydraulic cradle on the stern. Once launched, Stephen manned the centre console while Frank sat deep in thought.

The clue to the mystery surrounding the body in the boat shed would be to establish how she'd got there and why. Save swimming, there were few options for getting on to Rangitoto Island, with access limited to public ferry, private craft or vehicle, or helicopter. The island was separated by a creek from its neighbour, Motutapu Island, and a bridge linked the four-wheel drive track between the two. But there were few residences on Motutapu and only a handful of vehicles. Knowing all the residents, Frank was confident they would be a low priority in the investigation. If she'd arrived by helicopter or private craft then someone in the bay must know something, unless of course they'd left already. The time of death would be helpful, but he would have to wait for Forensics to determine that.

Across the water in the vicinity of the boat shed, people clad in PPE gear were swarming the crime scene like a host of snowmen.

"Where do you want to start, Frank?" Stephen spoke loudly over the noise of the motor.

A quick count revealed sixteen boats at anchor in the bay. "We'll need to talk to them all. But let's start with the furthest, just in case any decide to make themselves scarce. That way they'll need to pass us if we haven't already had a word with them."

Stephen eased the throttle forward until she was doing the five-knot speed limit. The first boat they approached was a sleek schooner named *Cruise Mode*. When they pulled up alongside, a deeply tanned man wearing boardies came up on deck closely followed by a bikini-clad woman. The couple looked to be in their thirties.

After greeting them, Frank asked, "How long have you been here at anchor?"

"We just arrived this afternoon. What's going on?"

"We're investigating a death. Have you seen any craft beaching over by the boat shed?" Frank pointed it out.

"No, sorry we can't help."

"See anything suspicious at all? Anyone acting strangely?"

"No."

"Where have you come from?"

"We left Westhaven marina around lunchtime today."

As an afterthought, he asked, "Do you recall any boats leaving the bay?"

"Sorry, I didn't take any notice. We've been walking on the island for most of the afternoon since we arrived."

"Would you mind giving me your names?"

They did and Frank noted the information down in his notebook. "Okay, thanks."

With a wave Stephen maneuvered the inflatable away towards the next target, a catamaran named *Twin Cat*. The couple, in matching hoodie towelling robes, were standing on the transom and appeared to be expecting them. Frank went through his questions again. This time the couple had been at anchor overnight but had not heard or seen anything of interest. They moved on to the next vessel while Frank jotted in his notebook.

A 70-foot launch called *Neptune* loomed on their starboard side, its forward deck littered with beanbags, kayaks and paddleboards. Loud music was playing, breaking the peace in the bay. Half a dozen men and an attractive young woman were milling about the aft deck, drinks in hand, giving the impression it could've been someone's work party. None of them appeared to have seen anything of interest and again Frank noted it down.

And on it went. They were down to the last handful of boats, and it wasn't looking like their efforts were going to produce anything useful for the investigation. An old Nova 28-foot yacht named *Nellie*, whose stained waterline and dull paint showed years of neglect, was at anchor not far from the boat shed. Although there was no sign of anyone, a small tender was tied to the stern suggesting someone was aboard.

As they approached, Stephen eased off the revs.

"Hello. Is anyone aboard?" Frank waited for a response, but none was forthcoming.

"Hello, anyone aboard?" It was louder this time.

A man appeared at the companionway entrance. On seeing the policemen, he seemed to blanch before scurrying back inside.

"Hello. Can we have a word?" Frank called again.

After a few moments he reappeared. His face was unshaven, his hair dishevelled, and his clothes looked like they'd seen better days. "I hear ya. What do ya want?"

"Just a few questions. How long have you been here at anchor?"

"Why?" The man raised his hand to shade his eyes and stared back at Frank.

"We're investigating a death. When did you arrive in the bay?"

"I don't remember. A couple of days maybe."

Frank's interest was piqued. "Can you be a little more specific?"

"The morning before yesterday." The man shifted his weight about. "That's right, it was two days ago."

"Where have you come from?"

"I was over at Motuihe for a few days. When that easterly came through. Before that I made my way up from the Coromandel." He crossed his arms. "As far as I know that's still legal, isn't it?"

"Mind if I come aboard? Frank asked.

"What if I do?"

Frank couldn't discern if the guy was in some way feeling guilty about something or being just plain obstructive. Occasionally he'd come across the type who had a deep mistrust of police. "It would suggest to me you've something to hide."

"Alright then, you can board."

Quietly to Stephen he said, "We'll tie up and you can back me up."

Once aboard *Nellie*, Frank asked, "Is there anyone else on board?"

"Nope. Just me."

"And you are?"

"Me name's Jerry. Jerry Ramsley."

"Frank Smythe, Maritime Police, and this here is Stephen Blackett, also with the Unit." Frank studied the man as he spoke. "What's your address?"

The man gave a lopsided grin, exposing his broken teeth. "*Nellie* is my home. Has been for some time now."

"Mind if I take a look around?"

"Of course I bloody mind." He looked down at his feet, before darting a sideways glance at Frank and then Stephen, then back at his feet.

"It will go better for you if you cooperate with us." Frank's voice had taken on a hard edge.

"Look then. But don't you touch me stuff." The man stepped aside, clearing the entrance to the cabin.

Turning to Stephen, Frank said, "Stay here." He took a last look at Jerry then moved past him and down the steps into the cabin.

The interior was as poorly maintained as the exterior. Woodwork needed a lick of varnish, food scraps and dirty dishes covered the galley benchtop. The bed in the forward cabin was unmade, its sheets looked like they'd not seen the inside of a washing machine for quite some time. Clothes were strewn about. The single bunks running aft under the cockpit seats were crammed full of all manner of tools and what could only be called junk. But there was nothing to indicate that a young girl had been aboard. And no evidence of blood. Still, the man was certainly acting suspiciously. Frank ventured back up the steps and into the cockpit where Jerry and Stephen appeared to be having a stand-off, each staring at the other.

"Have you seen any craft beaching near the boat shed over there? Maybe last night?"

Jerry looked out towards the boat shed before answering, "Nope."

"See anything suspicious at all? Anyone acting strangely?"

"Nope."

"What about any boats leaving the bay either yesterday or today?"

"You must be joking. Do I look like a nosey parker?"

"What about a helicopter?"

"Don't you get it? I've not seen a bloody thing."

"Where are you heading next?"

Once more Jerry's face broke into a lopsided grin. "Where's the wind going to blow next week?"

Frank eyed him curiously, raised his eyebrow and waited.

"I've no place special I need to be." Jerry shuffled his feet.

Frank didn't like it—there was something off about this sailor. Not getting anywhere with this line of questioning, he pulled a business card out of his pocket and handed it to Jerry. "We'll leave it there for now. If you think of anything you want to tell me, you can contact me on any of these numbers."

Once back in their inflatable and underway, Stephen said, "I'd put money on the fact he's hiding something."

"Something's not right with him. Hard to tell if he's just being obnoxious towards us or if he's involved in some way. His cabin was messy but no signs he might have had the girl on board."

"He seemed nervous all the same. The sort I wouldn't trust around my grandmother."

They approached the remaining boats, but the story was the same. No one had witnessed anything that might aid their investigation.

*

Frank and Stephen returned the tender to *Deodar III*. While aboard Frank took the time to make a call to update Andy Johnston, his immediate superior. What he liked about Andy was his hands-off management style allowing Frank to work autonomously. He'd been around too long to be micro-managed—it just wouldn't sit right. But this case was showing signs it could be significantly bigger than the usual cases the Unit dealt with, and Andy had appreciated the heads up and had asked to be kept updated.

Frank noted the tide was already part way up the ramp when he and Stephen approached the boat shed on foot. Jammie was still standing guard by the track.

Frank crossed the cordon and entered the little shed. A light had been erected that shone its yellow rays onto the child's body, casting an eerie glow over the waxen skin. Glenda, her face partially obscured by her PPE gear, was bending over her. Beside her Delia was taking notes and Joe was standing on the other side of the body with his camera in hand. Crouched by the door, Simon was busy dusting for fingerprints.

Glenda looked up at Frank. "Good, you're back. Take a look at this." She pointed to the girl's wrist.

Frank bent with his head close to Glenda's. On the inside of the child's wrist was a rudimentary tattoo of an eye and inside the eye were some sort of hieroglyphics. The tattoo was monochrome, the ink red, and was no more than two centimetres long. "Interesting. Do you recognise what those symbols are?"

"No, I haven't come across anything like it before. A specialist in linguistics at the university might know."

"Anything else?"

"Judging by the temperature of the body and the rigor mortis, the time of death appears to be more than eight hours and sometime in the last 24 hours. The blood splatter suggests she either crawled or was dragged up out of the water and into the shed. Once I have her in the mortuary, I can give you a more accurate time of death and confirm the cause of death. I have also found clear evidence that this child has been subjected to significant sexual abuse."

Frank exhaled slowly. "So, we're definitely looking at a crime scene."

"It appears that way. Although I'm fairly confident the sexual abuse didn't happen here. Did you find any witnesses aboard the boats in the bay?"

"No. It appears no one saw or heard anything—however there was one that acted somewhat strangely."

"Look we've just about finished here—there's not a lot more I can do outside of the lab. All the evidence has been bagged and we've got the photographs."

"Any fingerprints?"

Simon piped up from behind Frank. "I've managed to lift some partial prints from around the door, but we'll need to rule out the couple who found her."

"In their statement they said the door was ajar when they arrived, but he thought he may have touched it," Frank responded.

"Well, there's nothing more to be done here today." Glenda removed her gloves. "Could you please make the necessary arrangements to transport the body back to the mortuary? The sooner I can start on the postmortem the sooner we'll know what happened to the poor child."

Frank took a last long look at the girl. She looked so peaceful, as if sleeping soundly. Such a tragedy. Whoever did this to her would have to pay. No child should be subject to the horrors of sexual abuse. It was a crime that never ceased to evoke strong emotions, shaming him with what his fellow man could do, as if he was in some way responsible. He quietly vowed to bring whoever had harmed her to justice.

4

Frank arrived at the Maritime Police depot half an hour before his shift was due to start, and half an hour before his usual arrival time. All night he'd tossed and turned, unable to get the image of the young girl lying in the cold and dank shed out of his mind.

He'd wrestled with how he and Margie would've coped if told their baby girl wouldn't be coming home—ever. There would always be a void where once there had been play and laughter. A parent could never anticipate how they'd react in such circumstances unless of course they'd already been tested in that way—himself included. He could only imagine how angry he'd be if it'd happened to his own daughter, Jenny. He'd want to see the perpetrator strung up and quartered. Literally. Forgiveness would be hard. But then some fathers were the perpetrators, and that was something he also found unfathomable.

He helped himself to a strong coffee from the kitchen down the hall from his office and sat at his desk going over yesterday's notes. The couple that'd found the body had checked out okay and the search of the island had turned up a blank.

Jerry Ramsley, on the Nova 28 called *Nellie*, was definitely a person of interest. Could he have abused her and dumped her there? There was nothing to suggest he couldn't. And he'd come across as hiding something. Did he have the opportunity? He'd been in the bay and was on his own, so yes it was possible. Given the abuse, the motive was likely to be related to deviant behaviour. Was he the type? Quite possibly. However in Frank's experience, people were often not what they seemed and if you pigeonhole a person into a stereotype the chances were you'd end up misjudging them. Yet Jerry Ramsley was the only potential lead they had, if it could be called a lead.

The computer screen slowly came to life and he plugged the name Jerry Ramsley into the police database and immediately got a hit. The guy had been convicted of several minor offenses involving possession and dealing marijuana as well as petty theft. No records to suggest he was a known paedophile or had a history of child molestation, but what was recorded was only what he'd been apprehended for, meaning it certainly didn't rule it out. They'd need to keep a close eye on him. *Nellie* was not set up to take on an ocean, so the risk of him leaving the country aboard her was low and so long as he remained in New Zealand waters they could trace him. Nevertheless they would need to follow his movements. Frank made a note to contact Immigration to get an alert raised at the various ports of exit.

The postmortem was scheduled for this morning. The results regarding the time and cause of death and the full extent of the sexual abuse would help direct the investigation. Attending postmortems was something he'd always tried to avoid, finding them overwhelmingly intense, but for the sake of the victim he felt obliged to attend. With a bit of luck it wouldn't take too long.

His thoughts returned to the dead girl's family. Somewhere a mother or father must be missing their daughter. Or a grandparent, an aunt, uncle or some other family member. Someone somewhere must have loved that child and be looking for her, waiting on her to return home.

His friend and former colleague, Anahera Raupara, was working the Land Search and Rescue cases out of Auckland Central. Having partnered with her numerous times before joining the Maritime Unit when they both worked as detectives, he knew her to be a good operator. More recently they'd teamed up on a case where a yachtie, who happened to be an old sailing buddy of his, was lost in a man overboard incident. She'd be able to tell him if they had a missing person case open that matched the description of the victim.

He checked his watch and made the call which she answered on the first ring.

"You answered that like you were waiting for my call." Frank chuckled.

Her low-pitched laugh rewarded him. "Frank, it's good to hear from you. What's up?"

"The body of a young girl was found yesterday in an abandoned boat shed on Rangitoto Island. She'd been the victim of sexual abuse. The autopsy is scheduled for later this morning, so I'll know more about the time and cause of death then, as well as her age and ethnicity. But she looks Asian to me and my guess is she's around twelve years of age. Do you have any missing persons on the register that fit that description?"

"None come to mind, but I'll take a look through the database for you."

"She could have come from anywhere, not just Auckland. We have yet to ascertain whether she died at the scene or if her body was dumped there."

"I can check the national database and get back to you."

"Thanks. I owe you one." Frank picked up his pen and rolled it around his fingers. "How's the family doing?"

"They are all good, thanks. Jim's work's going well. Rangi still lives for volleyball and Piri his music. It's amazing how two kids from the same parents can be polar opposites. How're your lot?"

"Much the same. Margie and I have gotten used to being empty nesters. It took us a while after Brian and Jenny left home." He chuckled again. "We did waste a lot of food not having teenagers eat everything in the kitchen but now we seem to have adapted."

Again her low chuckle came down the line. "I know what you mean. My boys demolish anything and everything that's edible. Are you still enjoying the work in the Maritime Unit?"

"For the most part, yes. The variety is good. These days it's mostly transporting prisoners from Waiheke, fisheries support, petty crime and education. I enjoy being out on the water and having the degree of autonomy we get here. No plans to move any time soon. What about you?"

"Much the same. I enjoy the mix of Land Search and Rescue work and the occasional case out of Central. I'm getting better at the work life balance—in fact you'll be pleased to hear I've been frequenting the gym again." She paused. "It's good to hear from you, Frank, even if it's for work. I miss our working together. And it's been a long time between drinks."

"You're right, it's time we had a proper catch up over a pint at Smugglers."

"Sounds good. Why don't we go back to meeting after work on Thursdays when it fits with the rosters. Let me know if next week suits and I'll clear it with Jim."

They ended the call and Frank stretched back in his chair, his hands behind his head. What he missed most about working with Anahera was her inquisitive mind, her innate intuition, and her easy-going countenance coupled with a strong sense of loyalty. A top cop and yet she stayed humble. And she loved her family, always managing to put them first regardless of how busy she was, giving them the time they deserved. She was one of a kind, a truly decent human being.

His email pinged and he turned to his computer. It was from Joe and contained attachments of the photos taken at Rangitoto yesterday. The first was a wide angle shot of the boat shed and the surrounding area. A series of close-up shots of the blood splatters followed. The next showed the girl's body and Frank stared at the screen for a long time until his eyes no longer focused on the image. His shoulders hunched over the keyboard, and he let his head droop. During his time in the Force there'd been all manner of crime and countless victims, but the younger the victim the deeper it cut him. The world could be a cruel place.

He roused himself and went back to the task at hand. A series of close-up pictures of bruises, cuts and scrapes were next. When a close-up picture of the tattoo popped onto the screen he stopped. It was strange that a child would have a tattoo. The stylised eye and the markings inside it were unusual and distinctive and he felt certain it carried a message of some sort. He did a quick google search, trawling through some tattoo sites, but didn't find anything that came close to resembling it. He stood and went over to the window. Staring. Blankly at first. The harbour slowly came into focus, glistening in the early morning light with Rangitoto Island in the distance rising from its watery bed up to its crater. How a child got to be lying dead and abandoned on the island, with boats at anchor in the vicinity but no witnesses, was a mystery. Instinct told him that the tattoo had something to do with it.

His mobile rang and when he saw it was Anahera, he quickly answered it.

"Kia ora Frank. Anahera here."

"That was quick. What have you got for me?" He breathed in a deep breath and waited.

"I'm afraid it's not great news. I've checked the missing persons list and there aren't any girls of Asian ethnicity aged twelve years currently unaccounted for. It appears her absence hasn't been reported." She added more quietly, "I'm sorry it's not better news."

"We can't pinpoint her exact age. She appeared undernourished so she could be older or equally she could be younger than she appears."

"I checked for minors regardless of age."

"Hmmm." Frank sat down at his desk and picked up his pen. Tapping it, he looked at his screen again. "She had a strange tattoo on the inside of her wrist."

"What do you mean strange?"

"Just hold the line and I'll email the picture to you." He moved his mouse and tapped the keyboard. "You should have it now. Have you ever seen one like it?"

"It's just coming through ... hold on ... must be taking the long route around the globe." The line went quiet. "No, that's a new one on me. Damn it Frank, who would tattoo a child?"

"That's the question I've been asking. Could it be gang related?"

"I've no idea." She paused again. "It's possible."

"What about the symbols, ever seen them before?"

"No, but maybe they're some sort of alphabet?"

"I think I might try the university. Someone there might know." Frank considered the image again. "What do you think the eye symbolises?"

"Eyes are for sight. Could it be a threat that someone is watching? Or maybe a target, like a bullseye? Or something to do with a higher power? Healing? Protection?"

"Well, if it was protection someone failed her abysmally!" Realising his tone was sharp, he added, "Sorry, I'm not angry at you. I just hate to see a child treated badly—and this child not only had her innocence taken but also her life."

"I get it Frank, no need for an apology. Could the tattoo be symbolic of some sort of spiritual thing?"

"I just don't know. But someone must be looking for her. I'd better go but do us a favour and call me if anyone registers her missing."

"Can do Frank."

He hung up just as he received a callout from Despatch. It had been reported that a recreational boat was fishing in the Motuihe channel and pulling in and keeping undersize snapper. Frank grabbed his life jacket from his locker and joined the crew who were running a check over the rescue bridge—an essential piece of kit that rolled out as it was inflated using a dive tank, much like the blow-out whistles found at a child's party.

With well-practised actions, it didn't take long to get underway. The inner harbour and Gulf were calm under the large high pressure weather system that was straddling the country. Frank was on the helm and *Deodar III* cruised along at 32 knots, making good time. The craft in question was an 18-foot runabout called *Gone Fishing* and it wasn't difficult to find. Two males in their mid-thirties were standing in the cockpit holding fishing rods. Once alongside, Frank put *Deodar III* on the dynamic positioning mode, a recent system upgrade that kept her holding in a particular position. He left Dick in the wheelhouse and went to stand at the port side rail on the forward deck.

Frank waved to the men. "How's the fishing going? Catch anything?"

One of the men grinned. "Yep, I reckon we've got dinner for the next couple of nights."

"What are you catching?"

"Snapper mostly, one gurnard."

"Mind showing us the catch?" Frank asked.

The men looked at each other before looking back at Frank. The man spoke again. "They're in the fish hold. All legal and we've not yet caught our limit."

"Mind if one of our sergeants comes across for a look?" Frank smiled to put them at ease. "Just a routine check."

The man nodded.

Dick was at the wheel and Frank signalled to him. He skilfully brought *Deodar III* stern to stern and Jammie leapt across. He looked in the hold under the cockpit floor on the other boat and went about measuring the fish. Once finished he signalled Frank a thumbs up indicating all was well. Frank waited for him to come back on board. The majority of the snapper were only just long enough to be keepers with one or two being marginal. Jammie let them off with a warning.

Since they were passing Islington Bay where the boat shed was located, Frank decided to call in and see if Jerry Ramsley and *Nellie* were still there.

As they entered the bay, the crew grew unusually quiet. Frank assumed they were also thinking about the girl found lying in the boat shed. The silence was broken by his phone buzzing.

"Frank? It's Glenda Downey, Forensics."

"Hi Glenda. What's the news?"

"Just letting you know I'm about to conduct the autopsy on the boat shed child."

"We are out on *Deodar* but could be back at base in half an hour. I can come over to the morgue as soon as I get in, if that suits."

"Perfect. In the meantime, I'll get it underway." The line went dead.

Ahead of them was the old fishing trawler and beyond her a flotilla of anchored boats stretched across the bay. Over on the shore the derelict boat shed stood surrounded by police tape marking out the crime scene. They cruised through the assortment of boats to *Nellie*. This time Jerry Ramsley was up on deck and saw them coming.

"What do yer want this time?" he growled across the gap.

"Good morning. We were in the vicinity and thought we'd pass by to see if you've remembered anything that might help us with our enquiries." Frank watched him closely.

Jerry remained poker faced. "You harassing me? I might just make an official complaint."

"Just doing our job." Frank smiled, hoping to reduce the tension.

"I got yer business card. If I have something to tell yer, I'll call you."

The visit had served its purpose. Nellie and her skipper were still in the bay. Frank nodded to Dick and the *Deodar III* headed back to base.

*

Frank's trip over to the morgue was like driving through a long and dark tunnel as he was filled with dread over what he was about to witness. The sight and smell of rotting flesh was something he would never get used to. Intuitively he knew that the only way to deal with the autopsy was to try and forget that the body was once a person. If he had faith in a higher power then perhaps it would be easier to view a body as no longer having its soul and therefore mere flesh. It was one of those activities where he admired anyone who could be totally detached and unemotional when working with a body. Frank was just not wired that way.

Frank's senses were on high alert when he quietly entered the autopsy room. The combined smell of formaldehyde and human waste hit him in the stomach. Sounds of metal on metal along with a rustling of paper PPE gear echoed about the cold chamber. Glenda, dressed in her white overalls with a plastic apron, was in the centre under a bright light and alongside a stainless table on which a naked corpse lay.

She pulled the sheet up to cover the slight body and stood up straight. "Frank, you can kit up over there and then I'll take you through my findings." Her voice was remarkably upbeat.

Frank removed his police issue cap and put the disposable jumpsuit on over his blue police overalls, followed by the booties, mask and bonnet. When he joined her at the stainless slab, he noted the stainless bowl with various instruments including a small circular saw sitting on a table beside her and he was thankful he'd skipped breakfast.

"Welcome to my world, Frank." The corners of her eyes went up with a hint of a smile behind her mask which moved with her cheeks.

"Can't say I like being here." Frank was working to maintain his calm. Having the familiar notebook and pen in hand helped. "What have you found?"

"Firstly, I put the time of death somewhere between eighteen hundred hours and midnight on the evening before she was found." Her friendly manner had given way to professionalism. "And I can confirm the cause of death was secondary drowning. She must have been in the water and somehow made it into the shed before she died. Her lungs contained salt water."

"Are you saying she may not have had help getting into the shed?"

"That's for you to determine. Either she got herself out of the water and into the shed or someone helped her."

Frank jotted down some notes—the tactic wasn't just for recall. "Okay. What else?"

"There are numerous cuts and scrapes, particularly around her knees as you saw, but also on her arms and abdomen. The knees are bruised and swollen. I found pieces of oyster shell and grains of scoria in the cuts. They could be self-inflicted if she was able to crawl from the water's edge to the boat shed or she could have got them while being dragged. If the latter was the case, it's not clear if it was done maliciously or by someone trying to help her."

"So, there may not have been a crime that took place in the boat shed."

"That's right. Sorry I can't be more helpful." She sounded genuinely apologetic. "There's one other thing though. She has sustained significant damage to her genitalia and has extensive scar tissue consistent with multiple rapes over a long period. She would be one of the worst cases I've seen."

Frank was quiet as he absorbed this new information. "What age do you think she is?"

"I'd put her at twelve years of age. And I'm reasonably sure her ethnicity is northern India or Nepalese. I will get DNA tests run to confirm this."

"Anything else?"

"She is severely undernourished. And she hadn't eaten a meal in several days." Glenda shook her head. "This child has been through hell."

"What about the tattoo? Did you find any other markings?"

"No others. I haven't seen a tattoo like that before—and we get to see many in here. Most unusual to have one on a child." She paused. "One thing though, it's a fairly new tattoo."

"Interesting." He made a note. "I've not managed to find any clues as yet to its meaning."

"Has she been reported missing?"

"No, or at least not as yet."

"I'll complete my report today and will send it through."

The stench was beginning to get the better of him and Frank thanked her before making a hasty exit.

Back in the safety of his car, he put through a call to Andy Johnston and gave him the update. Andy agreed that they needed to ascertain how the girl got into the shed and whether anyone else was involved. Frank undertook to contact the ferry captains who were on duty the day she was found as well as the previous day. There weren't too many visitors to the island, so he was confident they'd remember if the girl had been on the ferry.

He opened his window, filled his lungs with fresh air and let the smells of the morgue blow off him.

*

Even though his office was a sanctuary, the cold and sterile morgue had left Frank distracted and lacking in focus. A series of eyes looked at him from the pad on which he'd been doodling. They were all similar to the one depicted in the girl's tattoo. The pencil moved backwards and forwards, shading in the latest one.

It was clear that this case was no longer a Maritime case and Central would be wanting to take it over. But he wasn't ready to let it go. Not yet. It felt personal, like he was connected. And yet it was for this very reason that he'd left the regular detective work and transferred to the Maritime Unit. His habit of letting things get personal had brought on excessive anxiety. He'd promised Margie he wouldn't do that anymore, and he hadn't; the anxiety attacks now ancient history. But this case felt different. He wanted to find where she'd come from, how she'd got to the island and who'd abused her. He wanted to be involved.

The team were busy aboard *Deodar III* carrying out routine maintenance, a never-ending task but one that gave them pride and a sense of ownership which added to the team being a tight unit. After making himself a coffee, he stood sipping it at the window looking out over Rangitoto Island.

If he couldn't find any evidence that the girl had been on the ferry, then they'd need to take another look at Jerry Ramsley. It might be worth pulling him in for questioning and seeing if anything turned up. It was important that they kept track of him and his movements. One option was to install cameras at the boat shed and wharf to give surveillance footage of the comings and goings of boats around Islington Bay. That would allow them to follow the man's movements, but only for as long as he stayed in the bay. How useful that might be was debatable, given the deed had been done and it was unlikely to turn up anything now.

He sighed deeply. It was no good procrastinating. The ferry captain still hadn't been spoken to and it was now a priority while the events of the last day were still in recent memory. After getting the name and number of the skipper who'd been rostered on the previous two days from the ferry company's head office, he tapped the number into his phone.

"Todd Brown."

"Todd, it's Frank Smythe of the Maritime Police Unit. Is now a good time to talk?"

"Sure Frank. How can I help?"

"The body of a young Asian girl approximately twelve years of age was found in a boat shed in Islington Bay yesterday afternoon. We believe she'd been lying there for around a day. Do you recall any young

Asian girls among your passengers around that time, either travelling on their own or with someone?"

"No, sorry I don't recall any, the crew might. But we have CCTV coverage now, so you can check that. The feed can be accessed at the office."

"That's good news. One of us will be down within the hour. Thanks Todd."

Thankful for the opportunity to put the autopsy behind him and focus on something else, Frank decided to go down to the ferry operator's office himself.

Given there were only two return sailings to the island each day, it didn't take long to scroll through the CCTV footage for the three days leading up to the time when the boat shed girl had been found. No children fitting the description of the girl were among the assembly of passengers, either travelling on their own or with someone. The obvious conclusion was that she must have gone over by other means.

Jerry Ramsley had just become a more significant person of interest.

5

Back at the Police Maritime Unit base Frank sat at his desk, coffee in hand, thinking through the case. Secondary drowning could indicate an accident. If someone was guilty of abusing the girl, it was highly likely they wouldn't want to be connected to her. And if that was the case, instead of calling emergency services they could have panicked and disposed of the body by hiding it in the disused boat shed where it could have remained hidden for a long time, had the photography students not been curious. He needed to know if Jerry Ramsley was known to be associated with an Asian girl and if he was capable of kidnapping.

He placed a call through to the senior constable in Coromandel, Larry Cook. After the preliminaries he got straight to the point.

"I'm after information about a Jerry Ramsley. Lives aboard a Nova 28-foot yacht called *Nellie.* Has some form for minor offenses. Have you come across him?"

"Yeah, I know Jerry. Had a mooring here in the harbour for a long time. Prior to that he lived in a small bach up the way—in a fairly remote part of the Coromandel. Built his yacht up there himself, and he was at it for years. I was involved when we busted him for growing and selling marijuana. Had quite the set up." He paused. "I have to say, he always came across as having a chip on his shoulder. You know the type, anti-authority and angry at the world."

"Was he known to have a relationship with an Asian child?"

"Not that I know of. What's on your mind, Frank?"

"We have a case of a dead Asian girl who's been sexually abused, and he was in the locality where she was found. He acted suspiciously like he had something to hide when we questioned him as a potential witness and he's our only person of interest at this stage. Was there ever any hint of paedophilia or sexual perversion?"

"No, can't say there was."

"Would you say he is capable of kidnapping?"

"I couldn't say. He's an odd one, no question about that. But kidnapping is a serious offense and way more so than the petty crime we pulled him in for. I'm afraid I can't help you very much. But you're welcome to him on your side of the Gulf." He chuckled into the phone. "Do you want me to ask around and see what I can find out?"

"That would be good, thanks."

Frank ended the call and sat staring at the phone. Was he missing something? In his mind he went over the shreds of information they had relating to the boat shed case. While Jerry Ramsley acted strangely and happened to be in the bay, there was nothing linking him to the case. And if he was guilty of disposing of the girl in the boat shed, why hang around in the bay? Unless he thought the body wouldn't be found. A more likely alternative could be that it wasn't Jerry at all but another boat who'd been in the locality and slipped out before the body was found. Without witnesses they had nothing—just one suspicious character who'd acted like he was hiding something.

*

Johnny Ingram was skipper aboard *Taniwha II*, one of the fleet belonging to Sea Cleaners. It was another calm and sunny day on the harbour. Days like this reminded him why he'd given up a perfectly good career of twenty years in the bank to join an organisation that took crews, sometimes volunteers included, around the Waitematā and Manukau

Harbours and Hauraki Gulf to remove rubbish from the water, estuaries and beaches.

From the very first time he'd heard about Sea Cleaners, their mission was like a magnet, drawing him to them. It wasn't just the appeal of days out on the water, but he was an avid environmentalist and a keen fisherman. The idea of plastics in the ocean due to his generation of consumers was frankly maddening. If his life was going to make a difference, then he had to be part of the solution. And he liked that through Sea Cleaners, they didn't just remove tonne after tonne of plastics and rubbish from the waterways around Auckland, but they also went into schools and educated the next generation. For the first time in his working life, he was satisfied he was doing something truly meaningful.

This day his deckhand was Les, an amenable young man who worked well and without complaint, regardless of some of the rubbish they got to handle, and whose company Johnny enjoyed. Their allocation this shift was the shoreline starting at the lighthouse on Rangitoto Island round towards Islington Bay.

"Take a look at this—disgusting!" Les called over the noise of the 250-horsepower outboard that was gently idling away. He held a long boat hook in one hand and a sodden and soiled disposable nappy in his other gloved hand for Johnny to see.

Johnny shook his head. "Some folks just don't get it. Why they'd dump something like that into waterways is beyond me."

"We should fine people if they're caught littering. I hear some countries do that and it's enough of a deterrent to make their streets cleaner." Les dropped the nappy into one of the green compostable bags in the cockpit.

"Lock them up would be my vote." He watched Les take the net and scoop up some more plastic. "My brother went to a place called Sikkim in the north of India where you were locked up if caught dropping litter.

He said the streets were completely devoid of litter, even though the rest of the country was covered in it. It proves it works alright."

"The trouble is there wouldn't be enough space to lock all the offenders up."

"Very true." Johnny turned his attention back to the rocky shoreline.

Rangitoto could be tricky as it was surrounded by shallow waters with hidden mounds of scoria that had flowed down from its volcano as lava during the last eruption. Thankfully Sea Cleaners were equipped with a small fleet of Stabicraft, a robust and stable design which were perfectly suited to the task with their solid aluminium hull.

"Are you coming to the celebration drinks on Friday?" Johnny asked.

"Sure, wouldn't miss it for anything." Les wiped his brow with the back of his hand. "It's hard to imagine we've picked up fifteen million litres of rubbish since we started in 2002—it's quite a milestone."

"Sure is. They say it's enough to fill six Olympic-size swimming pools. That's a lot of pieces of plastic—makes you proud to be a part of it." Johnny scanned to port. "Should be a good turnout."

"I hope the media cover it. We sure could do with some good publicity to raise awareness and make people think twice before dumping in their own backyard." Les leaned on the aluminium gunwale and pointed to something in the water. "What do you reckon that is?"

"Hard to say. Hold on and I'll bring us in closer."

The object was gently swaying with the tidal movement some fifty metres off their port side. Johnny brought *Taniwha II* round while Les stood ready with one of the large hand-held nets. As the gap closed, they could make out a small body lying face down in the water with long strands of black hair ebbing and flowing around it. The posterior was up and the limbs down in the water. It was wrapped in what appeared to be pink silk pyjamas.

"Cripes! It's a body! Should I net it?" Les asked, the colour draining from his face.

"No, that's a job for the police. I'll call it in and we'll have to wait for them to get here." Johnny took off his cap and raked his fingers through his thinning hair. "It doesn't look like it's going anywhere. I'd say it's snagged on a rock."

"It's no more than a child," Les said, his voice barely audible over the idling engine.

Johnny picked up the radio handpiece and called the emergency channel. Within minutes they received a message back asking them to stand by until the police boat *Deodar III* arrived. They dropped the anchor and *Taniwha II* bobbed quietly alongside while they carried out their gruesome vigil.

*

Frank had just finished talking to Larry Cook when he received the emergency call out. He checked his watch—it was getting late in the day—prompting a silent curse that a call out at this time would make for a long shift. All thoughts of any inconvenience vanished when he heard the nature of the emergency. Another body had been found, washed up onto the western shore of Rangitoto Island. Details were few and he leapt to his feet and grabbed his gear bag from the locker room on his way out.

Dick, Stephen and Jammie were aboard *Deodar III* finishing up their maintenance tasks for the day when he found Stephen applying anti rust to the engine bolts.

"There's been another body found out by Rangitoto. Alert the others and have them ready to depart immediately," Frank ordered.

Stephen put down his brush and wiped his hands on his blue overalls. "As good as done, Frank."

Within minutes *Deodar III* was free of her mooring lines and slicing smoothly through the water. She passed the Devonport Ferry Terminal to port, the Ōrākei marina to starboard, and on past the Devonport

Heads. Rangitoto Island lay directly ahead of them. Frank put the binoculars up to his eyes and adjusted the dial to bring the image into sharp focus. In the distance was the black aluminium hull and hard top of a Stabicraft. As they neared her, the branding for Sea Cleaners became clear on its forward hull, and he could just make out the nets and boathooks standing to attention along its stern.

"That's her, straight ahead," he instructed Dick who was on the helm, and immediately he felt a surge as Dick increased their speed to a nick over 40 knots. Within minutes they were approaching *Taniwha II* and Dick reduced their speed to an idle as Jammie put fenders out along their port side.

Frank hailed them from the port rail and Johnny pointed to the water off his stern. What appeared to be a small body was face down in the water. "Easy, Dick. The body is in the water just five metres off their port quarter," Frank called out to Dick. "We'll launch the tender and use the Stokes Litter to pick up the body."

Deodar III came to a stop alongside *Taniwha II*, and Dick called, "Virtual anchor engaged."

Two men were standing among green rubbish bags that were scattered on the cockpit floor aboard *Taniwha II*. "Johnny, good to see you again," Frank called across the gap between the two boats.

"Frank, I'm sure glad to see you." Johnny's face was partially hidden under a low cap and sunglasses. "I'm afraid we've found more than we bargained for."

"Something you could do without. How long since you found the body?"

"No more than half an hour ago—we called it in immediately. When we found it, it looked just as it is now. We figure it must have come in with the tide." Johnny shook his head. "Poor thing. I never expected this when I came into work today."

"Okay, we'll tog up and take it from here. You boys can get going. Thanks for standing by. We'll call you if we need anything else." Frank turned to Stephen and Jammie who were now standing next to him. "As soon as you're ready, we'll launch the inflatable."

Wearing their PPE gear, Stephen and Jammie placed the yellow litter on the RHIB tender and lowered it into the water while Frank stood watch, silent and unmoving, staring down at the child lying in her watery grave.

They recovered the body, strapped it onto the litter and gently brought it back on board to lie on the aft deck of *Deodar III*. Seeing another young girl made his heart sink. Her long black hair was tangled, the eyes just slits in her swollen face. Her arms were twisted as if broken but the legs lay straight, the bare feet puffed up like bear's paws. Her extremities were covered in abrasions. As with the boat shed girl, she was swaddled in ripped silk pyjamas that clung tightly to her bloated torso and limbs. Frank looked away, unable to take in the grotesque body any longer, only vaguely aware of Stephen covering her with a sheet.

Jammie moved quickly to the side rail where he deposited the contents of his stomach. There was no shame or recriminations, no merciless ribbing; they'd all done it at some point. This was no time for bravado. Nothing was said for a long time. There simply were no words.

Dick climbed down the steps from the wheelhouse and stood with them, his cap in hand. Giving the corpse due respect.

Eventually Frank pulled disposable gloves from his pocket and slowly pulled them on. He bent down to carefully pick up the girl's enlarged right arm from under the sheet. When he turned it over, what he found confirmed his suspicions. A tattoo had been inked in red on her inside wrist. It was of an eye with symbols in its centre, very similar to the one on the boat shed girl. These children were connected. The air escaped from him in a long deep sigh. This was no coincidence.

Two dead girls. Each with trademark tattoos. Both young and probably both Asian. Frank guessed this one was younger than the other child, maybe nine or ten years old. To his knowledge neither had been reported missing. These girls must be missed by somebody—someone somewhere knew something.

Turning to Stephen, he said, "Help me get her into a body bag."

Stephen, his face solemn, nodded.

"Dick, give Despatch a call and let them know we're bringing her in."

Dick walked slowly yet purposefully into the wheelhouse to make the necessary arrangements.

With a heavy heart, Frank helped Stephen zip the corpse into a body bag before joining Dick in the wheelhouse. An undertaker would be waiting for them when they docked back at base to transport her to the morgue. Knowing this was now beyond what their unit was equipped to handle, he called Andy to give him a heads up.

It was customary in the Unit to not leave a body alone out of respect, so Stephen volunteered to stand with her on the way back to base. The trip went quietly. The mood in the wheelhouse was sombre, the usual banter absent, as each was lost to their own thoughts.

A small welcoming party awaited them on the wharf when *Deodar III* approached the base. Andy stood with the undertakers. Once moored, and after Frank had instructed the crew to make *Deodar III* ready for the next shift before leaving for the day, he went to see his Senior Sergeant.

"Andy, I didn't expect to see you down here." Frank put out his hand and shook Andy's.

Although a good-natured guy, Andy's natural expression was neutral and difficult to read.

"Frank, looks like there's more to this than we first thought. I've had a chat with Brad Smart. We've agreed the investigation of the body found on Rangitoto and now this latest one best fits with Brad's CIB team at Auckland Central." Andy lowered his voice. "As the attending officer you've done your job, Frank. But Central are best placed to identify the victims and find their families, and to discover whatever happened to those girls that led them to end up out there and why."

"I expected that'd be the case." Deflated, he looked past Andy to the volcano that was Rangitoto in the distance.

"The media are going to be all over this. The body in the boat shed had only minimal coverage, what with the conflicts overseas and the election. But two dead children will cause a feeding frenzy among the piranhas. We need leads and we need to show we're on top of this."

"Understood."

"I've told Brad you'll head over and brief his team. His assistant will be in touch to set up a meeting."

"That I can do."

They stopped and stood in silence as the stretcher bearers carried the small body in its casing off *Deodar III* and along the wharf to the waiting hearse.

"What're your thoughts regarding Jerry Ramsley? Worth another look?" Andy asked, after the hearse rear door was shut.

Frank looked back at his boss. "I'm thinking that. He's shifty but perhaps just one with a chip on his shoulder. He's had previous run-ins with the Police and several petty convictions. Nothing to suggest child abuse." He sighed. "Still, wouldn't hurt to bring him in for questioning. I could've sworn he was hiding something."

"I suggest you hold off until after you brief Central. No doubt they'll want you to deliver him to them. What's the chance he might scarper?"

"I've been thinking about that. He maintains he lives aboard, and she's definitely not fitted out for an ocean passage, so he wouldn't get far. We could install cameras around Islington Bay but by the time the techies do that, he could well have moved on to the next anchorage. I think we just keep an eye on him."

"I suggest you put that in your report. The sooner he's brought in the better."

"I'll write my report ready for the handover before I call it a day."

"Then I'll leave you to get on with it." He placed a hand on Frank's shoulder. "Thanks Frank."

Andy left Frank wondering if it had been the right decision to transfer from Central to the Maritime Unit. Most of the time he loved the work. But he'd taken a slight demotion in rank when he made the sideways shift from detective to sergeant before attaining his position as Police Coastal Master. The work in the Maritime Unit had little call for real detective work and he missed that. But life often came down to trade-offs, and he certainly didn't miss the stress that came with his old work.

*

Frank arrived home to find a note from Margie letting him know she was out with her workmates and would be home late bringing takeaways for their dinner. His head was still spinning with images of the dead girls.

A cold beer was waiting in the fridge, which he opened before settling in on the couch to watch the television news. Other than the election coverage, the news of late was all bad and it was relentless, with the focus on wars in Ukraine and Gaza, seemingly more devastation worldwide from floods, hurricanes, tornadoes and wildfires, and rising crime rates at home. Some positive items would help to balance its negativity. The deceased girls hadn't yet made the news. With plates warming in the oven, he sipped his beer and let the sports news wash over him.

Margie entered the room to find him still stretched out with his feet up on the couch.

"I've brought Indian for dinner, hope that's okay." she said, coming over to peck him on the forehead. "How was your day? It had to have been better than yesterday."

"It wasn't any better. We had to recover a second child from out at Rangitoto. This one had drowned and washed up on the shoreline. She'd been in the water a few days judging by the mess the body was in. The thing is that this girl seems to be related to the boat shed one."

"Do you think there might be a mass murderer out there with a liking for young girls?"

"I doubt it, but it's a bit too early to say what's going on. Poor young Jammie seemed to take it hard, had a good old chuck."

"Maybe you've seen too much in your time and it's hardened you." She twisted her shoulder length brown hair and popped it up into a bun, holding it with a hair tie she had wrapped around her wrist.

"I never get used to seeing corpses, that's for sure." Frank sat up. "And when I think of those poor children, I can't help but imagine what if they were ours? How would I react? How would we cope?"

"Best not think about that. Our kids are safe and sound," said the ever-pragmatic Margie.

"Let's not talk anymore about the case, I'd rather switch off. Tell me about your day." He got up and followed her into the kitchen where he stood watching her take the plates out of the oven. Dressed in her everyday loose-fitting top and tights, she made them look stylish simply by the way she carried herself, even though she was under average height. She had a zest for life and lived it to the full doing everything at pace as if to try and squeeze as much into her day as possible.

"Nothing to report really. Just parent teacher interviews and then a group of us celebrated the end of another round of reports with a drink after work." She began dishing the takeaways onto the hot plates.

"Sounds better than my day." He came around behind her and put his arms around her waist and nuzzled the back of her neck, feeling her relax into him.

"Why Frank Smythe, you're a romantic at heart for all your tough exterior." She pretended to be surprised. "What would the *Deodar* boys think if they saw you now?"

"That would be their problem. Wine?" he asked letting go of her.

"Yes, thanks. Why is it that everyone seems to think that because you're married to a cop you want to hear all the goings on in their families and neighbourhoods. Like who's been burgled, who's cheating on their wife, who's been abused. I get sick of being cornered. Sometimes I just want to hear the good stuff about what's going on in the neighbourhood. Do you know what I mean?"

"In that case you should be thankful you're not married to a funeral director."

"Imagine being continually asked about cadavers when you're out." Margie giggled. "You know, like did Mrs So-and-So really have implants?"

Frank found Margie to be a tonic and despite the day, he was able to relax and simply enjoy her company.

6

Frank was in the lunchroom chatting with the Harbour Master at the start of his shift when Andy found him.

"Morning Frank. I've just come off the phone from Brad Smart at Central and he's requesting a meeting with the two of us at three p.m. this afternoon." Andy went over to the bench and helped himself to a coffee.

"What's it about?" Frank asked, having already guessed the answer.

"He wants you to give the handover of the Rangitoto girls' case."

"No problem. It's one hell of a case—I hope they get to the bottom of it real quick. Whoever is responsible needs to be nailed."

Just at that moment, Frank's phone rang.

"Frank here." He nodded to Andy who left the room with his coffee mug in hand.

"It's Glenda from Forensics. Thought you'd want to know I've scheduled the autopsy of the child found out at Rangitoto yesterday for one p.m. today. Do you want to be present?"

"Not really." He dreaded the mere thought of it, especially given the state of the body when found. "But I will come over."

"This one isn't going to be pleasant. You might want to come in towards the end, say two p.m.?"

"Will do. Thanks."

"Oh and Frank, it may be best to skip lunch."

"I might just take your advice."

"What are you doing out there anyway, Frank? Two dead girls in as many days?"

"Nothing to do with us. We just respond to the callouts."

"Well, let's just hope there aren't any more." Glenda paused. "See you this afternoon."

Frank went to his office, once more disturbed by the prospect of the autopsy yet eager to learn the outcome of Glenda's investigation.

With barely time to warm his seat, he received a callout to escort a prisoner who was a methamphetamine cook from Great Barrier Island back to the city. Situated on the outer limits of the Hauraki Gulf, the island was large and provided protection to the islands and waters of the Gulf from the Pacific Ocean. Sparsely populated and too far to be a commuter island like Waiheke in the inner Gulf, it was a magnet for those who wanted a secluded lifestyle away from the populous. But it also attracted a few who for criminal reasons wanted anonymity.

Dick, Stephen and Jammie were already on board when Frank stepped off the wharf and on to the transom of *Deodar III*. Its twin engines were already warming up. He joined Dick in the wheelhouse and took over the controls while Jammie cast off. The day was cloudy, the sea had a slight swell, and the wind was a pleasant ten knot westerly. In no time they were making their way up the Waitematā Harbour towards the waters of the Hauraki Gulf. Having cleared Bean Rock, Frank opened her throttle and they cruised along at a comfortable 34 knots, gently bouncing on the foils from one swell to the next.

Being mid-week and outside the school holiday period, they encountered only a handful of recreational boats out enjoying the day, which they sped past leaving them to rock gently in their wake. After just an hour and a half *Deodar III* approached Tryphena Harbour at the southern end of Great Barrier Island, its bush clad hills a reminder of why Aucklanders flocked across the gap every summer to holiday in the many bays and harbours surrounding the island. The scenic tracks through lush native bush, abundant fisheries and safe harbours were just a few of the attractions on offer.

Frank recognised the ample figure of Dave Watson in his blue police uniform waiting on the wharf as they quietly cruised towards it. Beside him was an unkempt man wearing handcuffs. Once Jammie had tied the mooring lines, Frank disembarked and shook Dave's hand.

"Good to see you again, Frank." Dave flashed an easy grin that creased his weather-beaten face.

"Dave, always a pleasure. And I understand you've got some special cargo for us?" Frank eyed the handcuffed man who was scrawny with a pock-marked face and unblinking wide eyes—all typical hallmarks of meth addiction.

The man scowled, showing missing teeth.

Dave looked amused. "There's a reception party waiting for him at Central, so you'll have to take extra good care of him for me."

"You can trust us to do just that."

The prisoner was taken on board and cuffed to a rail in the sick bay. After a quick chat with Dave about the state of the policing on Barrier, *Deodar III* threw her mooring lines and cruised back to base.

*

Once again moored alongside the wharf in Mechanics Bay, Frank left the crew to off load the prisoner and hand him over to a constable from Auckland Central while he prepared for his visit to the mortuary.

As he navigated the streets, his spirit sank as if facing his own certain demise and the feeling just wouldn't shift. Knowing it would be hard given the state of the child's body when they recovered her, it took all his inner strength to steel himself.

On arrival, he cleared security and found Glenda, covered from head to foot in disposables, transferring a body from the gurney to the chiller.

"Frank, you've just missed the autopsy. I've finished and was about to write up my notes." Her eyes were bright in the space between her mask and bonnet.

"Can't say I'm sorry about that." The pervading stench was sending his stomach into somersaults.

"Give me a few minutes to clean up and change out of these scrubs, then let's meet in my office where we can go over my findings." She exited the room before Frank had a chance to respond.

Glenda's office was next to the lab. Everything seemed to be clean and orderly. Two computer screens and a keyboard were the only things on her desk; no papers, no folders, no pens, nothing else that hinted of the work done there. In the corner was a filing cabinet with a single photo in a pewter frame showing her together with a man in front of the Eiffel Tower. An air freshener dispenser also sat on top of the cabinet, but it was no match for the prevailing formaldehyde odour. He took a seat and waited.

Glenda breezed into the room, all smiles. Her good humour despite the gruesome task she'd just undertaken wasn't lost on him, causing him to marvel at her resilience. Dressed like the professional she was, her pale green blouse and black slacks with high heels wouldn't have looked out of place in a corporate head office.

"Good Frank, I'm glad you came over. Sorry you missed the show. But I can tell you it wasn't pleasant."

Frank took out his notebook and pen. "I'm happy to hear it first hand, no need for me to see it."

"Let's get straight to the point." Glenda looked at her notes. "This Jane Doe is younger than the last … I would put her at nine years of age. Like the boat shed girl, her ethnicity appears to be Indian or possibly Nepalese, but we will confirm that with a DNA test."

"Could they be sisters?"

"I don't think so, but again a DNA test will confirm that." She put her pen in her mouth and absently chewed the end while studying her notes. "The cause of death was drowning, not secondary drowning like the first girl. I estimate the time of death to be sometime around 72 hours ago, or approximately two days in the water before she was discovered. These times are as good as I can give based on the state of the body, so allow for an error margin of plus or minus six hours at best."

Frank flipped back through his notebook. "You put the first girl's time of death within the same twelve-hour period. Could the two girls have been in the water together?"

"I can't say. There's no evidence to prove that was the case from the autopsy." Glenda looked up at Frank. "That's one for you to work through."

Frank made a note to check the tidal flows.

"The tattoos are almost identical bar some slight differences in the hieroglyphics."

"Interesting, there must be a meaning behind them." Frank frowned as he considered this.

"That would be my conclusion. They seem to be significant and it's clear they link the two girls together."

"Has this child also been the victim of sexual abuse?"

Glenda took her time answering. Her voice trembled as she said in what was barely more than a whisper, "She has suffered considerable sexual abuse in her short life." Glenda chewed her lip and stared down at her notes, as if struggling to keep her emotions under control.

Frank put his notebook and pen down on the desk and took in a deep breath, letting it out slowly. "Those poor girls."

They were silent for a minute.

"What kind of monster does that to children?" Glenda spoke forcefully through clenched teeth.

"The sort that we lock up." Frank's voice was equally firm. "He or they will not get away with this. Trust me Glenda, they'll have the full force of the law to contend with. And when we put them away, it won't be a holiday where they're going to be spending their days rotting. Other prisoners hate child molesters, so they're bound to get a bit of natural justice inside."

"I hope you catch them."

"We will, I promise. Was there anything else?"

"Only that she too was showing signs of being malnourished, just like the boat shed girl. There are a lot of similarities between the two cases. You'll get the full details in my report."

They finished up and Frank drove back to base. Although thankful that he'd missed the autopsy, his mood was far from upbeat as he absorbed the new information.

*

The mystery surrounding the two dead girls and how they both came to be in the vicinity of Rangitoto Island was perplexing. From the autopsy results it appeared that they'd been in the water within a day of each other. The tattoos made it more than a coincidence, meaning it was highly likely that they'd come from the same place.

A series of marine charts were filed away in the filing cabinet and Frank thumbed through them before selecting a large-scale chart showing the approaches to Auckland that included Rangitoto Island. With his computer he opened a file of tide tables on one of his desktop screens and on the other screen he pulled up the localised weather report for the days prior to the boat shed corpse being found that included the size of the swells. He removed his chart plotting paraphernalia from the top drawer of his desk and neatly laid them out on the chart.

The precise movements of the corpses leading up to their discovery would not be easily determined, as there were numerous variables. But if he could only show it was possible they had been together it would help progress the investigation.

With a pencil, he marked the exact locations of where the girls had been found, the time and date when they were discovered and the estimated time of death for each one.

The obvious place to start was with the most recently found corpse, the girl who'd drowned. Making the assumption she'd entered the water at her estimated time of death and only just snagged on the rock at her final resting place around the time she'd been discovered, he began the tedious work of plotting her possible movements. At best it would contain a large degree of error, but it was all he had.

It was a safe assumption that the body had floated with the tides. The channel had strong flood and ebb tidal flow of one to two knots with a tidal vector bearing 170 degrees. Fortunately the windage had been a consistent ten knot westerly over the period and the swells had been minimal. Drag allowance was minor due to her comparatively light weight.

He lightly pencilled in the tidal movements for the period between her time of death and discovery by Sea Cleaners, allowing for windage and drag, working his way backwards hour by hour. His initial results showed the area of water where she could have drowned was north of the Rangitoto Channel but with such broad assumptions it was impossible to pinpoint the exact locality.

Ripping the top sheet off the pad he'd been scribbling on, he scrunched it up and threw it at the bin. He went over to the window and stared out at Rangitoto. If she'd been snagged on that rock for a period of six hours, then the whole scenario changed dramatically showing she could have come from somewhere up the Waitematā Harbour. And neither of those scenarios tied her to Islington Bay where the boat shed was located or to Jerry Ramsley on *Nellie* and his alleged movements. The scenarios were so complex and the assumptions so wide, there just wasn't enough to go by to reach a satisfactory outcome. The Search and Rescue computer modelling programme would handle the scenarios better than his old-fashioned approach, and he made a mental note to ask someone more computer savvy than himself to put it through the models.

Following a quick check of the time, he cleared his desk and grabbed the case file before rushing off to find Andy.

*

Detective Inspector Brad Smart was waiting for them when Andy and Frank entered his office at Auckland Central. He immediately got to his feet and came around his desk to greet them, towering over both Frank and Andy.

"Andy, Frank, glad you could both make it." He shook each of them by the hand.

"Hope I'm not too late for the party." The familiar voice brought a smile to his face as Frank turned to see Anahera enter the room, grinning like the Cheshire Cat. Dressed in a navy shirt and slacks and carrying a notebook, she had a relaxed air about her.

"No, we've yet to make a start." Brad grinned back at her in his good-humoured way. "Come on in. You of course know Andy and Frank."

"I sure do. When did we first work together, Frank?" She smoothed her short straight brown hair back from her face.

"Must be at least ten years ago now. As I remember, you were just a fresh-faced detective when I was chosen to be your gnarly old partner who'd been around the block a few times."

"I was pretty green back then, but you showed me the ropes." Her smile caused the dimple in her left cheek to become more prominent. "And for that I owe you."

Once the pleasantries had been concluded and refreshments ordered from Brad's assistant, they took their seats around the coffee table in the corner of the room.

Brad cleared his throat. "I've asked you all here to go over the case of the two girls who were found dead on Rangitoto Island. Such a terrible tragedy." He ran his hand over his crew cut fair hair and leaned back in his seat. "Frank, how about you bring us all up to speed?"

"Sure." Frank opened the folder he'd brought and carefully laid out several photos of the deceased on the desk before opening his notebook. "The body of a young Asian girl aged twelve was found in an abandoned boat shed on Rangitoto Island two days ago by two day-visitors to the island. Their stories checked out and we're confident they were not otherwise involved. The autopsy showed she'd died of secondary drowning. Time of death is estimated to be between 18 hundred hours and midnight the prior evening. She had bloody scrapes, bruises and swelling to the limbs and torso consistent with crawling or being dragged over the rocks and there were spots of blood on the ground from the water's edge to the shed. She appeared under-nourished. Two things of particular interest. The first is that she'd sustained significant sexual abuse over a prolonged time. The second is that she had a tattoo of an eye with some sort of hieroglyphics in it on her wrist. We interviewed those at anchor in the Bay and no one claimed to have seen or heard anything. However one individual did act somewhat suspiciously, one Jerry Ramsley, and we've been keeping a watch on him."

"Any clue as to where she'd come from? Clothing?"

The door opened and coffees arrived. Frank waited until it was once more just the four of them. "No. The only way to get onto the island is by ferry, boat, helicopter or vehicle driven across the causeway from Motutapu Island." Frank shook his head. "I've ruled out the ferry, helicopter would have made a commotion and alerted all the boats in the bay to its activity and we've no sightings of one. As you know there are only a handful of residents on Motutapu and I believe they're unlikely candidates, but they still need to be ruled out. However, the most likely option is via boat—unless of course she swam there."

"You say Asian. Any idea what part?" Anahera's look was intense with large brown eyes that were free of makeup.

"Indian, possibly Nepalese. DNA tests are being carried out." Frank drew a breath. "She appeared to be wearing pyjamas made of a plain silk material, and not patterned as most Kiwi children usually wear."

"Interesting, sounds like something foreign children might wear." Anahera said it more as a statement than a question. "What about fingerprints on the shed?"

"They were unable to get any clear prints according to the Forensics' report. Then yesterday a second corpse turned up." Frank looked down at his notes. "Sea Cleaners were doing a routine clean up on the western shore of Rangitoto when they discovered the body of a girl, thought to be aged nine years of age, also Indian or Nepalese, also showing signs of significant sexual abuse, also with the same or similar tattoo, also dressed in what looked like pyjamas, and undernourished. The autopsy showed she'd drowned."

"Time of death?" Brad asked.

"Thought to be in the water 48 hours plus or minus six hours."

"Within a day of the boat shed Jane Doe. Could they have been in the water together?" Brad sipped his coffee while looking intently at Frank.

"The location they were found in suggests otherwise, although until we know more it can't be ruled out at this stage. And we don't know how Jane Doe One came to be in the boat shed."

"And do you think this suspicious character in the bay was involved?" Brad asked.

"Again, it's too early to say. He's a bit of a vagrant, lives aboard. Could just be he doesn't like the police—he does have some form for minor offenses."

Brad turned to Andy. "I'm sure I don't need to tell you to have your boys keep a close eye on him. In fact, it might be best to pull him in for questioning before he takes off."

"You needn't worry, we're onto it." Andy sounded defensive.

Slightly amused at the hint of a turf war, Frank added, "Last time we checked he was still in the same anchorage. I've alerted all ports of exit, and he's not rigged out to go beyond the coastal waters. His vessel is only capable of five knots at most, so he won't get far."

"Good." Brad sat back in his chair. "Any idea where the deceased girls came from? Have they been reported missing?"

"I looked up the missing person register and there've been no Asian minors reported missing in recent days," Anahera answered.

"They must have come from somewhere—bodies don't just appear out of fresh air." Brad's tone was verging on cynical.

The room was silent.

"Not your fault of course. What about the tattoos? Any progress regarding their significance?" Brad asked.

"Not as yet—several ideas but nothing concrete."

"Okay, thanks Frank." Brad looked pensive. Then clearing his throat, he said, "The reason I asked you all to come today is to set up a team to work this case. There is enough in common between the two dead girls that I think it's fair to conclude we are dealing with a crime involving both girls. Anahera, with your experience working as a detective and in Land Search and Rescue, I want to assign you to this case."

"I'm in." Anahera sat forward in her chair.

Frank looked at Anahera and nodded encouragingly.

"Andy, can you spare Frank to work the case alongside Anahera? They've a good track record working as partners in the past and I think Frank's knowledge of the maritime side would be invaluable in this case." Brad looked at Andy.

Andy looked from Brad to Frank and spoke directly to him. "What do you say, Frank?"

Surprised by a sudden surge of adrenaline, Frank answered, "I'm definitely keen to work on this one—I want to see justice done for those poor girls."

Andy looked back at Brad. "We've a full complement of staff in the Unit at present, so we could spare Frank and have him seconded back to Central. I'm guessing that's the best way to run the investigation."

"That's settled then. I'll make an office available and whatever resources you need. I want to see this one wrapped up before we find any more bodies." He stood up, indicating the meeting was over. "One more thing, the media are going to be all over this, and they will probe for new angles and any hint of news to keep it live for some time. We need results."

The message was clear and didn't require a response. Frank quickly finished his drink in a single gulp and followed Andy and Anahera to the door.

Standing outside Brad's office, the three of them were talking when Anahera's phone rang.

She answered it immediately. "Kia ora."

A pause.

"Yes, I'm his Mum. What's up?"

Frank watched as her face clouded over.

"Are you sure?"

She shook her head in disbelief.

"Okay. I can come in ... Yeah ... Okay, see you then." She hung up and held onto the phone, staring at it.

"Is everything okay? You look like you've had a shock," Frank said.

"It's Rangi. I've got to go to a parent meeting over at the school."

"Is he okay?"

"He's gotten himself into some trouble—I'll know more after the meeting." She crossed her arms. "It's just so unlike him ... there must be a mistake, he's always so good."

"Quite likely just a mix up then." Andy smiled reassuringly.

"Bound to be," Frank agreed. "You know your Rangi—he's never been any trouble. When you look at what some parents have to deal with, I reckon you and Jim have had an easy ride. And it's all credit to the two of you."

"All the same, this is new territory. It's the first time I've been called into the school for a meeting with the Principal." She chewed her lip.

"Best you get going then. I'll see you in the morning. I'm looking forward to cracking this case, and the sooner the better before the body count rises," Frank said by way of a goodbye.

They parted company with Andy and Frank returning to the Maritime Unit's base in Mechanics Bay.

7

Anahera hurried back to her desk. Thoughts of the new case were pushed to the back of her mind as she grappled with the news from the school. The Principal had said hardcore pornography was involved, but it was hard to get her head around it as she hadn't seen any signs that Rangi was even remotely interested in girls let alone porn. He seemed so young and innocent and from an early age he'd always been compliant. Being a school representative in sport had meant so much to him that she couldn't believe he'd jeopardise it. As both a policewoman and a mum she'd always prided herself on being especially aware of what her boys were up to, her work arming her with insights over and above those of most parents. There must be some mistake. She decided to call Jim.

Jim answered her call. "What's up?"

"Did you hear from the school?"

"Which school? Why?"

"Oh, I thought you would have." She paused. "It's Rangi. He and some mates were allegedly caught with some porn. I find it hard to believe. The school Principal called and asked me to come in for a meeting with him and Rangi. I don't know all the details but am afraid he might be stood down. I'm just about to leave—can you meet me there?"

"Too right I will. If he's guilty he'll get what's coming to him." Jim's anger resonated through the phone.

They agreed to meet outside the school and Anahera grabbed her bag and made a mad dash to her car. It pained her to be dragged into what she imagined would be a school disciplinary meeting, so much so that she put her foot down and sped through town—something she usually took care not to do. Being a cop meant she should set a good example. When she arrived at the school, she recognised Jim's white utility parked outside and she pulled up behind it. Jim climbed out and she could see he was bristling.

"He's going to be grounded—it'll hurt when he can't play for his volleyball team." He pursed his lips.

"Jim, let's just hear what they have to say. Remember you're innocent until proven guilty." She tried to make her voice sound calm even though she too was seething.

They walked into the reception and were shown to the principal's office where they found Rangi, his shoulders slumped, sitting outside. As they approached he looked up and on seeing both his parents tears sprang to his eyes which he quickly wiped away with the back of his hand.

"Rangi, what's all this about?" Jim asked.

Before he could answer the door opened and Neville Harris, the Year Ten Dean and Rangi's volleyball coach, emerged. He was an athletic man in his mid-forties who devoted a lot of his personal time to training teams in volleyball and rugby and to his credit he'd turned the school into one with a reputation for its sporting success, up there with the private schools who could boast greater resources and long sporting histories. He was popular with the pupils, having long since earned their respect as a good teacher and fair-minded dean. His was the gym where the cool kids liked to hang out and Rangi worshipped him. But today he didn't look at his coach, instead he sat in sullen silence with his head hung low.

"Thanks for coming in, it's good you could both make it in at such short notice."

They shook hands with Neville before being ushered into the office.

The principal's office was large with dark mahogany panelling and high windows that let in natural light. An oversized wooden desk with green leather inset on top sat in front of a high-backed leather chair. A series of frames exhibiting both diplomas and class photographs were hung on one wall and on another was a bookcase with a lot of weighty looking tomes and some trophies. Its austere decor would be intimidating to even the toughest of teenagers and Anahera guessed it might be the reason why it hadn't been modernised.

Tom Flinnagan, the Principal, who resembled a bulldog with a flattish face and slightly flared nostrils, was waiting for them inside. He offered them seats at a low table in the corner of the room. Anahera and Jim took a seat with Rangi between them as if offering him their protection.

Tom loosened his tie and cleared his throat. "Thanks for coming in and I apologise for not being able to give you more warning. It pains me to have to host this meeting, but we do not and will not tolerate this sort of behaviour in our school." He looked at his dean. "Neville will spell out the details that have led to this meeting."

"I'm sorry to have to be the one to report Rangi was using a phone during maths class and not paying attention. That in itself breaks a school rule. Brian Oates, his maths teacher, caught him scrolling through pornographic images and videos—many were of teenage girls. I have confiscated the phone. When asked he claimed he was sent the pictures by one of his friends. We look very dimly on behaviour of this sort."

Tom cut in. "What do you have to say, boy?"

Rangi hung his head. "Nothing."

"So you are guilty of possessing pornography at school?"

"Yes, Sir," Rangi mumbled.

"Speak up boy."

Rangi lifted his head, his eyes now defiant, and answered, "Yes, Sir."

Anahera cringed at his attitude.

"Where did you get it?"

"I can't say, Sir."

"What do you mean you can't say?"

"I can't say."

"Can't or won't say?" Tom shot back.

"C-c-won't say," he mumbled.

"Do you understand there will be consequences for this?"

"Yes, Sir." Rangi scowled.

Stunned, Anahera watched her usually enthusiastic and articulate son show the sullen traits often associated with other boys his age.

"Would you please leave us? Sit outside the door while I speak with your parents."

Without another word Rangi slunk out of the room, looking less staunch now.

Anahera caught a look from Jim and could see he was struggling to keep the lid on his anger. She too was finding it hard to sit and listen to the recriminations, as though she'd been the guilty one. It just didn't fit. She was used to coming to the school and receiving glowing reports of academic and sporting prowess leaving her filled to the brim with motherly pride. But not this. This was alien territory.

When the door closed, Tom looked at Anahera. "Rangi has always been a good student—his teachers tell me he works well, does his homework, and has good attendance. I can tell you he's generally well behaved. And he's an asset to the volleyball team as you'll be aware—I'm told he's never missed a training. This episode seems out of character for him. And I am mindful that there are other boys involved, including his friend Stephen who we believe to be the one who obtained the material and circulated it to the group of boys."

Anahera had been holding her breath which she now released slowly as she stole a glance at Jim who was staring at Tom, his face set in a stern grimace.

"But." Tom emphasised the word. "But pornography is a problem not to be tolerated. Of late the school has been dealing with a run of cases where boys have been found in possession of indecent material and it's a trend that we want to nip in the bud so to speak. The board has been made aware and are fully supportive of our response to clamp down. I'm sure I don't need to tell you that access to pornography is all too easy with the use of smart phones and the internet. A recent study showed that 75 percent of boys have viewed porn by the time they are 17 years old with 25 percent watching it regularly. You will also be aware that it can affect relationships and lead to deviant sexual behaviour." He paused his monologue to draw breath.

Feeling decidedly uncomfortable, Anahera was reminded of her own time in the principal's office for skipping classes.

"We don't believe Rangi has been involved in creating porn, although the subjects were teenage girls. But pornography is a scourge that we want stopped in this school and we are taking this offence very seriously."

Anahera felt she was melting under his gaze. Her cheeks burned with the shame of her son's misdemeanour.

Neville took over. "Rangi is a good kid, loyal to his friends as you saw from his reactions. A fitting punishment could be to stand him down from the volleyball team, but we are heading into the regional champs and he's one of our star players. If he can stay out of trouble and keep up his training and schoolwork, he stands a good chance of attaining a scholarship to one of the American colleges. That's an opportunity not many get."

Anahera looked at Jim who was looking decidedly more relaxed.

"We have considered standing him down." Tom paused. "But given his good record to date, I propose we give him detention and a warning. We strongly suggest you agree to have him see the school counsellor to gain an understanding of the issues surrounding porn—it certainly won't do him any harm."

"Thank you." Anahera breathed it out. "Of course we'd be happy for him to have counselling."

"We appreciate your leniency and want you to know that we will not be tolerating this behaviour at home." Jim looked at Anahera who nodded in agreement. "There will be consequences."

"Here, this belongs to Rangi." Neville held a mobile phone out to Anahera who slipped it in her bag.

Rangi was called back into the room and as he hung his head, he was given the news, and the meeting was concluded.

*

Anahera and Jim were waiting in the kitchen for Rangi when he came in after riding his bike home. They'd sent Piri to his room to do his homework.

Jim waded straight in, his face dark. "Who gave you the porn?"

"I don't want to say."

"It will go better for you if we have some open and honest discussion. Now I'm going to ask you again. Where did you get it?"

"Stephen."

"Why didn't you tell Mr Flinnagan?"

"I don't rat on my friends."

Anahera looked at her son and for the first time saw him as the teenager he'd become and not the child he'd always been.

"How long have you been accessing porn?" she asked.

"It's my first time."

She studied him carefully, unsure whether to believe him.

"Well, let it be your last!" Jim barked.

Rangi looked at him defiantly. "It was only a few dumb pictures! What's the big deal?"

Anahera stepped in before the situation became explosive. "Rangi, pornography is not a healthy option."

"Whatever!"

Bristling, she carried on. "Perhaps you're still too young to appreciate how pornography can become a habit and gives a warped view of sexual relationships. It could affect your future ability to love someone intimately."

"Yeah, yeah!" Rangi turned to walk away.

Her anger raged like a volcano as she grasped this new sullenness, while images of the deceased girls flashed through her mind. "Just a minute young man. Have you considered the subjects of the porn? These girls are all victims. Victims, Rangi. Sometimes they are forced into it and it can have a lasting impact on their lives. I see it at work. By partaking in it, you're promoting the activity. What if it was one of your cousins and lecherous boys were ogling her? How would you feel?" She now had his full attention. "Would that be okay?"

"No."

"Well think of each one as somebody's sister or cousin."

He suddenly looked unsure of himself.

"Rangi, you need to exercise your maturity and say no to porn. Don't be a sheep and follow your friends. Always stand up for what is right." Jim softened his gaze. "If you want to talk, you can always come to me. It's natural to be curious but there're right ways and wrong ways to deal with it. Talk to me—don't forget I was once a young man."

Rangi looked his father in the eye. "You and Mum are always busy."

"Don't give us that. One of us always makes your games. Are you aware the school considered standing you down from volleyball team?"

"They wouldn't!"

"They would and they could if you're caught again," Jim answered sharply. "Did you also know that Mr Harris thinks you stand a chance at getting a scholarship to the States if you keep working hard?"

Rangi's eyes opened wide. "Really?"

"But if you are stood down for porn it will go on your record, and you can kiss goodbye to any scholarship."

"I didn't know."

"Alright," Jim acknowledged. "Your Mum and I need to decide what the punishment will be. But first, what do you think it should be?"

"I don't know," Rangi mumbled. "I guess you could take my phone off me?"

"Interesting thought. Go and do your homework while we discuss it," Jim said.

After Rangi left, Jim poured two glasses of wine and handed one to Anahera.

"What do you think?" he asked, coming to sit next to her on a barstool at the breakfast bar.

"I think he makes a good point: confiscating his phone would be good punishment. I say we take it for four weeks."

"That'll hurt, but it's a fitting punishment given the circumstances."

"When did he become interested in girls? I thought he still considered them a waste of time. He's growing up, Jim. It seems to have snuck up on us."

"I know what you mean."

She toyed with her glass, turning it in her hand. "This is all I need at present. Did I tell you I've been given a new case? Frank and I are to team up on the one with the two girls that drowned out at Rangitoto. There are similarities that link the girls, including the fact that both suffered horrific sexual abuse. I'd only just gotten out of the meeting about it when I took the call from the school."

"That was bad timing—sorry you've had to deal with this today." His eyes were full of concern.

"Pornography is just the beginning—it's like opening the manhole cover to the sewer. Where to from here? And think of the models, they are the victims."

"Let's not get it out of perspective. Most boys dabble in it at some stage. You heard the statistics—75 percent by the time they're 17, but only 25 percent turn it into a habit. It's part of them satisfying their curiosity about sex. The main thing is to see it doesn't develop into a habit."

"That doesn't make it right."

"I'm not saying it is. You know I hate it as much as you do. The fact that people are making a truckload of money out of it is just plain wrong."

"You're right. They're the real villains." Anahera took a sip of wine and let it linger on her palette. "How do we control it to ensure it doesn't become a habit for Rangi?"

"I honestly don't know. He cares a lot about his sport and that may be the deterrent he needs."

"Access is way too easy."

"Not having his phone for a while will help."

"Don't be naïve, you know internet access is everywhere," she snapped, before drawing in a deep breath. "Sorry Jim, just feeling the heat."

"You're right, access is easy. We're just going to have to trust him."

"There is software that screens out porn—maybe we could think about that when he gets his phone back."

They lapsed into silence.

"It was such a shock to be called in there today." She ran a hand through her hair.

He reached over and put his hand on her shoulder. "We'll get through this. It's just a bump in the road. He's not a bad kid—you know that."

"I didn't like his attitude in front of Tom Flinnagan. I thought him insolent." She frowned. "Have we done something wrong?"

"I don't think so. He's just being a fairly typical adolescent teenager, feeling his way and dealing with surges of testosterone."

"Let's not normalise porn, Jim. It's not okay." She sounded annoyed.

"I didn't mean I condone it. You should know that."

"Sorry Jim, but I just hate the thought that our son is part of the problem by helping to create the demand for that stuff." She slowly sipped her drink. "Do we need to change what we're doing?"

"Maybe." He looked at her thoughtfully. "Perhaps I need to give him more of my time, one on one. Perhaps take him out for a dad adventure? I haven't done that for a long time."

"He'd love that."

As Jim went off to find Rangi and break the news about the phone ban, Anahera prepared the vegetables for dinner, finding cold comfort in the rapid action of the knife on the chopping board.

8

The following morning Anahera trudged up the stairs to her new office, caught in a maelstrom of emotions. The incident with Rangi was a shock and she'd not slept well between her concern for him and the images of the dead girls that had filled her head.

Young, vulnerable, defenceless girls. Men could be such monsters, and she didn't want to be guilty of raising another one. That her own son had been caught with porn, the subjects of which were minors, was appalling. Now Rangi had taken the first step in what could be a very slippery slope and rarely had she felt this angry.

Time and again children were the subject of abuse. Her spare hand made a fist that she would gladly use if it meant saving one child from violence. What could possibly lead to the depravity that caused one human, usually with more strength and more power, to abuse another who lacked the ability to effectively fight back. She'd seen it too often in the Force. Children harmed by the very hands that should nurture them. Children being treated as chattels. Children hung out to dry by family who should be protecting them. The world was so unfair.

It wasn't surprising when one of these children lashed out at the world and got themselves in trouble. But Rangi? He didn't fit this profile—she and Jim had made sure of that. He had no excuse for bad behaviour.

Yes, she'd gladly taken the case—how could she not. Together with Frank, they'd track down the people who'd done this. It would be her mission to see justice done for these girls. She sucked in her cheeks as she considered this. Someone had to care enough about them to see their lives weren't lost in vain—that through their deaths others might be saved.

The thing she liked most about her work was that she was in the business of saving lives. Recognising the familiar strategy brought a slight smile to her lips. Maintaining a focus on the positive outcomes had helped her cope with the evil she'd encountered virtually daily throughout her career.

Working this case with Frank would be satisfying. He was a good detective with instincts she could trust, and he could be relied on to have her back. Theirs was an easy-going relationship. Both worked hard but with good humour and mutual respect.

And he didn't cuss like so many of their workmates, a trait they shared. Her cheeks warmed with a flush as she recalled the slap her mother had given her when she'd come home from school feeling especially grown up as she tried out some of the new words she'd learnt. Her mother had said, "None of that rubbish round here my girl. Have some self-respect—and show some for your tikanga." Anahera had gone on to drill that same message into her own boys.

When working cases involving children, her maternal instinct never failed to kick in, almost always making them personal. Raising her own kids, Rangi and Piri, was her most important job—which was why she felt so deeply betrayed by Rangi. Ever since they were born there was nothing, short of murder, that she wouldn't do to keep them safe. Even if it meant laying down her own life for them if that was what it took to protect them.

Finding missing children and reuniting them with family was incredibly rewarding when working in the Land Search and Rescue Unit. Most of the time. Except when they went home to a place where Anahera instinctively felt they weren't safe. And often that would be in the hands of a father, brother, uncle, stepfather or mother's partner, and less common were those cases where the mother or some female figure was doing the abusing.

Most of all she abhorred the cases of sexual abuse, and especially those involving young children. Almost certainly they'd be scarred for life. No matter how much counselling and rehabilitation they received the memories would always be with them, affecting all their relationships. The offenders deserved nothing less than castration, but luckily for them she wasn't the law maker.

Rangi. Was she overreacting? Jim was probably right when he said that most boys looked at porn at some stage. As much as she hated to admit it, porn was almost a rite of passage into adulthood. The good kid was still inside Rangi and he did care about his sport. She had to believe it wasn't too late to stop it from escalating. And she couldn't let it affect her work.

She opened the door to the room that had been allocated to her and Frank for the duration of the case. They'd used this room before and it hadn't grown any more spacious. It could have been a janitor's cupboard with just enough room for two desks, corresponding office chairs and the all-important whiteboard. She placed her bag under one of the desks and went to find a coffee.

*

Frank called into the Maritime Unit to collect the few personal items from his desk. He found the crew in the locker room and shared with them the news of his secondment. Following some good-humoured ribbing insinuating he had swapped the Unit for a cushy number off the water, he left the Maritime Police base in Mechanics Bay and drove over to Auckland Central.

His new temporary office was on the first floor. Cursing his bad knee and lack of fitness, he traipsed up the steps and arrived at the office out of breath.

Anahera, who was already at her desk setting up her computer, turned and on seeing him, flashed her teeth in a wide grin. "What sort of time do you call this? It's not slackers' hours here like at the Maritime Unit you know. You're back in the real world now."

He laughed. "Can I get you a coffee?"

"No, I've had mine already. Feel free though."

Frank left her and minutes later was back with a mug of steaming caffeine infused drink. "Now to business. Shall we go over what we know again?"

"How about we get our workstations set up before we look at the workflow?"

"Good idea." He dropped the bag he was carrying and removed his jacket. "How did it go at the school yesterday? Was Rangi all right?"

Anahera appeared to freeze. "Yes, no, I don't know."

"Is everything okay?"

"He was caught looking at pornographic material." Anahera added, "The subjects were only teenagers."

"Oh, sorry to hear that. It's out of character, isn't it?"

"Sure is. He says it's the first time." She straightened up and ran her fingers through her hair. "The school was really good about it and he knows he's on thin ice. I just hope the message really sank in."

"He'll be fine, you'll see."

It took time to set things up just the way they each liked to work and to source the stationery they needed. After a while Frank took the lead by going over to the whiteboard where he picked up a blue pen and wrote *Boat Shed Jane Doe* on one side and *Jane Doe Two* on the other.

"Let's start by how Boat Shed Jane Doe might have got there." He wrote down *How* and drew a line out to it.

Anahera had pivoted in her chair to watch Frank at the board. "Okay. So, you've already ruled out the ferry?"

"Yes, I've been through the CCTV footage for the days leading up to her discovery and there was no sign of the victim. We can easily eliminate a helicopter and vehicles from Motutapu Island—I can check those. That leaves private vessels, and of the boats visited immediately after the body was found, the only suspicious person was Jerry Ramsley on his yacht *Nellie*."

"Could she have swum out there?"

"Highly unlikely. It's a long way from the nearest point on the mainland." He wrote the various means of access to Rangitoto on the board, then crossed out the ferry.

"Okay. What about this Jerry Ramsley guy, what made you think he was suspicious?"

"He appeared to be hiding something, and he made it clear he didn't like being visited by us. His answers to our questions were evasive and it felt like drawing blood out of a stone. And he has form for petty theft and marijuana."

"But not sexual related offending or kidnapping?"

Frank shook his head.

"Did you look inside his boat? Do we know there are no more girls there?"

"Yes I did, and no there weren't."

"And no signs girls may have been on board?"

"Not that I could see. It's small and the inside of the saloon was a mess. I could get Forensics to go over it, but we've nothing that suggests he was involved apart from a feeling." Frank checked his notes. "I talked to Larry Cook, the Senior Constable in Coromandel and he's unaware of Jerry having any associations with an Asian girl. He's going to do some digging for us."

"I think we should bring him in for questioning, and the sooner the better. What about other boats? Could there've been another boat in the bay that'd left by the time you got there?" Anahera asked.

"Good point. I did ask the boaties we talked to if they'd seen any other boats in the bay, but no one could recall any. The thing is when you're anchored in a bay, you're not close to the next boat like in a caravan park. It's easy to simply not notice other boats—and they tend to come and go all the time."

"Secondary drowning means she'd been in the water and had taken water into her lungs. Can we assume she was alive on arrival in the boat shed? If someone wanted to dispose of her from a boat, why would she have been in the water? Why nearly drown?"

"Perhaps we're thinking too narrowly. What if she was already dead when she was put in the boat shed? What if someone put her there to dispose of the body?"

"Feasible. But that doesn't explain the second girl's body being washed up. And if the boat shed girl's body was hidden there, why secondary drowning?" Anahera asked.

"Maybe it's more innocent—accidental. What say she nearly drowned trying to swim, after all, many people can't swim, especially new immigrants. And she succumbed to secondary drowning after being rescued and whoever she was with panicked and tried to dispose of her in the boat house."

"Okay, I could buy that." Anahera spoke slowly. "But that would suggest she was with someone who didn't want to be linked to her."

"True. If it was kosher you'd think they would have reported a drowning." Frank played with the pen. "And then there's the sexual abuse. If the person was guilty of inflicting that on her then they could well want to distance themselves from her."

"That brings us back to your man Jerry Ramsley." Anahera tucked a lock of wayward hair behind her ear. "Do you think he could be a deviant?"

"Possible. He's our only person of interest at this stage. I'll arrange for the boys on *Deodar III* to bring him in." Frank wrote the name on the board.

"What about the second girl? How did she turn up where she did?"

"Given she drowned, we know she was in the water at the time of death and at the time of discovery she'd been in the water for two days."

"So where could she have come from?"

"I've looked at that. I tried to plot her potential course given tidal flows, windage, drag and swell conditions going backwards from where and when she was found. But there are so many variables and assumptions that at best it's a very broad-brush approach."

Anahera laughed. "Don't tell me you did it by hand on a chart?"

"Nothing wrong with that." He feigned being hurt by the remark. "Good old-fashioned navigation got Aotearoa New Zealand discovered."

"And look at what good that did. But let's not go there."

He laughed and then became immediately serious. "Jane Doe Two was snagged on a rock when found, and we don't know how long she'd been caught there. That puts her entry into the water anywhere from the shipping channel north of Rangitoto to the Waitematā Harbour."

"Could Jerry Ramsley have been in either of those places before anchoring in Islington Bay?"

"Not according to him, but it's not impossible." Frank paused. "The trouble is if the tide was opposite when she got snagged, that is if she'd been on that rock for longer, then she could've come from Devonport, the Viaduct, Westhaven marina, the port, our base at Mechanics Bay, and anywhere in between—we couldn't rule out her having drowned anywhere along that stretch of waterfront. It's impossible to say where exactly. All the same, and to satisfy myself, I'll get it run through a maritime search and rescue computer model."

Anahera frowned and played with her pen. "Let's consider how the girls might be linked."

"The tattoo is a good place to start. What does an eye signify?"

Anahera tapped some keys on her keyboard while Frank wrote *Tattoo* on the board.

Leaning into her screen, she said, "Let's see ... sight or vision, watchfulness, higher power, all-seeing, all-knowing, evil eye, protection, health, good fortune, enlightenment, just to name a few."

"Whoa, slow down! I can't write that fast."

"Here're some more ... light, perception, clairvoyance, a gateway to the soul." She sighed. "Not surprisingly it's been used through the ages and in many different cultures to symbolise different things. It's endless. I think we need to find an expert who can shed some light on it. No pun intended."

"Someone at the university?"

"Yes. I'm happy to track down someone in the anthropology department and see where it gets us. They should also be able to put me onto a hieroglyphist who could identify the markings inside the eyes."

"Wow, so who went to the right school? A hieroglyphist? Where did you dredge that one up from?" He laughed loudly.

Anahera rolled her eyes and grinned at him "I bet you can't spell it. But seriously, why would anyone tattoo young girls' wrists?"

"Gang insignia?"

"Possibly, I haven't seen it before though." Anahera googled gang insignia New Zealand, but nothing came up that even remotely resembled the tattoos.

"It could mean ownership, like claiming possession of an object."

"That was what I was thinking. A brand, like Maximus in Gladiator." She smiled, increasing the crease of her dimple. "I loved that film—Russell Crowe was awesome!"

"Trust you." Frank laughed heartily. It was so good to be working with Anahera again. "Or maybe it's a spiritual thing, like wearing a cross. A belonging to an ethnic group or religion."

"Perhaps a family insignia, like a crest."

"That concept is quite feasible. It would be like tattooing Rangi and Piri to show their whakapapa."

"That's not a bad thing, at least not in our culture. I think the chat with the anthropologist should help us understand its meaning." She turned back to her screen. "How about we make a start. What say I tackle the eye and track down an anthropologist while you check out those other possible transport modes for the boat shed girl. You could also check in with the residents on Motutapu Island. Maybe they spotted something that's significant in the bay around the time of death for the boat shed girl."

"I'm good with that. I'll also arrange to bring Jerry Ramsley in for questioning."

"And I'll check the missing persons' register again." She looked Frank in the eye. "Let's get going. The sooner we crack this, the sooner whoever's responsible is locked away and prevented from doing it to any other victims."

"I'm with you on that."

Frank sat down at his desk and called the base. *Deodar III* was out on a call, so he arranged to meet them at Mechanics Bay later that morning. Rather than bring Jerry Ramsley into the city, they'd question him on board *Deodar III*.

While he waited, he called Air Traffic Management, the air navigation service provider who were responsible for managing the air space around Auckland. As expected, no logged helicopters were operating in the vicinity of Rangitoto Island during the period between the time of death of the boat shed Jane Doe and the time she was discovered, nor the 24-hour period prior to her estimated time of death.

Frank looked across at Anahera, whose desk was positioned adjacent to his own to maximise the space in the small office. She was intent on her screen, her head tilted forward and every now and then making a rapid burst of taps on her keyboard.

"As I thought, we can rule out the boat shed girl being taken out to the island by helicopter," he said.

Anahera looked up at him. "Mm-hmm."

"How are you getting on?"

"Nothing yet. Just scrolling through information on illustrated eyes."

"I'll contact the residents on Motutapu so we can eliminate them. There's only a small handful living out there and most of them are Department of Conservation workers."

"I thought it was farmed."

"It is. Most of it is a recreational reserve that's run as a farm. And there's a camp there for school trips and kids' holiday camps. A lot of planting of native trees has gone on out there in a partnership between government and Māori, and it's now a pest-free island. The populations of native birds, including endangered ones, are increasing, making it an important conservation asset and a real success story—hence the presence of Department of Conservation staff."

"Mm-hmm." Her eyes had already drifted back to her screen.

Frank busied himself finding contact numbers for the Motutapu residents. A short time later he'd spoken to them all and as expected they were unable to assist with his enquiries—no one had seen or heard anything. And all, without exception, were able to account for their time over the period in question.

That left transport to the island by private vessel. He looked up at the whiteboard and stared at the name Jerry Ramsley. While still early in the investigation, he was their only person of interest, the basis of which was flimsy: strange behaviour and in the right place at the right time. Their only hope was that something would come out of a formal interview—it might just rattle him enough to make him say something to incriminate himself. The sooner they interviewed him the better, before the trail grew cold.

Beside him Anahera continued to be absorbed in her research.

With so few leads, he flicked back through the notebook to his handwritten scrawl of the interviews with the boaties in Islington Bay on the day the boat shed body was found, hoping he might find something he'd overlooked. But there was nothing. In need of a break and a boost, he left the office in search of coffee-to-go from a café down the street.

*

So engrossed in her google search, Anahera was only vaguely aware Frank had left the room. Endless databases contained a multitude of eye images. Of most interest were tattoo sites. If she could find the same stylised version it might lead them to the artist. And if they found the artist who'd tattooed the girls, it might just lead them to their family members or guardians. There can't be too many young girls getting a tattoo, so a tattooist should be able to recall them and the circumstances around them being there.

A mug of hot drink was thrust in front of her, and she looked up to see Frank holding it out to her.

"Kia ora Frank, you're a life saver. Thanks."

"I thought you might need it." Peering over her shoulder, he asked, "Any luck?"

"Not as yet. You wouldn't believe how many artistic impressions there are of an eye. Or how many tattooists operate around the greater Auckland area."

"I had a brief look myself but gave up fairly quickly. I didn't have the time then to do what you're doing now. You deserve the coffee."

"If it's a coffee when I haven't got anything positive to report, what'll it be when I do?" she said with a wry smile. "My shout next time."

"I'll hold you to that." He sat down at his desk. "I've arranged to go out to Rangitoto and interview Jerry Ramsley. We leave in an hour's time. Do you want to come? I thought we could conduct it on board *Deodar*."

"Definitely. And it would be good to see his boat—it might help to get an overall impression of the guy."

"That's what I thought. And I knew you wouldn't turn down the opportunity to joyride aboard *Deodar III*."

"Not when you chose her as your partner over me." She tried to look hurt.

"No contest. She'd be hard to beat even for you—powerful, reliable, hardworking, and never questions her orders—I couldn't ask for more." He laughed.

"Not much of a contest then." She laughed with him, relieved to have a break after her time digging. "Well, I can't wait to meet this Jerry Ramsley. He sounds like a real charmer. Let's hope we can make some progress there. Meanwhile, I'll make an appointment for tomorrow to see an anthropologist. The eye means many different things to different cultures, so talking to an expert should speed things up."

She picked up her phone to search for the contact details of the Anthropology Department at the University of Auckland. It was only then she realised she hadn't thought of Rangi all morning.

9

Deodar III was waiting for them when Frank and Anahera arrived in Mechanics Bay. His old crew were rostered on with Dick at the helm. Within minutes they were free of their mooring lines and heading out into the shipping lane.

The trip across to Islington Bay was easy, the weather still benefiting from the high-pressure system providing light winds and negligible swells. Although somewhat hyped in anticipation of the forthcoming encounter with their prime suspect, Frank relaxed amid the light-hearted banter in the familiar surroundings. Anahera, dressed in a no-nonsense white blouse and straight navy skirt, sat on the bench seat behind the helm engaged in deep conversation with Stephen.

They passed a ferry laden with Waiheke passengers then turned into Islington Bay, slowing down to the five-knot limit as they approached the old rusty fishing trawler anchored in the middle of the bay. An anxious moment passed when Frank thought *Nellie* had gone, but she'd been obscured from sight behind a 50-foot gin-palace.

"Bring her alongside, Dick, then we'll tie up at the wharf and ferry him over in the inflatable."

"Aye aye boss." Dick stood at the open window beside the helm seat and switched to the spring-loaded mouse to steer them in. The mouse was a relatively new techy toy that enabled him to control the boat with a twitch of the wrist and would be the envy of many a boat owner.

Frank moved to the starboard gunwale and Anahera came to stand at his side.

Pointing ahead of them, he said, "That's the boat shed where the Jane Doe was found."

"It looks nothing like a tomb." She stared at the little shed nestled among dark rocks under a pōhutukawa tree, its peeling paint and the water licking halfway up its ramp. "Poor thing."

Dick eased *Deodar III* to sit off *Nellie*'s port rail.

"Jerry Ramsley, are you on board?" Frank called across the gap between the two boats.

He waited.

Jerry's head popped up in the companionway. "Yeah, what do ya want?" He scowled when he saw Frank.

"We just want to have a chat with you about the day leading up to the girl being discovered in the boat shed. You might be able to help us with our enquiries."

"I told ya, I didn't see nothin'!"

"We'd still like to go over it again. How about we tie up at the wharf and one of the boys can come over and pick you up in the tender."

Jerry scowled again. After a long moment that felt like a standoff, he answered, "Yeah, alright."

Deodar III motored the short distance to the wharf where Stephen and Jammie secured her mooring lines before launching the inflatable. The tender's motor whined as they crossed to *Nellie* where it bobbed about next to her stern while Jerry Ramsley climbed on.

Back at the police launch Jerry stepped onto the transom and Stephen escorted him up the steps to the aft deck where Frank and Anahera waited.

"Jerry, thanks for coming across." Frank put out his hand and Jerry reluctantly shook it. "Meet my partner, Detective Anahera Raupara."

He looked her up and down but didn't offer his hand.

She met his gaze but neither offered her hand nor said the customary *pleased to meet you.*

Jerry looked around the boat, his eyes wide. "Nice boat. Mind if I take a look around her? I'm guessing I own some of her given I've paid a share of taxes in my day."

Choosing to ignore his remark, Frank said, "We'll go down to the saloon, it's comfy down there and we can have that chat."

Before going down, Frank took Stephen aside and asked him to take Jammie and search the foreshore around Islington Bay and Gardiner Gap to look for anything that might be related to the case. It was a long shot given the initial search hadn't turned up anything, but something may have washed up and they would have the time while Frank and Anahera undertook the interview.

Anahera led Jerry through the sick bay which doubled as the prisoner holding area and down into the saloon. Frank followed, comfortable in the familiar setting. Being a catamaran *Deodar III* was beamy, allowing for a spacious room with windows on three sides making it light and airy. The galley was under the forward windows and crew sleeping quarters were accessed from aft of the saloon. Between the cabins six steps led up to the wheelhouse.

Jerry looked around and whistled. "Bit flashy for a police boat don't ya think?"

Frank ignored the comment and gestured to the wine-coloured seats around the table where they sat down with Anahera and Frank taking pole positions either side of Jerry.

Frank put his notebook and pen on the table. Anahera looked at him and he nodded, indicating Anahera should take the lead. Given Jerry's attitude towards her, he hoped she might just rattle him enough to uncover the truth. This small interaction came from years of working together and would've been imperceptible to anyone else.

Anahera took out her phone and asked, "Mind if we record this? It's the normal procedure." Without waiting for his response, she tapped the screen and put it down. "Interview commenced at 13-0-6-hours." She eyeballed Jerry with a steady gaze. "Please state your name and address."

"I didn't know this would be a proper interview," he whinged. "Do I need a lawyer?"

Anahera's voice was smooth as silk. "You're not under arrest. We just want your witness statement relating to the young girl found deceased in the boat shed." Then as if an afterthought, she added, "Presuming you've nothing to hide, it shouldn't take too long. Now, your name and address, please."

This time Jerry complied, and Frank had to hand it to her—Anahera was a good operator.

"Can I call you Jerry?"

"I guess so."

"Jerry, when did you arrive in Islington Bay?"

"I don't rightly recall now."

"Try to remember—this could be important."

"Maybe four days ago I guess." He looked at Frank. "I told ya when you came over to my boat that day."

"Are you absolutely sure?" she asked.

"I dunno. See I'm retired and days don't mean nothin' to me. It's all just one long holiday."

"I believe you're aware that the body of a young girl was found in one of the boat sheds here in Islington Bay. What do you know about that?"

"Only that he ..." He jabbed a finger towards Frank. "He came asking me about it. Looked through my boat too."

"Did you see anything suspicious in the bay prior to that time?"

He sneered. "Yeah, a wigwam for a goose's bridle."

"Anything else?"

"This police boat came in and out a couple of times."

"Did you notice any boats in the bay with a young Asian girl aboard?"

"Was that what she was?" His rugged face twisted in a grin displaying several broken, dead teeth. "Nah, I don't take much notice of what others are doing. Figure it's their own business."

"Did you notice anyone leaving the bay?"

At this, he sniggered. "What? You must be joking. Boats leave bays all the time. Of course I don't know what boats left. You lot are..."

Frank cut him off. "Have you been in the Rangitoto Channel or Waitematā Harbour in the last week?"

"Nope."

"Do you have GPS on board?"

"Ha! I've no need for them fandangle things. I'm a sailor, been sailing since I was a boy."

Catching a look from Frank, Anahera asked, "Where did you anchor the night before you came into Islington Bay?"

"Home Bay."

Frank cut in. "I thought you told us you were at Motuihe."

Jerry's eyes shifted from one to the other. "Yeah I was. And then I took shelter at Home Bay before deciding to come here."

Frank watched him closely, but he gave nothing. Motuihe Island to Home Bay to Islington Bay was a bit of a zig zag but not improbable if time and destination weren't important.

"I notice you've had a few run ins with the police in the past. Would you like to tell us about those?" Anahera picked up the questioning.

"I knew you were angling to get around to those. Bet you already know all 'bout them, be on your records. So you won't be needing me to 'fess up."

"How about we hear about them in your own words," Anahera pushed.

"Alright, alright. So I was caught growing a little weed in the Coromandel, nothing much." He crossed his arms. "Who doesn't deal in weed over there?"

"Anything else?"

"I made a mistake and accidentally stole a bottle of whiskey from a bottle store. Forgot to pay."

"And the dealing?"

"Yeah, yeah. I sold some weed to an undercover cop. Lousy trick to play if you ask me."

"Where do you plan to head next?" Anahera asked, changing tack.

"There and back to see how far it is." He looked smug, as if enjoying himself.

Anahera glanced at Frank, and he could sense her frustration. They were getting nowhere.

Frank asked, "How long have you been living aboard *Nellie*?"

"Eight months, give or take a few."

"Do you live on your own?" Frank watched him closely.

"Yep." He looked at Anahera, his face breaking into a lopsided grin. "Women are nothing but trouble."

"Have you had anyone else staying on board?"

"Nope." Jerry looked from Frank to Anahera and back to Frank. "You can't get me on that one. I ain't done nothin' wrong. I never saw that girl. I've just been at anchor mindin' me own bloody business, that's all. Now if ya don't want to charge me with anything I'd like to go back to *Nellie*."

Anahera sucked in her cheeks but maintained her outward calm. "Interview ends at 13-20-hours." She picked up her phone and turned off the recording.

Frank closed his notebook then stood up to lead Jerry back out the way they'd come in.

While Dick ferried Jerry back to his own boat in the inflatable, Frank sought out Anahera.

"What did you make of that?"

"He's a creep, but there's nothing to suggest he had anything to do with this." She let out a long sigh. "We've got absolutely nothing."

"I agree. We're no further ahead. Without a single shred of evidence there's insufficient justification to search his boat. Without a GPS on board and no witnesses, we only have his word for where he's been." Frank scratched his head. "We can't detain him without just cause."

"I reckon his sort would likely go us for harassment."

"You could be right—he's a real smart arse. We need something on him. If only we could catch him in a lie." He sighed. "Let's take a look at where Jane Doe One was found so you can see the scene for yourself."

They disembarked and walked the track around to the boat shed. The perimeter tape blew in the breeze and the scene looked just the same. Frank pulled out a pair of disposable gloves and put them on before stepping over the tape and leading her to the little shed.

"I can see why it attracts photography students." Anahera had stopped to take in the landscape. "It's lovely."

"Come over here." Frank carefully clambered over the rocks to the high tide mark near the ramp, and pointing down he said, "This is where we found some splotches of the victim's blood. They're no longer visible but they led up to the boat shed door."

They walked on to the side door of the boat shed, which was still ajar.

"This door was partially open like this, and the body was lying in the middle of the floor." He pulled the torch from his belt and turned on the light before stepping inside.

Anahera followed. They stood in silence out of respect for the child who'd finished up in this shed.

Eventually Anahera whispered, "Such a tragedy. If only we had more of a lead."

"Perhaps we should appeal to the public. The deaths have been getting a lot of airtime. Someone out there must know who they are or where they came from and if prompted, they may just come forward." Frank too spoke quietly as if not wanting to disturb the ghosts.

"You're right of course. Even if the guardian doesn't want to come forward, someone else may have noticed they're absent, like a neighbour or schoolteacher." Anahera continued to whisper. "I'll ask Brad to put out the press release. He seems to like being in front of the media."

"Come on, let's get going. We can show you where the second body was found on our way back to base."

They strolled back to *Deodar III*, slowly. Each deep in thought.

"I can't shake the thought of that young girl lying in the boat shed, dying from a lung-full of salt water. That is unless she was already dead and had been left there." Anahera shook her head. "Disposed of like an object that isn't worth diddly squat—what a shocking thought."

"I was thinking the same. What drives a person to do that?"

"Fear? Arrogance maybe? Someone who didn't give a toss or had no respect for her?" She tossed her head to move the hair that'd fallen over her eyes.

"We're still thinking someone was involved other than the victim. But we've got no evidence of that."

"It's a fairly safe assumption given we're on an island. How could a young girl get here all on her own? And with two girls, both horrendously abused, there's got to be someone."

"You're right of course. Maybe through the media plea a witness will feel compelled to come forward."

"I hate to say it but right now we need a miracle."

They were back aboard *Deodar III* when Stephen and Jammie returned reporting that their search was futile. It was as expected.

After leaving the bay they followed the shore around, passing the ferry terminal on the southern coast before cruising to the western coastline beside the Rangitoto Channel. Dick reduced their speed and coasted in close to the island. Having reached the targeted GPS coordinates he engaged the virtual anchoring to keep her stationary.

Frank took Anahera out to the gunwale and pointed to a spot just off their port bow. "See that dark rock just visible under the surface? That's the spot where we recovered Jane Doe Two."

Anahera scanned the seascape around them, her eyes returning to the rock. She stood leaning against the rail. And a minute of silence passed.

"We need to find a clear lead." She was speaking quietly. "We owe it to these girls. This is all so wrong—it makes me angry."

"I've still to ask someone to run her potential movements through the computer model to see if they can get a more certain picture of where she might have gone into the water." He shook his head. "But don't get your hopes up—I think it's an impossible task."

"I'll also do another check of the missing persons register. But I do have an automatic alert out, so it's unlikely they've been reported missing. And after this length of time, I doubt their absence will be reported." She inhaled a deep breath of the sea air. "It's time we got back to the office."

Deodar III docked in Mechanics Bay and Frank left Anahera in the lunchroom making some calls while he went to see about getting the computer modelling done. One of their techies, Shari, was at her desk when Frank entered the large open plan office where most of the Unit's staff were based when ashore. After explaining what he was after she agreed to run it for him.

*

Anahera walked out to her balcony, a bottle of Corona in hand, and leaned on the balustrade. Her boys were in bed, the domestics were all done, and it was when she'd normally relax and have some down time with Jim before bed.

Their house was on a rise and looked down over the roofs of suburbia. Despite the light pollution, a full moon illuminated the view such that she could even see the silhouette of a stray cat walking across her lawn.

The dead girls plagued her. She paced, sipping her beer. The tattoos were distinctive and linked those girls together. It would be up to her and Frank to find out who they were, where they'd come from, how they'd got to Rangitoto Island, and more importantly, who'd abused them.

She continued to pace.

The sliding door opened behind her, and Jim asked, "What's up?"

"Just thinking about the new case."

"You're pacing, and I haven't seen you do that for a while. Are you worried about it?"

"The new case is brutal Jim. The sexual abuse those poor drowned girls endured was just horrific. And we've not made any progress with the alleged suspect—I met him today and he's a creep, no question. But we have no real leads. Not a one. Zilch. I feel like I'm failing those girls. I need to uncover what actually happened to them, who abused them, and see justice done for their sakes."

"Hey, don't take it so personally."

"Easy for you to say. This falls on my shoulders."

She stopped and turned to him.

"And if the case isn't enough, I'm also worried about Rangi. His attitude seems to have changed, moodier somehow. Having him involved in porn is just too close. Whoever abused those girls may well have started with watching child porn on screen before escalating into the real thing. I don't know how much emotional capacity I have in the well to deal with it."

"Let me worry about Rangi. It's just the first strike for him and we'll get through this. Remember it could've been worse—imagine if he was on drugs."

"Worse for who Jim? Certainly not worse for the girls that were the victims."

"Point taken."

"I need to devote my energy to solving the case—and to solve it fast for those young girls before whoever abused them gets away with it. Even if we nail our person of interest, it's going to be difficult to prove. I only hope that luck will be on our side." She sipped quietly and watched as a satellite tracked across the night sky. "I'm meeting with an anthropologist in the morning and I'm hoping he'll help by throwing some light on the meaning behind the tattoos. And maybe with a bit more luck some member of the public will come forward with something worth following up."

"Try not to take this one to heart. You weren't responsible for what happened. And you were never their guardian angel. Remember you are just part of the team attempting to get justice done." He put his arms around her and drew her to him, his tall strong body dwarfing hers.

"But if we don't get a lead soon there won't be any justice for those poor girls. You know how it is Jim, with each passing day memories fade and it becomes that much harder to get a conviction. And those children deserve one."

"You can only do your best with what you've got. Nothing more. And I know you and Frank are the best cops to solve this case." He kissed her. "You know you're an asset to the CIB. You bring empathy and compassion that's hard to find in a male dominated workplace. But you mustn't let it become personal or it'll destroy you. You're tough, no question, but everyone has limits. And I hate seeing you stressed out."

"I'm okay—no need to worry about me." She snuggled into him, wanting to absorb his strength. "But they said the signs of sexual abuse were as bad as they get. And they're just children, Jim. The youngest was only nine years old and the other twelve. I can't begin to imagine the pain that children their age must suffer each time they're raped. Their young bodies aren't yet developed and aren't ready for sex. And that's just the physical pain. There's the emotional pain as well. And I doubt they would have the maturity to deal with it—not that it's easy when you're older, of course it's not. I don't want to minimise the impact of rape for anyone." She released a deep sigh. "But it breaks my heart to think what they've had to endure."

"I hear you. When I consider how some people behave and what they inflict on those they can control just because they're bigger, stronger or more powerful, frankly it makes me question humanity."

"Thank God you're not like them."

"I don't imagine we'd still be married if I were." He chuckled. "Your tolerance level would be zero."

With her head resting against his chest, she finished her beer.

IO

Anahera waited patiently in the foyer of the Faculty of Arts campus at the University of Auckland to meet Professor of Anthropology, Duncan McLaughlan. Around her groups of students were milling about and a steady stream of people flowed up and down the wide staircase that led up to the floor above. In one corner an intense game of table tennis was being played.

The pornography issue was distressing and to do her job, and do it well, she recognised the need to compartmentalise it. This strategy was a familiar one that worked well when juggling the stress over things on the home front and that which comes with a big case. When at work she needed to have her full wits about her.

"Detective Raupara?"

She turned to see a short and wiry man approach, his eyes darting from one group of students milling about the foyer to another. His brown tweed jacket over a cream check shirt with a brown and orange tie, along with the grey trousers that barely came down to his ankles, pegged him to the world of academia.

"Kia ora. Professor Duncan McLaughlan?" She extended her hand to him. "Please call me Anahera."

"Pleased to meet you." He shook her hand. "Follow me—we can talk in my office."

Duncan turned quickly and led the way up the stairs. He was the proverbial energizer battery, taking the steps two at a time and talking continuously while constantly surveying their surroundings, all of which was at a rapid pace.

Anahera quickened her pace to keep up with the professor. Three flights of stairs later they went through a series of doors and corridors before stopping outside an office. He used his key card to open the door to a small office overflowing with books and papers.

Duncan cleared a pile of loose papers from one of the three chairs in the room and indicated for her to sit down. He sat on an office chair behind the cluttered desk.

"Now what can I do for you?" His speech was rapid and his eyes intense behind his thick glasses.

"We are investigating a case involving two dead children," Anahera began as she extracted her notebook and pen from her bag.

He leaned back in his chair and tapped the fingertips of his right hand onto the tips of the fingers on his left in a rhythm as if playing a wind instrument. "Ah yes, the case that's been in the news."

"That's right. As yet we've not been able to find their next-of-kin or guardians."

He raised his long hairy eyebrows. "And why the interest in anthropology?"

"Although found in different locations and at different times, both girls had a tattoo on their wrist, and I was hoping you might be able to shed some light on that for me." She pulled out a photograph of the boat shed girl's tatt and placed it on the desk. "We believe the girls' ethnicity is Asian and we're waiting on the DNA results to pinpoint what part of Asia."

Duncan leaned forward to peer at the photograph. "Interesting. Interesting."

"Do you recognise it?"

"Not exactly, but you've come to the right place. My specialty area is Southeast Asia. In Hinduism, Buddhism, Taoism and Theosophy the eye is important. All reference a third eye with several of the cultures depicting it as a coloured red dot on the forehead. It represents knowledge, wisdom and enlightenment."

He spoke so rapidly that Anahera struggled to keep up with her notes.

"Legend has it that the Hindu god Shiva opened his third eye after being shot with an arrow by Kama, the god of lust. Angry that he'd allowed himself to be tempted by him, Shiva burned Kama to ashes. Awakening one's third eye became a metaphor for achieving inner clarity."

"I don't understand how the red dot relates to the symbol of the eye in the tattoos."

"Yes, yes." He spoke impatiently. "The red ink used in the tattoo could be significant. The colour red is often associated with strong emotions, such as passion and love, and with energy and power."

Anahera stopped writing and looked up. "Power?"

"Yes, it also signifies prosperity and wealth, making it popular for business logos where companies are superstitious and want to attract fortune and success. The goddess of wealth, Lakshmi, is typically drawn in red attire." He paused. "Because of its importance, the colour red is used in various rituals, traditional ceremonies and festivals. You'd be familiar with the use of henna."

Anahera didn't stop her writing. "Ah-ha."

"There is also the concept of the evil eye. It is in many religions and is thought to go back to Mesopotamian times. In the Hindu religion it is called *Nazar* and can be in the form of envy or jealousy, where it is thought to be borne like a curse by those who are bearing the brunt of the envy or jealousy. They believe it manifests as negative energy, causing failure and disaster."

"Do they really believe someone can do this with a simple look?"

"Yes, but there are rituals they perform to ward it off. Fascinating stuff. One technique is with salt—they carry a small amount around the affected person in a clockwise direction and then they dispose of it. A second method is to burn cloves and have the smoke spread around them to cleanse and purify. And then there's a water method whereby some water is taken around the affected person while chanting then it's thrown onto a hot surface and the resulting steam is thought to be the evil energy being burnt away."

He picked up the photograph, holding it close as he studied it. "I don't recognise the eye symbol exactly—it appears to be stylised and could be just the artist's own impression."

"That would suggest the same tattoo artist did both tattoos."

"Possibly. The symbols inside the eyes are interesting. Let me check a reference book." He went to the bookshelf that covered the end wall and stood frowning, hands on hips. Then he picked out a thick hard-covered book and returned to his seat. After flicking through the pages he stopped and said, "Yes, I thought so. The symbols are Brahmi script, an ancient Indian writing system. They each represent a number."

Anahera pulled out a second photograph taken of the tattoo on Jane Doe Two's arm. "And these?"

"Yes, yes—the same script but a different number."

"Why would these symbols be inside an eye?"

He shook his head enthusiastically. "I really don't know. It's not something I've come across before."

"Who still uses Brahmi symbols?"

"They're no longer in general use—more an artifact for language enthusiasts. It was once an important language, arguably as old as the first century, that gave rise to a number of languages in various language families around Asia."

"Do you have any hunch at all as to what the tattoos might mean? And the meaning behind the numbers? Are they consecutive numbers?"

Anahera silently urged him to come up with some nugget as he considered her question.

"No, I couldn't say for sure. But these numbers are not in sequence. A lot of attention is paid to auspicious moments in time and perhaps the different numbers somehow are unique or special to each child."

They were silent while Anahera finished her scribbles. "This has been incredibly helpful, thanks. Before I go is there anything else that comes to mind about those images?"

"I can't think of anything. It's a most interesting case."

Anahera pulled out a business card and put it down on the desk in front of him. "If you think of anything else, please call me."

The halls were busy as they walked back to the ground floor. Duncan talked incessantly of matters unrelated to the case but Anahera scarcely noticed, lost as she was in her own thoughts about all that she'd learned.

*

Frank had spent the morning following false leads. The media request for witnesses to come forward had sparked a feeding frenzy and the hotline that had been set up especially to receive the calls had begun to ring with people reporting having seen young Asian girls. Auckland being such a cosmopolitan city, they'd fully expected to get a lot of false sightings. The problem was that each one had to be followed up and given appropriate due diligence, using up precious resources.

All calls were taken by Cara Harris, a constable who'd been assigned to the case. She screened out the obvious crank calls before forwarding the remaining messages to Frank, who'd spent much of his morning chasing red herrings. There had been young girls, seen on their own or in pairs, spotted in the city centre, on K Road and Queen Street, down around the Viaduct, on the Domain, at the bottom of Dominion Road, around nearby suburbs, and still possible sightings were coming in. But nothing linked two pyjama-clad Indian or possibly Nepalese girls, to Rangitoto Island, the Gulf or any boats.

Frank had just got off the phone to another member of the public who'd responded to the call for witnesses when Anahera returned from her meeting at the university.

"Thank goodness you're back. That was another caller with potential information. This time they remember seeing two Asian girls walking arm in arm at the viaduct on Sunday. Could've been anyone! How did you get on?"

Anahera sat down at her desk and opened her notebook before updating Frank with what she'd learned. Finishing, she said, "Although we're no further ahead, I'm even more convinced that the tattoos are significant and symbolise something that is key to this case. Perhaps the key. How soon do we get the DNA tests back?"

"The turnaround for the lab results has been running at around ten days. While that will confirm their ethnicity, I think it's fair to say they were Hindu Indo-Asian judging by what you've learned."

"The symbolism was meaningful to whoever organised to have them tattooed, and that's who we need to find."

"As soon as the phone calls slow down, I'll organise for Cara to take the tattoo photographs around the city's tattoo shops to see if anyone recognises the artwork," Frank said.

"Have you considered they may not have been tattooed in this country?"

"It's a possibility, but they were recent tattoos and given they were in Auckland it may well be worth the effort to start here. But point taken—if they were recent immigrants they could have been tattooed overseas."

"There must be someone here who knows them. They can't have come into the country on their own." Her dimple deepened as she pushed her jaw forward resting it on her right thumb, stroking it with her forefinger.

"I know that look." Frank grinned. "It usually comes before something ingenious. What are you thinking?"

"It was what you said. We haven't checked immigration. Two minors wouldn't have come in on their own and if they're immigrants then there will be records of their guardians or next-of-kin." She smiled at him. "How about I do that while you continue chasing up the alleged sightings."

Frank laughed out loud. "I think I just drew the short straw."

"You call it, I don't mind doing either."

Just then Frank's phone rang. He mouthed, *It's okay.*

"Detective Frank Smythe speaking."

"I heard the call for information about the two dead girls. Such a tragedy." The caller was a woman, her diction crisp and clear.

"Yes, it is. Could I have your name and contact details please."

The woman complied and Frank entered them directly into the computer.

"Do you have information about a possible sighting?"

"I don't know. My husband told me not to call as I shouldn't be a busybody. But I felt if I could help ..." Her voice trailed off.

"Go on."

"You see I saw a man with a young Indian girl last Saturday. We were walking the dog along the waterfront in Devonport, near the museum. He was pulling her along by the wrist and it appeared she didn't want to go with him." She lowered her voice as if conspiring with him. "She seemed frightened."

"What was she dressed in?"

"I'm pretty sure she was in jeans and a pretty blouse with puffed sleeves. Flowery I think."

"How old would she have been?"

"It's hard to say now, but maybe a young teenager. Could've been younger."

"Any distinguishing features?"

"Not that I remember."

"And the man. What did he look like?"

"He was also Indian. I couldn't describe him now. Nothing stood out."

"Anything else?"

"Not that I recall."

"Thank you. You've been most helpful. If we need anything more, we'll follow up with you." He ended the call.

"Any useful information?" Anahera asked from her workstation.

"An Indian girl with a man in Devonport last Saturday. Could have been any child with her father. No pyjamas." He groaned.

"Not worth following up then," Anahera said. "You know we only need one lead to blow this thing wide open."

"Well, I only hope it comes through soon before I go completely mad."

The phone buzzed again.

"Detective Frank Smythe here." He pulled his keyboard closer. "Please can you give me your name, address and phone number?"

He typed the information into the database he had open on the screen.

"Do you have information regarding the dead girls?"

"Yeah, I reckon so." The male voice was gruff.

"I'm listening."

"Me and my wife live in New Lynn. And I know we're a long way from the waterfront near Rangitoto Island, but I see young Asian and Indian girls from time to time, at a house across the road where a lot of men come and go. We think it's a brothel of some sort, maybe a drug dealer. Either way, there seems to be a lot of night-time activity there. It's the talk of the neighbourhood."

"What's the address?"

He gave it as Frank tapped the keys.

"And what age would you say these girls are?"

"Hard to say, but teenagers, and far too young to be serving in a brothel!" The voice expressed his indignation.

"What else can you tell me about them?"

"Not much. They seem real shy, scared maybe."

"And what about the adults that live there?"

"There's a woman, friendly type. Looks European, with deeply tanned skin and long frizzy hair that's dyed different colours."

"And the visitors?"

"Men of various ethnicities and ages. All sorts really. Mostly at night but some during the day." The caller paused. "Don't get me wrong. We're not nosy neighbours, it's just that you don't want a brothel on your street. It affects the tone of the neighbourhood as well as our house values."

"What type of clothes do these girls typically wear?"

"The sort of clothes you'd see in a nightclub." He added hastily, "Not that I spend time in nightclubs. It's just what I imagine they'd wear."

"Can you be a little more descriptive?"

A woman's voice was instructing in the background. He said, "Brightly coloured tank tops, short skirts, shoes with heels—that sort of thing."

"Anything else?"

"Not that I can think of just now."

"Thank you for your call. If we need anything more I or one of my colleagues will get back in touch."

The call ended and Frank decided to pass the information on to Puawaitahi, the child protection multi-agency whose mandate was to investigate child abuse and neglect. While the city council was responsible for leading raids on illegal brothels, if criminal activity was involved then the matter was referred to the police. Although the information hadn't been substantiated, he sent a brief email outlining the information received.

Frank pushed back in his seat. Roughly 160,000 Aucklanders identified as Indian ethnicity. Identifying actual sightings of the deceased would be nigh impossible. It would be like standing in the middle of Times Square during rush hour and chancing to see an old school friend. Still, they might get lucky.

In the background Anahera was speaking into her phone when Frank received another call.

"Detective Frank Smythe."

"I'm ringing in response to your request for information on the two girls that drowned." A man, his voice held a relaxed air.

Again, Frank entered the contact details.

"Please explain why it is that you think you can help us with our investigation."

"I own a forty-two-foot launch named *Whatsup*."

Frank sat up straight. "Go on."

"I was out at Mansion House Bay, Kawau Island, at the weekend. There was a yacht at anchor there with what appeared to be an Asian family on board. Might be nothing—the reason I noticed is that we don't often see Asian sailors on recreation yachts."

"Did you see the name of the yacht?"

"*Big Blue*. And I remember her canvas and hull were blue."

Frank went through the other questions, seeking answers that might link the people on board to the deceased. But there was nothing that suggested the dead girls had been on *Big Blue*. However, it would be worth following up with her owners.

When he'd finished the call, he asked Anahera, "Any luck with Immigration?"

"Not as yet—I'm waiting to hear back. How about you?"

Frank told her about the calls.

"It's almost lunchtime. Let's take a break and go find something to eat. I could murder a steak and cheese pie!"

"Good idea, I'm more than ready for that." Frank stood up and grabbed his jacket. "It's so frustrating that we've so little to go on."

"It's still early days."

They left the office to take refuge in a nearby café.

II

The next morning Anahera rushed into the office, bag slung over her shoulder and two coffees-to-go in her hands. "Kia ora! Sorry I'm late Frank. Had to sort out gym gear for the boys and drop them off at school. The traffic was bumper-to-bumper the whole way with roadworks and cones everywhere." She placed one of the coffees on his desk. "And I had to queue for these, seems like half the downtown office dwellers were out on the hunt for a coffee."

Frank had looked up as she'd breezed in. "What's this? A peace offering?"

"Something like that." She sat down at her desk and busied herself booting the computer and arranging her things. "Did I miss anything?"

"No. The owner of the vessel *Big Blue* checks out. An Indian family and their girls aren't missing. And Cara is making a start collating a list of tattoo studios. The trouble is there're some that don't operate out of a shop and tracking them down may prove difficult—especially if they're not listed with the IRD. She'll work on the list this morning while manning the hotline. I expect those calls will start to tail off now."

"I'll chase Immigration again."

"Good." Frank pushed back on his chair, crossed his arms and looked up at the ceiling. "I've been thinking."

"I'm glad one of us has. What's on your mind?"

"I think we need to push harder with Jerry Ramsley. There's something very shifty about him. The trouble we have is there're no witnesses to verify his story and no way to know whether he was in the vicinity where the second Jane Doe might have gone into the water. We only have his word for it. A witness is needed in order to rule him out."

"Or rule him in. He certainly acted like he might have something to hide." Anahera considered this for a moment. "What if he had both girls on board for some perverse purpose."

"How would he come to have two Nepalese-looking girls on board? He's obviously Caucasian himself, so unlikely to be blood relations—although they could be related indirectly. We don't even know if the girls are related to each other."

Anahera stood up and began to pace their small office as if the answer lay in each step. "Let's assume they're sisters or at least known to each other. What if he knew their mother or guardian and was taking them for a holiday on board *Nellie* when they fell overboard and drowned?"

"For starters, it's not school holidays. And even if they took the time off school, it still doesn't add up because they'd have been reported missing if it were legitimate."

"Okay then. What if the girls were escorts?"

Frank shook his head. "Too young."

Anahera stopped pacing and looked at him. "It's possible—there are plenty of sick people out there. What other reasons could he have had?"

"He could have kidnapped them."

"Possible. But again, they'd have been reported missing." She sat back down.

"So should we assume that given they weren't reported missing, it was consensual for him to have them aboard?"

"I think so, otherwise they'd have been missed."

"But if they were aboard for legitimate reasons, surely he'd have reported the drowning incidents to the police or in the very least to the emergency channel."

"Unless he was scared."

"True but let's think this through. Let's assume they were on board *Nellie* and he had permission from their guardian or guardians, so at this stage nobody is missing them. Perhaps he picked them up from the Coromandel before making their way to Islington Bay, as he said."

"Okay."

"Now the wind has been a prevailing westerly for the last week and to come around the south of Motutapu through the Motuihe Channel would've required a lot of tacking or use of the motor. I'm guessing he doesn't use the motor much, being a live-aboard, meaning he'd have preferred the easier route which would have been to sail north of the island through Rakino Channel and as close to the wind as he could and then come down through the Rangitoto Channel and run downwind to Islington Bay. If I'm right, that puts him in the area that Jane Doe Two could have drowned. Then round into Islington Bay where Jane Doe One was found."

"Then why the drowning?"

Frank shook his head. "I don't know—it doesn't make a lot of sense."

Brainstorming with Frank energised her and was something she'd missed since they'd gone their separate ways in the Force. That thought was immediately followed by a guilt pang given two girls had lost their lives. She went to the whiteboard and picked up a pen. "I think we're pretty much agreeing that the actual drownings could well have been accidental and not murder. Agreed?"

"Quite possibly. I just can't see any reason why the girls would be purposely disposed of in that way. There would be better ways, for example why so close to Auckland when they could be taken further out to open water where the bodies might never be found."

Anahera wrote *accidental drowning vs murder* on the board and underlined the former. "Okay, so I reckon there're four main questions to answer. The first is, where did the girls actually die? The second is, how did the girls get to Rangitoto Island? Who transported them there and what were they doing out there? The third is, who abused them? And the fourth is, what is the link between them? That may come down to the meaning behind the tattoos. But I think we have to assume they are linked and that they were together at some stage during their final journey. Did I miss anything crucial?"

"Sounds reasonable to me." Frank spoke slowly.

Anahera wrote the questions on the board. "Let's consider the first question. Where did the girls actually die? Were they already dead and someone transported them out there to dispose of the bodies? Or did they drown out there?"

"I think it highly unlikely they would be taken out there to be disposed of. If the motive was disposal, surely they would have taken them further out where they wouldn't be found. And it doesn't explain why one drowned and was found washed up on one side of the island and the other was found in the boat shed, where they could be discovered at any time."

"That logic sounds reasonable. So, let's assume for now that the girls were alive when out there." Anahera jotted *Drowned near Rangitoto* on the board under the first question. "That leads us to the second question—how did they get there?"

"We've ruled out the ferry, helicopter and land vehicles. That leaves us with private boats."

"Or ships, they could have jumped from a freighter," Anahera interjected. "Or even a passenger ship."

"That's entirely possible too, given the currents that could have brought Jane Doe Two into her final resting place from the shipping lane." Frank sat staring at the board. "But it doesn't explain how the boat shed girl got to Islington Bay."

"Given her cause of death was secondary drowning couldn't it be feasible she got herself there?"

"I would have thought that unlikely—it would take a mammoth effort from somebody suffering salt water in the lungs. But I agree, let's not entirely rule it out."

Anahera wrote *Ship or Private boat* under the second question. "So, we have either ship or private boat of some sort. What if they were on board a ship or private boat and were being abused, making them so scared they jumped in the water to escape. Perhaps Jane Doe Two couldn't swim and drowned while Jane Doe One managed to reach shore and somehow got herself to the boat shed where she succumbed to secondary drowning."

"The alternative is that whoever took them out there pulled Jane Doe One out of the water, but she later died causing the person to panic and dispose of her in the shed."

"That also sounds plausible but would rule out the ship." She finished her coffee and tossed the empty cup in the bin.

"Why might they have been on a private boat? Given the abuse, should we assume they were being used and abused on board?"

"So, we might be looking for a pervert or a pervert and his friends aboard some sort of private boat."

"This brings us back to Jerry Ramsley. We need to rule him out." Frank picked up his phone. "I think I'll ask the Maritime boys to cruise the bays and talk to boaties asking if anyone remembers seeing *Nellie* last week. If we can confirm he lied about his movements and track him to the Rangitoto Channel we may just have our answer."

"We still don't know who the girls were or why they were on board or who abused them, but it's a start."

Frank made the call.

Anahera checked her emails and found one from the Department of Immigration. There was no record of the girls having come in through one of Aotearoa New Zealand's ports of entry based on the photos and identikit pictures she'd supplied. Either the deceased girls must have been living here for some time, perhaps born Kiwis, or had been smuggled in. They were no closer to identifying them.

Just as Frank got off the phone to the Maritime Unit, Brad entered the office looking very formal wearing a white shirt and tie under his police jacket instead of his usual open-necked shirt. He seemed to be wearing the stress of the job in deep creases on his face. "I'm about to go into a media briefing and I need a progress report."

Frank glanced at Anahera who took the cue, saying, "There's not a lot to report. We've been back out to interview the person of interest on board the small yacht in Islington Bay, but we've nothing to pin on him at this stage. However, we're working to see if his movements check out." She drew in a deep breath. "We're still waiting on the DNA analysis. There's still no missing person's report and no records of the girls having come through Immigration. No leads have come out of the media appeal. I've spoken to an anthropologist at the university who has led us to believe the tattoos are of Indo Asian significance and their meaning may be key to the case. And we've started the search for the tattooist." She smiled at Brad.

"In other words, you're no further ahead." Brad's blue eyes bore into her.

"That's a bit unfair," Anahera shot back, smile now gone. "It's still early days."

"I've got the media climbing all over me on this one. Nobody likes dead children especially when there's been foul play. Nor do we want people thinking there's a serial killer out there. We need to make some progress. Today. And we need some positive PR. I'm counting on you two to come through for me—don't let me down."

Although the youngest Detective Inspector in the region, Brad had earned the reputation for being a good cop and fair-minded, which was why this outburst caught Anahera off guard. Past successes had made her proud of her own competence, particularly when partnering with Frank, and she took the criticism personally.

She snapped back, "We're doing our best Brad. We've only been on it a couple of days. And we're doing it by the book. We want this conviction as much as you do, and when we lay charges, we want them to stick."

"What about the suspect? How close are you to applying for a warrant to search his boat?"

"He's more of a person of interest. We don't as yet have anything that would convince an issuing officer to grant a search warrant." Anahera sighed. "We're working on it."

"Well don't let me stop you. I want you to keep me posted with any progress." He rubbed a hand over his snowy number two cut. "In the meantime, I'll have to feed the media something."

Brad turned on his heel and she could hear his footsteps all the way down the hall.

"You handled that well." Frank was grinning at her. "I thought you were going to smack him one."

She grinned back. "It felt that way too. But seriously, that wasn't the usual Brad. He must be under a lot of pressure."

"I suspect the cuts the government announced are adding to his frustration. I wouldn't want to be in his shoes."

"There're never enough cops on the beat, and it doesn't help that crime statistics are on the rise."

"Let's hope the *Deodar* boys come up with something soon and we track down the tattooist. We certainly could do with a break." With that he turned his attention back to his computer.

Anahera sat staring into space, seeing nothing. They had to be missing something. Why would those two girls be with someone like Jerry Ramsley? It just didn't make sense. Legally they were too young to be escorts—the mere thought made her stomach churn. No matter how hard she tried, she couldn't come up with a plausible explanation. If they had been on *Nellie* with him, it couldn't have been for innocent reasons because the drowning incidents hadn't been called in. And if he'd somehow taken them, why wasn't there a missing person's report?

Without any clear leads, she felt she was gridlocked in a busy intersection with no way forward, no way back and no turns available.

Frank's voice broke through her thoughts. "I'm going to go with *Deodar III* to look for a witness who may have seen *Nellie*'s movements. I want to be directly involved and conduct the questioning myself. I'm placing my bet on finding a witness to discredit Jerry Ramsley's statement." Frank picked up his jacket and moved towards the door, his notebook in hand. "Why don't you chase the DNA results, perhaps they can give a preliminary result."

"Can do Frank. Good luck with finding someone who remembers him."

Before he'd even left the office she was placing a call to Forensics, who gave her a contact for the lab where the testing was being done.

She dialled the lab and made her request to the receptionist, Jenny Chan, who offered to find out if the results were out, promising to call her back.

Ten minutes later her phone rang. "It's Jenny Chan. You were asking for the DNA results for the two drowning victims?"

"Yes, we're especially interested in their ethnicity and relationship to one another."

"Please understand we've only got the raw results as there's not been enough time to write the full report. However, I can tell you they are most likely of Nepalese parentage. They could of course have been born in Aotearoa New Zealand to Nepalese immigrants."

"And could they be sisters or related in some way?"

"There is no blood relationship between them—definitely not sisters with 99.9 percent certainty. We'll complete the report and send it through in the next couple of days."

"Okay, thanks for your help." Anahera ended the call.

*

Deodar III was primed and waiting when Frank climbed onto the transom and made his way to the wheelhouse. On this occasion Dick and Stephen were the crew. Frank had taken the time to stop by his old locker and change into a pair of his Maritime Police blue overalls and life jacket.

"I see you've been demoted back to the Unit, Boss?" Stephen quipped with his freckled face creased in a grin.

Frank looked at the face that was partially covered with an overgrown handlebar moustache. "And I see you've still not found your moustache trimmer."

Dick, seated at the helm, guffawed loudly.

It was good to be back.

"About today. We're looking for someone to help us confirm the movements of Jerry Ramsley and his boat *Nellie* in the days prior to our first meeting with him." Frank looked from one man to the other. "I figure there'll be a boat still out on the Gulf somewhere who has been in anchorages where *Nellie* has been and who may remember seeing it."

"Where do you want to start?" Dick asked.

"Let's start with Motuihe Island and then Waiheke Island's northern side and around to Man O'War Bay."

Stephen performed the deckhand role releasing the mooring lines and soon they were making way towards Motuihe Island at a rapid 36 knots. Frank went and stood at the port gunwale, breathing the sea air deep into his lungs. It was just the tonic he needed after the frustrations of the case. As they cruised past Islington Bay, he grabbed a pair of binoculars but couldn't make out the outline of *Nellie*. It was likely she was hidden from view behind the old rusty trawler's hull.

No boats were anchored at Motuihe, which wasn't unusual given the wind direction. They carried on towards Oneroa Bay on Waiheke. There were a dozen boats at anchor. As they approached the first one, he hailed a middle-aged man and woman who were lounging in the cockpit of their Beneteau 430 yacht. The couple stood up to watch as Dick brought *Deodar* alongside and held her there.

"We're after any information about the movements of a Nova 28 yacht called *Nellie*. Have you seen her in your travels?"

"No, sorry." The man replied.

"Did you notice any boats with two young Nepalese girls on board?"

"No. Is this to do with the girls that drowned at Rangitoto Island? It's all over the news."

"Yes, we're trying to track down their movements."

"Terrible tragedy. Good luck with your search."

"Thanks. Enjoy your day." Frank gestured to Dick to go on to the next boat.

All but two of the boats were occupied and no one remembered seeing *Nellie*. Frank was beginning to feel the frustration of the last two days creep back over him like a big grey cloud.

They left Oneroa and picked up their speed briefly before slowing for Little Palm Beach. Only three boats were anchored there and again the answers were the same. Next stop was Onetangi Bay, but still no luck. They made their way east stopping wherever they found boats at anchor. Eventually they came into Man O'War Bay, a popular anchorage for recreational boaties, with a vineyard on the shore and a reasonable walk to Stony Batter where gun placements stood as a memorial to the home guard in WWII. More than twenty boats graced its bay and again they stopped by each and every one. But no information came forth that could help them with their enquiry. A few boats were anchored along the shoreline that ran south of Man O'War and in behind the mussel farm, but the answer there was the same. Next they circumnavigated Rotoroa and Ponui islands, but still no luck.

Coming into the wheelhouse, Frank said, "Okay Dick, I think we'd best call it a day. I suggest we take a cruise around the Waiheke southern coastline and check out those bays before returning to base."

Te Wharau Bay was situated on the southwest corner of Waiheke Island. Although shallow, there was enough depth to provide a sheltered anchorage in westerly winds. An old H28 was at anchor and as *Deodar III* drew near an old timer came up from down below. He had the weathered look of a sailor and was sporting a full grey beard that would have done Father Christmas proud.

"Ahoy!" he shouted across the gap to Frank.

"We're looking for information regarding a Nova 28 named *Nellie*. Have you seen her sometime in the last week?"

"She came into Home Bay last weekend when I was there. Stayed a night and left. Why?"

"Could you be more precise about which night?"

"Let me see." He counted on his fingers. "Yes, it would have been Saturday night."

"Did you see who was on board?"

"I spoke briefly to the man when he came past, he was a bit gruff but likeable enough. Came over from Coromandel."

"Was there anyone else on board?"

"Not that I saw. Could've been down below."

"Did he say anything else? Like where he was going?"

"No, we didn't really have a conversation."

"Did you see which way he went when he left the anchorage?"

"No, sorry."

"Okay, thanks. You've been very helpful."

The witness had corroborated Jerry Ramsley's story, but it remained unclear whether *Nellie* had gone via Rangitoto Channel or Motuihe Channel.

It was getting late when Stephen tossed the mooring lines over the bollards at Mechanics Bay. After coming up with a plan to continue the search to the north the following day, Frank thanked the boys and with heavy feet walked slowly up the ramp and into headquarters. He didn't partake in the usual locker room banter but instead walked out of the building and straight to his car. Once home he cracked a Steinlager and sat sipping it on the deck until Margie got home.

*

After Frank left, Anahera continued to follow up with the public who'd contacted them following the appeal but drew blanks with each caller.

Eventually she took a break and went to see Cara Harris, the constable assigned to helping them with their investigation. Cara was young, sporty and gave off a clear 'don't mess with me' signal not only in the way she walked and held herself but also in her staunch attitude. Anahera thought her the type of woman who would thrive in the tough police environment.

The constable, in regulation police uniform with her long mousy hair pulled back in a braid, was at her desk in the open plan office. She looked up as Anahera approached.

"Hey Anahera."

"How's the tattoo artist search going?" Anahera asked, smiling at the policewoman who was at least ten years her junior.

"Getting there. I'd no idea how many there are around Auckland." She pointed to her screen and Anahera peered over her shoulder to read the list.

For the next hour or so Anahera helped Cara complete the list before strategizing the most efficient way to speak with each one. Armed with printed photos of the tattoos, Cara took a squad car out to begin the hunt.

Frank called to let her know *Deodar*'s search had turned up only one sighting but nothing that would help get them a search warrant.

Back at her desk, Anahera was packing up her things for the day when her phone rang.

"Detective Anahera Raupara. How may I help?"

"I'm Detective Tania Jones. We haven't met but I'm with Puiwaitahi, the child protection multi-agency, representing the police. I received the tip-off from Frank Smythe regarding a potential brothel in New Lynn." Her accent was distinctly Kiwi.

"I'm listening."

"I wanted to thank you for the intel. We've had the house under surveillance ever since we received Frank's email. We believe underage girls are working there and we think drugs may be sold on the premises. We're preparing for a raid later this evening. It will be a joint effort between Council, due to it being in breach of a by-law regarding its location, Immigration, IRD, and us. We're striking fast to avoid losing them because these operators sometimes move from place to place in order to stay under the radar."

"I appreciate your feedback. It's always good to know when there's a positive spin-off to an investigation."

"I know what you mean—that's why the call." She paused. "I assume you're working the case of the drowned girls?"

"We are but it's slow going. We've got no clear leads and only one potential suspect at this stage."

"Well good luck with that. I'll let you know how the raid goes."

The call ended and Anahera checked her watch. It was home time, and it couldn't come too soon for her. It'd been an infuriating day, and she left the office hoping tomorrow would be more productive.

12

Anahera walked along the street looking at the names on shops and above doorways. She and Cara had divided up the list of tattoo artists and because of their concentration in the proximity of Auckland Central, they'd each set off on foot to cover their share of the list. She was convinced the key to solving this case lay in finding the artist. Numerous tattoo shops were in the central business district and many more were dotted around the suburbs. It was going to be a mammoth task.

Somewhere in this group of shops was a tattoo studio and she checked her list again. A narrow door between two shops advertised the name she was looking for. She opened it and climbed up the dingy stairs that had been the canvas for a graffiti artist.

At the top of the steps was a well-lit room with walls covered in a huge array of stylised pictures. There were traditional Māori designs, ferns, zodiac signs, butterflies, animals, reptiles, flowers, mythological creatures, and many more. One panel advertised a variety of fonts. Customers were spoilt for choice.

A small reception area with a couple of hard plastic chairs and some magazines on a low table was in front of a counter where Anahera rang the small bell. Behind the counter was an open space where a man sat on a low swivel stool beside a massage table where a woman lay, her bare arm extended. The tattooist, with disposable blue surgical gloves and a mask, was bent over the arm. A tattoo workstation was beside him covered in small ink bottles with a light extended out to illuminate the arm. The needle made a low buzzing sound as it moved forwards and backwards over the flesh, reminding her of pain endured during trips to the dentist.

The tattooist, his head shaven, looked up then muttered something to his client. He took his time finishing his line, before putting the needle down and coming over to the counter. "Yes?" he asked.

It was hard not to notice the colourfully patterned biceps that bulged from his muscle tee-shirt, an advertisement for his artistry. While not a large man, his muscular body suggested hours spent at a gym lifting weights.

Anahera flashed her badge. "Kia ora, I'm Detective Anahera Raupara. I'm looking for the artist who did this tattoo." She tapped the screen on her phone and showed him.

He craned his thick neck to look at it. "It's not one of mine."

"Have you seen a design like this before or do you have any idea about who might do this type of design?"

"No, sorry I can't help you." He made to move back to his job then paused as if thinking better of it. "Why do you want to know?"

"It's related to a case where we're looking to trace someone. Thanks anyway. I won't take any more of your time."

With a last look at the woman being inked, she left by way of the stairs.

The second tattoo shop that was on her list was only half a dozen shops along the street from the first one. She entered and asked the same question but once again she received a negative response. And so it went on—all morning she traipsed the streets showing the photograph to tattooists and each time she received the same response.

It was late morning by the time she returned to the station. Making a quick check of the missing person list confirmed the two deceased girls still hadn't been listed. Why they hadn't been reported as missing was beyond her. Surely after this time their absence had been noticed—if not by a guardian, then a teacher or a neighbour. There must be someone.

Frank had once again gone out with the crew aboard *Deodar III* to continue the hunt for a witness who could testify to *Nellie's* movements. He was determined to prove Jerry Ramsley had lied to them about the route he'd taken, and if he could do that, then it should be enough to get a search warrant. While Anahera hoped they'd had some better luck, she was becoming less convinced of Ramsley's involvement. It just didn't add up. Sure she disliked him, and yes he'd acted strangely. But nothing linked him to the girls.

She turned off her computer and stood up, stretching, before picking up her bag to go out to buy some lunch when her mobile rang.

She answered it on the second ring. "Detective Anahera Raupara speaking,"

"Anahera, it's Tania Jones from Puiwaitahi."

"Tania, you've just caught me. I was about to go and get some lunch." She put her bag down and pulled out her chair. "How can I help?"

"A courtesy call really. I thought you'd like an update on how our raid on the illegal brothel went this morning. After all you guys provided the tip off."

"That's thoughtful—I was wondering if it was helpful."

"It was. We managed to catch them before they were spooked and moved premises. An eleven-year-old girl was living there who's showing symptoms of being severely traumatised. A social worker is now working with her ..." Her voice trailed off. "But I won't keep you since you're off to lunch. And I might just follow suit. It's been a long day already."

"Why don't you join me? It would be nice to meet in person."

"That's nice of you, but I'm over at Grafton."

"I can wait."

"You know, I think I will—there haven't been too many opportunities to meet colleagues outside my team since I transferred up here from Wellington."

"How about we meet at the Crazy Horse Café in fifteen minutes?"

"Sounds good, I'll see you there."

After ending the call, Anahera called Frank for an update. *Deodar* had spent the morning covering the bays along the coastal route to the north of the Rangitoto Channel and up to the Kawau Bay area. Sounding despondent at the other end of the line, he told her they hadn't tracked down anyone else who remembered seeing *Nellie* prior to the boat shed girl being found. They would finish searching around the Kawau Island area that afternoon and be back at base later in the day.

Deeply frustrated by the lack of leads, she left the office.

*

Anahera walked into the Crazy Horse Café and looked about. Not seeing a lone woman, she chose an empty booth facing the door and sat down to wait. The café was a popular venue for office workers at the top of the town, with some tables out on the footpath. The cabinet was full of delicious looking food ready for the lunch crowd. The noise level rose as a steady stream of punters filled the small room, their chatter reverberating off the tiled floor and wooden walls.

A short time later a petite woman hurried in and looked around. Her hair was short with a bluish hue, and she was dressed in tight trousers, boots and a loose fitting brightly coloured top.

Spotting Anahera, she approached uncertainly. "Anahera?"

"Yes, and you must be Tania."

They shook hands before going up to the counter to order their food. Back at the table they sat facing each other and began with the usual small talk as one does when meeting someone for the first time. The other woman was warm and friendly, her smile lighting up her face as she talked. Anahera instantly warmed to her.

Once the weather, foot traffic and congestion topics had been covered, Tania said, "It's good to meet another woman detective up here.

I transferred here last year and have been so busy getting my head around the new unit that I haven't had a lot of time to socialise within the Force."

"Where did you come from?"

"I was stationed in Wellington—I met my partner while at police college and after graduating I stayed down there to be with him." Tania adjusted her glasses on her nose.

"What made you decide to move to Auckland?"

"Unfortunately, my partner and I broke up—in hindsight it was never going to work. Then the position in Puiwaitahi just happened to come up at the right time and I was ready for a fresh start. It's similar work to what I was doing in Wellington, so it was a no-brainer." She checked her phone before looking at Anahera. "Sorry, it's been a hectic morning. Have you always been based up here?"

"Yep, I'm an Aucklander through and through—I grew up and went through school here."

"How do you like working for CIB?"

"I love it. Most of my current workload are Land Search and Rescue cases and that can be quite rewarding. Finding people and reuniting them with their whānau is the best part—but we don't always get the ending we want." She paused as a waitress delivered their orders. "I'm not sure I could do what you do—I'd invest too much of myself in it. How do you cope?"

"Cases of child abuse and neglect are challenging—I think it's why I've chosen not to have children of my own. The hardest are when it involves the young defenceless ones, and where sexual abuse is involved. It can be a tough world out there for kids growing up and you do tend to get a warped view on life when you're seeing the worst possible situations on a daily basis." She took her time to chew through a mouthful of savoury. "It can be draining."

"I think I'd take each case personally—it'd get to me."

"To be honest, each one breaks my heart a little bit more. It's impossible to try and stay dispassionate." Tania toyed with her fork. "Knowing we are doing everything we can to get the best possible outcomes for each child helps. Our whole focus is to provide protection for them and that's front and centre in all our decisions. Now that we're taking a cross-agency approach things have improved, but it's still not perfect. I have to keep reminding myself it'd be a lot worse without our intervention."

"How often do you see underage children being exploited like with today's case?"

"My feeling is it's on the rise, but there's a surprising lack of hard data, just mostly anecdotal. It's not often we find under twelve-year-olds, but we do come across them from time to time. There's a sick market out there that drives the whole industry. Sorry if I sound like I'm ranting but having seen so many tragic cases I get angry just thinking about it. If the truth be known, I can tell you that from time to time I've fantasised about how I'd like to deal with those men who create that demand." Her voice had risen, drawing attention from the neighbouring tables.

Anahera watched the other detective, admiring her passion. "There's no need to apologise. It's pretty disgusting if you ask me."

"The child porn industry feeds and stimulates their deviant desires—it's impossible to stop its growth and the internet makes it so accessible. Child pornography, paedophilia and underage prostitution all blur together at the edges. It's so evil."

Suddenly Anahera felt like the wind had gone out of her. Her Rangi, part of the problem. The thought sickened her. She'd always assumed they were bringing their boys up to be good citizens. She and Jim would need to see to it that it didn't become an ongoing issue.

Unaware of Anahera's struggle, Tania continued her monologue. "We've had cases where underage sex workers were taking meth and working nights on the street and then going to school the next day." She shook her head. "Can you imagine it? Coming home after a night of selling yourself, then straight into your school uniform and off to school."

"That's terrible. Makes me glad I have boys and not girls."

"I can't blame you. Of late I've become particularly interested in the issues around underage sex workers. Partly because it's been overlooked for so long and we know so little about the trade. There's a real dearth of research in that area and I feel we're only scratching the surface of what's really happening out there."

"I hadn't realised."

"No, it's rarely talked about. You never hear about it in the media. But commercial exploitation of children must be our greatest shame as a society. Sometimes teenagers engage in the practice willingly for survival, without fully understanding the long-term implications and impact on their physical, emotional and spiritual health. But others are coerced into it by adults who stand to profit off their forced labour, and I find that abhorrent. Sometimes it's done for favours where the child is led to believe they have little or no choice, such as a false promise of protection or having a basic need met in some way. Often it's accompanied by drug use, and then it becomes a necessity to maintain their habit." She finished her savoury. "The children themselves are generally too young to deal with the emotions that accompany it, and they will often be riddled with shame thinking they are bad and that they did something wrong. Some will even crave the attention it brings them having never known the love of a caring family. It's such a mixed-up world."

"How many underage prostitutes are there?"

"Frankly we don't know. A survey turned up around 150 who were under the age of 16 years, but that was based on fairly flimsy data." She rolled her eyes. "To keep it in perspective, most of our cases are abuse and neglect at the hands of the caregivers, and those are bad enough."

"We get a lot of young run-away cases in Land Search and Rescue. That's an area where our work potentially overlaps. Some of these kids end up selling themselves on the street."

"Yes. One young teen I dealt with had left home at eleven to escape abuse at the hands of her father only to find 'sugar daddies' who paid her a meagre amount. When we found her, she was sleeping rough in a used clothing collection bin and living hand-to-mouth."

"Once rescued, do they ever recover from the trauma?"

"Not really. It's real tough for them. Too often they are introverted and view the world through a hostile lens." Tania picked up her cup and cradled it in both hands. "Enough about me and my work. Tell me about you—do you have family?"

"Yeah—my husband Jim and I have two boys. Rangi is our oldest and is at college already. He's ..." Anahera stopped. Sharing her boy's successes had always come easy to her. But today was different. Unsure whether to bring up yesterday's issue with her newfound colleague, she simply said, "He's sporty and overall seems to be doing well. Volleyball is his big thing and we're hoping he might get a scholarship to the States. Our youngest, Piri, is at intermediate school and is also doing well. His thing is music and that keeps him occupied. Mostly they're good kids."

"Nice. And what about work?"

"I've been pulled off the Land Search and Rescue cases to focus on the case of the girls found drowned out at Rangitoto Island. They were aged twelve and nine. The pressure is on, what with the story splashed all over the media this last week."

Tania nodded. "The tip off you gave us had something to do with that, right?"

"Yeah, I've been working the case with Frank Smythe. He's a good detective—we've partnered in the past and have had a pretty good track record together. But this case is different. As yet we've made little or no progress—it's so frustrating. Both girls had been sexually abused in the past. Nobody has come forward to report them missing. We put the plea out to the public—that's where we got the tip off for you—but it hasn't brought in any leads."

"Any suspects?"

"One person of interest, but we've got nothing concrete and he's probably a long shot at this stage. It's based more on a feeling rather than anything we can nail him on, not even circumstantial evidence." Anahera took her time to empty her cup. "Tell me about the raid this morning."

"Thanks to you, we surprised them. The place was set up with a bar in the lounge and the usual red lights were dotted around along with some fairly tacky decorations. We have a woman in custody who appeared to be running the place. Quite a stroppy Madam—she's refusing to say anything at this stage. A man was caught in the act with the eleven-year-old girl, and we have him in custody as well. The door to that bedroom had a padlock and the window had bars across it. I assume they kept the child locked up in there to stop her from running away. Two other girls, teenagers we think, heard us and scarpered through a bedroom window and over the back fence. We found wads of cash on the premises, alcohol and marijuana."

"How's the child?"

"She's with a social worker. As yet she's not uttered a word, just whimpers and stares vacantly. We're not even sure she speaks English." A stray tear formed in her eye and found its way down beneath her glasses until she wiped it away. "I can't imagine what she might have gone through. The child will have a medical exam as soon as she's up for it, but there's no question she was raped."

"That's shocking."

"Tell me about it."

"Was she the daughter?"

"No. The Madam is white and the girl Indian, or so we think."

Anahera leaned forward. "The girls that drowned were Nepalese."

Tania eyed Anahera closely. "Interesting. What do you know about them?"

"Pretty much nothing! It's so frustrating. We've really no idea who they are or where they came from. Nor how they got there. We put out the media appeal to try and find their guardians but so far it's been unsuccessful." Anahera checked her wristwatch. "Goodness, is that the time already? I need to go. I'm supposed to be checking tattoo studios, and there're so many of them. I've just spent all morning walking around the inner-city ones, and I have a constable doing the same. It's going to take the rest of the day and then some."

Tania's eyes widened behind her glasses. "Tattoos?"

"Yes. The deceased each had a tattoo and if we can find the tattooist, we're hoping they might be able to lead us to someone who has information about the girls. You'd think you wouldn't forget if you tattooed a child's wrist."

"What?" Tania sat up straight. "It wasn't an eye by any chance, was it?"

Anahera's heart skipped a beat. "You've seen it?"

"Just this morning—the child with the social worker has an eye tattooed on her wrist, with some sort of markings in the centre."

"Do you have a photo of the tattoo?"

"No, but I can get you one. Do you?"

Anahera opened her phone and pulled up a photo. "Did it look like this?"

"Yes, exactly like that." Tania looked stunned.

"Can I see her?"

"I'll have to run that by Sandie. She's the social worker assigned to the case. She'll be extremely protective of her—I've worked with Sandie a lot and she's one who cares deeply for all her clients. I'm guessing she won't let anyone near the child until she is out of shock and is being responsive." Tania shook her head in disbelief. "I would never have connected the girl in the brothel to your drowning victims had we not had lunch. How's that for luck?"

"I can't believe it! This might just be the break we've been waiting for—and we were the ones who fielded that call and passed it on thinking it irrelevant to our case!" Anahera shook her head while breathing out a long sigh. "Thank goodness you followed it up. But if you'll excuse me I really must dash. Don't forget to send me a picture of the tattoo. And please keep me up to date."

"Likewise, and I'd appreciate a copy of the photos of the tatts on your victims. I'll talk to Sandie about you visiting the girl."

Standing outside the café, they agreed to make lunch a regular occurrence before heading off in opposite directions.

13

Frank had just finished speaking with the owner of a Farr 1020 yacht when his mobile chirped and Anahera's number came up on the screen.

"You must be missing me—two calls in less than two hours. What's up?"

"I think the girls were being used as prostitutes. There's another one with the same tattoo found in a raid on a brothel in New Lynn." Anahera spoke quickly while sounding breathless.

"Whoa—slow down. What's happened?"

"Remember the tip we received in response to the appeal regarding New Lynn? The one where a caller was concerned there was an illegal brothel with underage girls in their neighbourhood and you passed it on to Puiwaitahi?"

"Yes, of course I remember. What of it?"

"They've had the place under surveillance and raided it early this morning. An eleven-year-old girl was there of Asian ethnicity and ..." She paused. "Frank, she has the same eye tattoo on her wrist!"

"Wow, that *is* great news!" The sun was beginning to feel warmer.

"The girl was in a room that had a lock on the door and bars on the windows."

It took a moment for him to digest the news. "Bastards! Who is she? Where did she come from?"

"I don't know—she's with a social worker. The bad news is she's traumatised and not yet speaking. I'm trying to get access to interview her."

"Who was her guardian?"

"A woman has been arrested who apparently ran the outfit, but it sounds like she's playing the silent card. Frank, this is the break we needed." Anahera sounded excited. "When do you think you'll be back in the city?"

"We're pretty much done here. We've not found anyone who can either corroborate or refute Jerry Ramsley's story."

"Do you think he might've had them on board as escorts after all?"

"Quite possibly, although that begs the question where did he pick them up. We need to interview the woman from the brothel."

"I'm already trying to set that up for this afternoon. What's your E.T.A?"

Frank checked his watch. "I make that 15-hundred hours. Tell me, how did you piece it together?"

"I've just had lunch with Tania Jones, a detective with Puiwaitahi, and it was a chance remark about checking out tattoo studios. We could easily have missed the connection."

"Good work. I'll see you back at Central. Keep me posted if there's any more news. And best update Brad—he'll be delighted to learn we're making some progress at last."

He ended the call and put the phone in his pocket, unable to contain the grin that had spread across his face as he joined the others in the wheelhouse.

"What's up, Boss?" Stephen asked from his perch at the navigation station.

Frank relayed Anahera's news to Stephen and Dick.

"So there were three girls and not two?" Dick asked.

"At least three."

"Sounds like you're close to closing this one. When do you suppose you'll be back in the Unit?" Stephen asked.

"At a guess I'd say give us a couple more days to get the answers and tie the loose ends."

"How did the girls get to Rangitoto Island from New Lynn? They're not even close, and New Lynn is nowhere near the harbour." Dick looked puzzled.

"That's the big question." Frank frowned. "This may be a whole lot bigger than we first thought."

"What about Jerry Ramsley? Still think he's involved?" Stephen asked.

"I honestly don't know. But they had to have had someone to transport them out to the island."

"It's sick using young girls in that way. It's hard to comprehend some of the evil that goes on in our own backyard." Dick shook his head.

"I know what you mean. But we'll see that the culprits are stopped and put away, and the sooner the better," Frank said with determination.

Flocks of sea birds floated contentedly over the chop, its peaks now whipped to white foam by the breeze as *Deodar III* made her way to home base.

*

Anahera was standing outside the interview room talking to Tania while waiting for Frank. The Puiwaitahi team had agreed to accommodate Frank and Anahera by giving them access to Scarlett O'Connor, the woman arrested during the raid of the brothel, in between their own interview sessions.

"I've contacted Sandie Tolkin, the social worker who's looking after the girl, and she said there's no chance of you seeing her until she's less traumatised. Effectively she said don't call her, she'll call you. Sorry, but I did try."

"I guess we'll just have to wait. Can we assume this girl is also Nepalese?"

"I think so, although the man we apprehended called her Harmony—not very Nepalese if you ask me. I let Sandie know that the two Nepalese girls found drowned had similar tattoos on their wrists and are therefore somehow connected. She's going to arrange for a Nepalese interpreter to speak with the child. We're hoping she'll open up when she hears her own language."

"How have the interviews with the prisoners gone?"

"Poorly. The client caught with Harmony is an accountant with a reputable company downtown. He got lawyered up and is terrified his name will go public. He wants to do a deal to get permanent name suppression in exchange for supplying information. It's not just about his name either—he's scared his wife and adult children will find out. I very much doubt if he knows much about the workings of the brothel though because he maintains he's a newish client. Thankfully the decision around whether to make a deal is above my pay grade."

"Why should he get special treatment? He should have thought about the consequences before becoming a perpetrator. I have no sympathy for the man." Anahera frowned. "Given there's no question he was guilty, I hope his name gets splashed across all the news channels. I hate seeing these guys get name suppression—they should be made to bear the public scrutiny of what they do."

"I couldn't agree more. He did however tell us that he'd recently been referred to the New Lynn house by someone at *Red Lights*, an adult nightclub he'd frequented a few times. We've yet to determine if there's a relationship between the two. As for Scarlett O'Connor, the other one we apprehended at the scene, she hasn't said much. It's early days but her lawyer has her plugged tighter than a cork in a bottle of champagne."

"There's only one remedy for that and that's to take it out forcefully and drink the bottle!" A familiar deep voice interrupted, ending with a chuckle.

Smiling, Anahera turned to see Frank join them. "Frank, I'm glad you made it. Meet Tania Jones, the detective with Puiwaitahi."

Frank and Tania shook hands.

"The prisoner is all yours," Tania said. "I hope you get further than we have thus far. I'll be watching from next door. When you're done, we'll have another go. Good luck in there."

"Thanks." Turning to Frank, Anahera asked, "Mind if I take the lead on this one?"

"Of course not, she's all yours." Frank smiled. "I'll play the good cop."

Anahera was feeling upbeat when they entered the interview room, confident they would soon have answers to end their investigation into the appearance of the two drowned Nepalese girls.

Two women sat at the table, heads together and speaking in whispers. One was dressed in a khaki singlet under a denim mid rift vest pulled together with a single button revealing a deep cleavage adorned with brightly painted wooden beads that hung around her neck. Her hair was long in tight multi coloured ringlets, and her face was partially obscured behind iridescent blue rimmed glasses that matched the paint on her long nails. The other woman was petite in comparison and smartly dressed in the corporate clothes you'd expect of a well-paid lawyer. They looked up when Anahera and Frank entered and took their seats across the table from them.

"I'm Detective Anahera Raupara and this is my colleague Detective Frank Smythe." Anahera looked expectantly at the two women.

"Prue Thomas of Thomas and Associates Law Firm." The smart looking woman reached across the table and shook their hands.

Turning to the other woman, Anahera said, "We have a few questions we'd like to ask, and we'll record the interview. Is that okay with you?"

The woman looked at her lawyer who nodded. "I guess."

Anahera began the interview by stating the time. "I believe you have already been read your Miranda rights. Is that correct?"

"Yeah." The prisoner scowled.

"Please state your full name and address for the record."

Scarlett O'Connor again looked at her lawyer before complying.

"We want to ask you about the Nepalese girl, Harmony, found on the property during the police raid. Could you please tell us her full name?"

Scarlett looked at Prue before turning to Anahera, her expression sullen. Silence.

"I advise my client not to answer that," Prue said in a voice that suggested a privileged upbringing.

"Can you tell us what your relationship to her is?"

Another pregnant pause before Prue repeated, "I advise my client not to answer that."

"Are you aware that in the last week two other Nepalese girls were found dead out at Rangitoto Island?"

"What on earth has that got to do with me?" Scarlett looked at Anahera, her eyes wide behind her glasses. "There're probably hundreds of Nepalese girls in this city."

"What does the tattoo on the wrist symbolise?"

Prue cut in before Scarlett had a chance to answer, saying, "You don't have to answer these questions."

"It's okay." Scarlett looked back at Anahera. "How should I know? It's just a tattoo. I bet most people in this city have a tattoo somewhere. Do you want to see all mine?" This time she cast a sensual grin at Frank who maintained his poker face.

"Do you know where Harmony got the tattoo?"

Scarlett laughed loudly. "I'm not her bloody minder."

"Then who are you to her?"

Prue cut in quickly before Scarlett could answer. "My client doesn't need to answer that question."

Scarlett stared at Anahera, her jaw set in a smug smile.

"How many girls do you look after?"

The question was met with a stony silence.

The line of questioning wasn't getting the responses Anahera wanted and she glanced at Frank, silently passing the lead to him.

"Scarlett, may I call you that?" Frank asked.

She nodded.

"Scarlett, here's the thing. The two Nepalese girls found out at Rangitoto Island were dead, drowned. They were only twelve and nine years of age. They too were tattooed with an eye on their wrists. All we want is to trace where they came from and notify their next of kin. Look, we're just asking you to help us find them." Frank's voice had softened, his eyes pleading as he looked at Scarlett. "Now you seem to be a reasonable person. Can you do that for us? Please?"

Anahera kept a straight face as she recognised the good cop strategy.

"I advise my client not to answer that." It sounded like an artificial intelligence voice.

"It's okay Prue, I've got nothing to hide." Scarlett gave Frank a haughty look. "I don't know those girls and I don't know anything about them being out at Rangitoto. Not my girls I'm afraid."

"Can you suggest where we might go to find someone who might know?"

Scarlett looked at Prue. "I'm through with this."

"You don't need to answer any more questions."

"Look, we're not trying to pin it on you. We just want to contact their legal guardians so they can grieve appropriately. We would *appreciate* your help." Frank emphasised appreciate.

"You deaf or something? I've already told you I don't bloody well know anything about that."

"What about the tattoo? Did Harmony already have it when you took her in?"

Scarlett's demeanour seemed to change as she stared at Frank, her eyes wide behind her glasses while chewing suggestively on her lip.

Anahera's patience was like sand running through the hourglass. "You're not helping yourself by refusing to assist the police in our investigations. Who are you trying to protect? Do you think they'd care about you?" She sucked in a deep breath to restore her calm as she waited, watching, only to be met with stony silence.

A minute passed. Scarlett shifted uncomfortably in her chair.

A thought struck Anahera. "Could *Red Lights* nightclub help us with our enquiries?"

Scarlett's face clouded over briefly before turning into a pout. She quickly turned to Prue, who stepped in with her standard monotone answer, "I advise my client not to answer that."

Frank nodded at Anahera who took the cue and ended the interview.

Outside the meeting room Anahera said to Frank, "Did you see the look that passed over her face when I asked about *Red Lights*? You know I may just have struck a nerve."

"Yep I caught that and thought she looked surprised. What prompted the question?"

"Something Tania said earlier, about the punter being referred to the New Lynn house by someone at *Red Lights*. I just had a hunch they could be tied up in some way."

At that moment Tania joined them.

"Are you done for now?"

"Yes, thanks. We'll let you know if we need any more time with her."

"I heard you ask about *Red Lights*. I'm wondering if Scarlett has any link to them. That'll be my next line of questioning."

"Any news on the girl?"

"Not as yet, but I promise to keep you posted."

Tania left to prepare herself for the next stage of the interview, leaving Anahera and Frank to return to Central. Soon they were standing outside Brad's office and Anahera rapped loudly on the door.

"Come in."

They entered to find him packing up his desk.

"Good, I'm glad you caught me. Take a seat." He gestured to the seats in front of his desk.

"We've just come out of an interview and wanted to give you an update," Anahera said.

"You're just in time. You've caught me getting ready to leave early for a change." He grinned good naturedly, revealing the old Brad. "The wife's wanting me to man the barbecue for a small dinner party she's got organised and I thought I'd build up some brownie points. Can never have too many."

"You'll be pleased to hear we've had a bit of a breakthrough," Anahera began. "One of the tip offs from the public appeal was a neighbour in New Lynn who thought an illegal brothel with underage Asian girls was operating at a residential address in their neighbourhood. We passed it on to Puiwaitahi and they conducted a raid this morning. A punter was caught with an eleven-year-old Asian girl in a room, goes by the name Harmony. The interesting development is that Harmony has the same tattoo on her wrist. We've just come out of an interview with the woman who allegedly runs the outfit, but she didn't give anything away. Turns out the punter was told about the New Lynn place by someone he met at the *Red Lights Adult Nightclub*. We'll follow up that lead in the morning."

"Good to hear there's some good progress at last. What is the girl saying?" Brad's blue eyes studied them both.

"Nothing at this point. She's under the care of a social worker and is traumatised. I have asked for access and am waiting to hear."

"Good. What do you make of it?"

Anahera looked at Frank, who answered, "We've not yet had time to discuss it in any great detail but obviously the cases have to be linked. We could be dealing with an organised crime ring."

"And what about the boatie you were following up?"

"As yet nothing."

"Do you still think he was involved?"

"I honestly don't know." Frank rubbed his chin. "We've pretty much ruled out helicopter, land vehicle and ferry. That leaves boats—and they could be private vessels or ships. The latter doesn't answer the question as to how the girls got to the island. Jerry Ramsley may be a person of interest but I'm not so sure anymore."

Anahera cut in. "We've not found the tattooist either and that's not for a lack of trying."

"Well then, keep pushing and stay close to Puiwaitahi. Oh, and keep me informed of progress—I will need to put out a press release in the next day or two." He looked at his watch. "Have a good night, you've earned it."

Anahera followed Frank out of his office feeling like she had her mojo back. Brad's high spirits were contagious, and the events of the day had left her confident they were closing in and now it was just a matter of time before they got those responsible. Her footsteps were light as she descended the stairs.

*

That evening Anahera sat in her favourite chair on the balcony. The long spell of clement weather had finally broken and the first spots of heavy rain were making a splatter pattern on the tiles beyond the shelter of the roof. She fiddled with the wine glass stem as the random pattern of splotches filled in to add a reflective sheen to the exposed tiles. A strike of lightning lit the sky followed closely by a crack of thunder. Another round followed.

Sheltered under the overhanging roof, she said to Jim who was sitting next to her, "Let's stay out here and watch the show. Isn't it beautiful?"

"Sure. You seem more relaxed. Good day at work?"

"Not bad. We had a small breakthrough on the case, but we're unsure what it means as yet. But that's not it. I was just thinking that with all that's going on in the world, we're lucky we live in a relatively stable country and not in a state of anarchy."

"You mean like Waterworld?"

"Something like that."

"We should be grateful we live under the rule of law." He reached over and squeezed her hand. "I'm proud of the work you do."

"I couldn't do it without your support."

They lapsed into silence. The storm continued to rage.

"I made a new friend today—we had lunch," Anahera said. "She's a detective and moved up here from Wellington. Her casework is child neglect and abuse for the multi-agency unit Puiwaitahi."

"I've heard of that initiative."

"I couldn't deal with those cases—it'd kill me. I admire her for her passion." She sipped her drink just as another bolt of lightning flashed across the sky. "She passed a comment about how perverts often begin with pornography, and I don't think I've ever felt so ashamed on account of Rangi. Have you talked to him today?"

"Not about that. He was complaining about not having his phone. I plan to take him out after volleyball practice on Saturday and we can have a chat then."

"Jim, we need to make sure he doesn't become part of the problem."

"He won't. Trust me."

They sat in silence, sipping their drinks, watching the storm rage around them.

"Life's a bit like this, isn't it?" Anahera looked at Jim. "You can coast along in the calm, enjoying the periods of sunshine. And then out of the blue a storm comes along. The lightning heralds the thunder and rain falls—stuff happens that's largely out of your control. But it doesn't last forever and eventually it clears up, the sun comes out and you move on.

After a while you can barely remember it. This business with the pornography is like the storm, isn't it Jim? We will get through it—and one day we'll look back and realise it was only a small hiccup."

Jim smiled at her. "You're right. Rangi has a strong foundation and is a good kid. Part of the problem is peer pressure—and we just need to help him navigate his way through this."

"We can do this Jim."

"Too right we can."

Mother nature continued her show, giving them a front row seat, content in each other's company.

14

Frank stood with Anahera outside the *Red Lights Adult Nightclub* door in an area of the city known for its clubs, massage parlours and adult shops. The sign that hung overhead had the name of the establishment emblazoned on it with a caricature of a buxom woman holding a tray with a drink on it. The image did nothing for him and he wondered why it was considered a drawcard for the club—they obviously had a different demographic in mind for their target market.

Stairs led up to the floor above and along the walls above the stairs were more caricatures of pole dancers in a variety of poses. A string of red lights lit the stairwell just enough to make out the steps. At the top of the stairs was a door into the nightclub manned by a large bouncer who wore a fitting black skivvy and trousers that highlighted muscles obtained by hours of disciplined training at a gym, making most people think twice before causing a commotion. The sort of guy who could maintain their poker face doing a good impersonation of nobody at home. But behind that blank expression Frank knew he was being scrutinised. In his ear was an earpiece. His face was devoid of expression, not even a flicker of cognition, as he sized Frank up.

The detectives each flashed their ID and walked straight past him without hesitation and entered the nightclub.

Inside was a large windowless room with a bar that ran the entire length of one side. It was the only part of the room that was well lit. Behind it was the usual array of bottles of spirits and liqueurs on glass shelves, more shelves displaying glasses, and a bank of fridges full of bottles. A good selection of beer taps was positioned along the bar. Two bar tenders, both blonde females wearing black uniforms that consisted of low-cut tops and extra short skirts with aprons that had a white frill around them, stood behind the bar looking bored. Bar stools along the length of the bar were unsurprisingly empty given the time of day, apart from one man who leaned on the bar looking sorry for himself. His suit was crumpled, his tie loose around his neck, and his hair dishevelled. A glass of clear amber liquid over ice sat on the bar beside him.

The main part of the room was illuminated with subdued light from red-coloured halogen downlights. A stage ran the length of the room opposite the bar and three poles were symmetrically located in a triangle, but the dancers had not yet begun their shifts. A few people milled about, looking more like staff than customers. In a booth near the stage sat three men all wearing suits, their heads inclined towards each other in deep conversation. One glanced sideways, and on seeing Frank and Anahera sat bolt upright, then said something to his friends who also looked in their direction.

Frank approached the bar tender and asked to speak to the owner or manager. She pointed towards the three men.

"Frank, look!" Anahera spoke in an insistent whisper beside him. "There, on the shelf beside the glasses."

Frank scanned the area behind the bar, then caught his breath. Sitting on the shelf was a gold frame and in it was a picture of a stylised red eye with hieroglyphics. It was the same style as the tattoos. Eureka! "Well spotted," he responded in a low voice.

"How do you want to play this?"

"For now, let's keep it low key and not mention the tattoos, just gauge their reaction to the drowned girls. There's something much larger at play here."

Frank strode over to the booth with Anahera at his side. The three men stopped talking as they approached, tensing their bodies, their expressions not the least bit friendly.

"Detective Frank Smythe." He waved his badge at them. "And my colleague here is Detective Anahera Raupara."

Anahera flashed her badge.

"Which one of you gentlemen is the owner?" Frank watched the three men closely.

The man with heavy gold bling and thickset glasses who'd spotted them first cleared his throat. "I am. What is it you want?"

"And your name is?"

"Chase Craddock."

Frank smiled to defuse the situation. "We're after some information about some young Nepalese girls. You have probably read in the papers that two Nepalese girls were found out near Rangitoto Island. We have reason to believe you might be able to help us trace where they came from."

"Why would you think that? How should I know?"

Frank ignored his questions. "Do you know a Jerry Ramsley? Perhaps he is a customer of yours?"

"Sorry. I don't recall the name." The man's flushed face remained expressionless.

"What about Scarlett O'Connor?"

The man looked momentarily indecisive before responding, "That name sounds familiar." He turned to one of the other men at the table. "Do you remember a person with that name? Did she work here?"

"I think she might have."

Turning back to Frank, Chase flashed a smile revealing a gold crown. "There, you have your answer. I can't possibly remember all the girls that work here. They come and go so frequently. It's so hard to retain them. You train a girl and then she up and leaves to dance for the opposition. It's a competitive business. Why did you want to know?"

"She may have a connection to the drowned girls." Frank felt their intense scrutiny.

"No, I can't help you. Sorry." Chase Craddock turned back to his friends as if dismissing the two detectives, then leered at Anahera. "Darling, if you ever want to make a smart career move, be sure to contact me. I would see you right with a spot pole dancing. You've got the tush for it."

"I'll keep it in mind."

Frank looked at Anahera who'd turned and was already walking towards the exit.

"Thanks for your time." He followed Anahera to the door and down the stairs.

They walked in silence for a few metres until confident it was safe to talk without being overheard.

"Were you tempted to throw it in for pole dancing?" Frank asked.

"Haha very funny," she said punching him lightly on the shoulder.

"What did you make of that?" Frank asked.

"Very interesting. The eye tells me they know more than he was letting on."

"I agree. It smells of an organised crime ring to me."

"That's what I was thinking—one dealing in underage immigrant sex workers. Let's get back to the office and I'll do some digging into Chase Craddock and see what I can turn up. With a bit of luck I might discover a relationship between the nightclub and the brothel in New Lynn."

"Good. And while you do that, I'll pop down to Mechanics Bay and get a list of all ships that were in around the period in question and chase Shari over the computer modelling for Jane Doe Two."

"We should talk to Brad and see how he wants to handle the nightclub. They're definitely in the middle of all this, that picture proves it. But just how they're linked is a mystery to me. Still, I can't help but feel that whatever it is, it's big."

"Hopefully a search of their premises will throw some light on the case. Let's see what you can uncover on Craddock before we meet with Brad and apply for a search warrant."

"I'll set up a time to meet with him."

They chatted about the case the whole way back to the office. Life had just become a whole lot brighter, reminding him why he loved detective work. To put these guys behind bars would be immensely satisfying and mean that the girls' deaths wouldn't be in vain.

*

Frank pulled up in the car park outside the Maritime Police building which also housed the Harbour Master and went to find Shari. As luck would have it, she was at her desk and looked up as he entered.

"Hey Frank. I ran that information you gave me through the computer model, but as you expected the results cover a large area and are probably not very useful. With so many variables it's impossible to say where the body could have entered the water with any degree of accuracy." She peered at him over her glasses. "Take a look at this."

He leaned over her shoulder to look at her screen. "Help me understand what I'm looking at."

"Let's start with Jane Doe Two. If the body drifted on to the rocks where it was located on the ebb tide, and assuming the time of death was when it entered the water, then the likelihood that the starting point was somewhere within the shaded circle here is 95 percent." She pointed to the screen.

"This shows that if those assumptions were true, then the most likely scenario would be off a boat somewhere just north of the Rangitoto Channel and close to the shipping lane." Frank rubbed his head. "Right?"

"Correct. But if you look at the circle shown by the lighter shading, the area increases significantly with the likelihood now 98 percent."

"Okay. That could mean she went in off Narrow Neck beach, or off a boat traversing that area. It does include a boat coming west through the Rakino Channel, which is what our person of interest may have done."

"That's right. Also, the area used to anchor freighters waiting to dock at the port is right in the middle of the grid—she could have literally jumped from a ship."

"Or a passenger liner waiting for clearance to dock at Queens wharf."

Shari's fingers flew over the keyboard with speed and accuracy, reflecting her youth and status as a digital native. "I can get the model to calculate the most likely area the body drowned based on the differing times the body could have arrived at the place where it was found using the tidal currents, windage and body drag. This one shows the difference had the body been snagged on the rock for one hour prior to being found. See how the area of likelihood changes? And now two hours. And three. And so on. If I overlay all these potential times the body may have snagged on that rock, we get this."

Frank stared at the screen. As he'd seen with his own crude calculations, the whole of the Waitematā Harbour, Rangitoto Channel and the approaches to Auckland were within the grid. "That certainly widens the net. I'm afraid it doesn't help us at all."

"I guess the most you can extract from it is none of these possibilities can be ruled out." She looked at Frank and adjusted her glasses. "I'm sorry it wasn't better news Frank."

"Not your fault. Thanks anyway."

Shari typed and another chart came onto the screen. "I ran a similar exercise with Jane Doe One, assuming she floated with the current and died once she'd arrived in the boat shed. I've also made some fairly broad assumptions around the likely length of time she might have been in the water before she would have succumbed to drowning. Here you can see the most likely route would have been from the Motuihe Channel, which is virtually in the opposite direction."

"Can you overlay the charts for Jane Doe One and Jane Doe Two?"

"I've already done it. Here you can see the likely areas each Jane Doe went into the water do not overlap at all—not even close."

"So, the conclusion would be that either they did not enter the water at the same place and time or Jane Doe One had help to get to the boat shed."

"There are two other possibilities that I've shown on this next chart. The first is Jane Doe One walked from the west side of Rangitoto Island around to the boat shed. But I would find that highly unlikely given how much salt water she'd inhaled."

"Yes, I think we should rule out the walk from the western side," Frank interjected. "It's just too far and very tough over the scoria. I'm guessing it would be near impossible for a young girl in her state. What's the second possibility?"

"She could've come ashore on the northern side, potentially at Gardiner Gap, and managed to walk the short distance from there to the boat shed."

"This seems more likely but why the boat shed? Why not one of the small baches in Gardiner Gap or near the Islington Bay wharf?" Frank nodded. "It doesn't seem to make sense."

"I can't help you with that."

"That means it's feasible the girls were together on either a ship or private vessel."

"It is only a guide, but yes, it's feasible. I hope this has helped." Shari smiled at Frank. "I'll send you the report."

Although it hadn't come as a surprise, it was disappointing that the modelling hadn't shown something more positive to go on. He took his leave and went to find the Harbour Master, who was in his office.

"Frank, come in. How're things going over at Central?" Brett Tripps was a stocky man with a full grey beard.

"Good but looking forward to getting back on *Deodar*."

"Well, it'll be good to have you back on this side. What can I do for you?"

"I'm after a list of all ships entering the Port of Auckland for the week leading up to when the Rangitoto drownings occurred."

"Give me the exact dates." Brett passed a notepad and Frank scribbled down the dates.

"Can you include dates any of the ships were at anchor waiting to dock and the exact locality at which they were anchored."

"Sure thing, Frank. I'm assuming this is important so I could get those to you within the hour."

"Thanks Brett, I owe you one."

With his mind solely focused on the case, Frank barely noticed the abundance of orange cones and roadworks that plagued the streets as part of the Council's drive to modernise the city and bring people into its centre. Once parked outside Central, he went to a local café and bought two coffees-to-go, thinking Anahera would most likely be needing one by now.

She was staring into her screen when he entered their office.

"Order for Raupara," he said, placing the coffee beside her.

"Frank, you're a lifesaver." She reached for the cup. "How did you get on?"

Frank ran through the computer modelling outcomes. He finished saying, "So in summary it's quite possible the girls had been together, and if that's right then they could have been on the northern side of Rangitoto Island when they went into the water with the most likely scenarios for Jane Doe One being either she beached on the north side and made her own way to the shed or she was taken there by someone. Alternatively, they weren't together at the time they entered the water. It opens up both being on either a ship or private vessel together. I've asked the Harbour Master for the shipping records. How about you?"

"I've fared better than you. I've done a little digging and the lease for the New Lynn address was taken out by a fellow who goes by the name of Grant Tate." She sipped her coffee.

"I was hoping it would be Chase Craddock."

"I investigated the ownership of the *Red Lights Adult Nightclub* and found that the building is under one company, the operation under another which employs the staff. Craddock's name is not on any of them. I did a bit more digging and found another layer of companies, one of which includes a casino. Then sitting over the lot is Cee Cee New Zealand Investments. And guess who owns that?"

"Would it be Chase Craddock?"

"Spot on. He owns the whole damn shooting match but has set it up so it's arm's length and has no direct connection to him."

"But no link to Scarlett O'Connor or the New Lynn address?"

"I've checked the directorships for each of the companies." Anahera giggled. "You won't believe it—we've got the link we need, Frank. Grant Tate is listed as a director of the company that controls the operation of *Red Lights Adult Nightclub*."

"With the tattoos on all three girls and in the picture at the club, and the link between the brothel and the club, we should be able to get a search warrant. Let's hope we find what we need to see the culprits rot in prison."

"What do you think we are looking at here? Illegal immigrants being forced to work?"

"With children involved, it's more likely to be a trafficking ring. We need to get a search warrant. I'll start the paperwork now."

They were sipping their coffees, relieved to have finally made some real progress when Anahera's phone bleeped.

"Kia ora. Anahera Raupara speaking."

Pause.

"That's great news. Yes, this afternoon works for me. Where is she?" Another pause.

"Thanks Tania, I'll see you there." She ended the call and looked up at Frank. "Harmony, from the New Lynn address, is speaking to an interpreter. I can see her later this afternoon, but you'll have to give this one a miss. They don't yet know how she might react to a strange male, given all she's been through."

"I'm not surprised."

"How about I call a meeting with Brad to let him know we're applying for a search warrant? I'll suggest the police prosecutor is also present," Anahera said, already picking up her phone.

*

Frank and Anahera found Brad sitting at his desk which was piled high with papers. He looked up and on seeing them said, "I'll swear there's a conspiracy to rid this country of its pine forests."

Frank dropped a copy of the warrant application on his desk and chuckled. "I can add to that paper mountain."

At that moment Pam Downer, a prosecutor with the Police Prosecution Service, entered his office. In her late-thirties, Pam was always well-groomed reflecting her professionalism and Frank knew her to be a capable lawyer who could be relied on to provide wise counsel.

"Take a seat." Brad stood up, gesturing to the chairs around the small table in the corner of the room. "I understand you've made good progress since we talked yesterday."

Frank gave a brief overview of the case for Pam's benefit and outlined their visit to the *Red Lights Adult Nightclub* and their brief interaction with Chase Craddock. Anahera explained the company structure and link to the address in New Lynn where the illegal brothel had been operating.

Frank finished by saying, "I've gone ahead and completed the paperwork for a warrant to search the premises."

Pam stopped her note taking and looked directly at Frank. "Let me be clear. The exact same figure as is tattooed on both your victims is also tattooed on the young girl found in the brothel and is the subject in a picture frame at the nightclub. Correct?"

"Almost. The stylised eye is the same but the hieroglyphics inside the eye differ slightly. We think they are some sort of identification system," Frank answered.

"And this man who took out the building lease for the brothel is a director of one of the companies owned by Chase Craddock and linked to the nightclub where the picture was found?" Pam sat poised with her pen in hand.

"That's right," Anahera answered.

"What is it you are hoping to find?" Brad leaned forward.

"Papers, files, anything that links the nightclub to the New Lynn address. As well as the names of clients who may have been given access to the girls. Also it's possible the girls' passports were being kept there." Anahera spoke quickly.

"Do you agree that it is now looking like some sort of organised trafficking ring at play here?"

"We're thinking that's the most obvious explanation," she said.

"There's a special taskforce operating that is looking into international human trafficking. I'll have a chat to them—they may want to be in on this one." Brad rubbed a cauliflower ear, a remnant of his time spent playing senior rugby. "In the meantime, I suggest we get the warrant but don't go in until I get back to you."

"Understood," Frank said, as Anahera nodded her agreement.

"Then I think you have enough to make the case for a warrant to be issued. I'll get onto it straight away." Pam closed her legal pad.

Brad stood up indicating the meeting was over and Pam hurried out of the office.

"Good work you two. And keep me informed," Brad said, returning to his mountain of paperwork.

Anahera and Frank returned to their own office.

15

Needing fresh air to clear her thoughts, Anahera opted to walk across town to the children's hospital where the child found at the New Lynn address was being treated. The clouds overhead held the moisture that had gathered from over the sea. They darkened with every step causing her to hurry. At first a few spots of rain dropped, and she wiped them from her face. But then it became a torrent that soaked everything in its path. Cursing her stupidity for not checking the weather and bringing a jacket, she broke into a run only to arrive at the hospital with her hair hanging in wet clumps and her clothes sodden.

First stop was the ladies' room where she sat on her satchel under the hand drier to dry her hair and shirt. She checked her image in the mirror, combed her hair with her fingers and straightened her clothes.

The ward was on the fifth floor. Choosing the stairs, she climbed steadily but not so fast as to raise a sweat. On entering the ward, the smell of cleaning products left her in no doubt she was in a hospital and yet the walls were painted in brightly coloured panels.

Tania was standing at the reception talking to a nurse. As Anahera approached, she ended her conversation and put out her hand to shake Anahera's. "You look like you were caught in a storm."

"I was, but you should have seen me before I dried off." Anahera laughed.

"It's good you could make it. Sangita is the girl's actual name, it seems Harmony was given to her only recently and she doesn't respond to it at all. From the little she's said, we believe she'd only been here a few weeks at most when we raided the place. She's awake now and talking a little although she's very fragile and not very trusting. Thankfully she seems to have developed a bond of some sort with the interpreter who is also Nepalese."

"That's understandable, given she's been betrayed by both men and women. It must make it hard to know who to trust—the default being to trust no one." Anahera pushed her damp hair behind her ears.

"How's your investigation going?"

"We've made some good progress at last, and it also affects your case." Anahera proceeded to update her with where their investigation had got to and in particular, about the *Red Lights Adult Nightclub* and what she'd discovered about Chase Craddock.

"You're one step ahead of me then," Tania smiled. "I'd like to be in on the search."

"We're applying for the warrant now—it should be a formality. There's a taskforce looking into human trafficking that the boss wants involved as well—he's asked us to wait until he's talked to them. I'll let you know when it's going down."

"Great, thanks." Tania led Anahera down the wide corridor to a closed door where they stopped. As if on cue, it opened and a motherly looking woman with a mass of grey curls and a generous figure stepped out wearing a bright top patterned with pink and blue flowers over jeans. Her well-rounded face smiled easily when she spotted Tania, revealing a perfect set of pearly white straight teeth framed in red lipstick.

"Sandie, meet Anahera Raupara, the detective I was telling you about," Tania said.

Sandie shook Anahera's hand before exchanging business cards. "Nice to meet you. Let's go into the family lounge so I can bring you up to speed before you meet Sangita."

Anahera and Tania followed her to a small room with walls covered in cartoon characters and a kitchenette at one end.

"Would you like a drink? There's tea and coffee here. I admit I'm dying for a cup of tea," Sandie said.

They each made themselves a hot drink before taking their seats.

"I think it important you understand Sangita's condition, that is apart from the physical scarring. I'm no psychologist but I will explain it as best as I can. Sangita has been severely traumatised. She has also been given cannabis and methamphetamine, the impact of those drugs on a developing brain is not to be underestimated." Sandie's look was intense as she studied Anahera. "And her ability to trust adults and especially strangers, men in particular, has been sadly challenged. Abuse of such a serious nature as she's been subjected to can negatively impact her mental health, cognitive function, the ability to form satisfying relationships, and her sense of self-worth. Her overriding response has been to hide inside herself, to withdraw completely from the physical reality." Sandie paused to sip her tea.

"Will she recover from it?" Anahera asked.

"It's going to take a long time for her to recover, and she may never fully recover. No two children are affected in exactly the same way, so there's no textbook answer for that. Moreover, children generally feel the impacts of childhood sexual abuse at different points over the course of their lifetime, and the ways they are impacted can change from childhood through to adulthood." Sandie paused. "What we are most concerned about is how she is now. We are trying to encourage her to take the first baby steps back to normality."

"So how is she doing?"

"Sangita has only just started speaking again, in Nepali, that being her native tongue. We haven't been able to ascertain if she speaks English or if she understands any English words at all. And we've got her to start eating again."

"That's good progress then, right?"

"Yes, it's progress but as I said, there's a long way to go. You must have heard of our hard-wired automatic response system that protects us when facing a traumatic event; that is fight, flight, freeze, flop or friend?"

"Only fight, flight or freeze."

"No matter. My point is, it's possible that in her case her brain's protective mechanism was to freeze in the face of abuse and because of the severity and frequency of the abuse, it now recognises similarities associated with her past traumas constantly—it could be a colour, smell, sound—activating her freeze response even when she's not currently in danger. In this way she is constantly shut down. If you combine that with her lack of trust and a total loss of family and community, it will give you a better understanding of where she's at."

"Wow, I really had no idea." Anahera wiped away the tears that welled up. "That poor child."

Sandie studied Anahera, as if deciding how much to say. "There is one other thing. Sangita's development may be impaired. We don't know how long the abuse has been going on, but it is possible it could affect her long term. She presents young for her age, extremely naïve despite what she's been subjected to."

"Will she be able to answer some questions?"

"Possibly—I can't say how she might react. But we have a very good interpreter who is with her now, a Nepalese woman whose name is Binsa Dahal. She's providing far more than expected and they seem to have already formed a bond, even though they only met this morning. She's really the first person that Sangita has responded well to. Binsa has worked for an NGO trying to prevent the trade in young Nepalese women being sold over the border to India, and she seems to have a real understanding of what Sangita may have gone through."

"Where did you find her?"

"She is currently attached to the Consulate of Nepal."

"Sounds like we're lucky to have her here."

"What exactly did you want from Sangita?" Sandie asked, picking up her cup.

"We're investigating a case of two Nepalese girls found out at Rangitoto Island. The first was in a boat shed and had died of secondary drowning. The second had drowned and was found washed up on the shoreline. Both girls were sexually abused and each had a tattoo on their wrist." Anahera tapped on her phone and held it up for Sandie to see.

"I recognise it, Sangita has the same on her wrist."

"We are trying to find out who they are and where they came from. We want to locate their next-of-kin or guardian and discover how they got to be at Rangitoto and who abused them. I believe Sangita may be able to help us."

"As I explained, you'll need to be sensitive to her situation. While I understand your need to solve the case for the two deceased, remember Sangita is living meaning her well-being must not be put at risk. It might be best not to mention they died, at least not so soon in her recovery. And I'd prefer you don't show her any photos of the dead girls or anyone else for that matter. It's still very early days. I can give you ten minutes with her, but no more. You do understand, don't you?"

"I understand." Anahera finished her coffee.

"I'll go and see if she is awake." Sandie took her cup over to the sink and rinsed it before leaving the room.

"The thought of what she went through sickens me," Tania said.

"Me too. I find it hard to comprehend. And judging by what Sandie said, it's not just now but the psychological impacts could continue for life. It's so unfair—she didn't ask for it but she's the one who will pay and keep on paying. No guilty verdict will ever change that."

"Those that stand to make profit only think of themselves and the wealth they're creating, the punters only think of satisfying themselves, and apparently no one gives any thought to the repercussions for the children. It makes me so angry."

They sat in silence. Anahera was processing what Sandie had explained when she was struck by an idea.

"Tania, please tell Sandie I'll be back in a minute."

Before Tania could reply, Anahera was already racing for the stairs. She bolted down them, barely missing an orderly who was on his way up, and exited the stairwell on the ground floor where she'd remembered passing a shop. There she looked at the array of toys and treats for children before her eyes rested on a selection of small soft toys. She chose a teddy bear with a friendly face. Once purchased, she rushed back up the stairs where she found both Sandie and Tania waiting for her outside Sangita's room.

Taking a few deep breaths to slow her breathing, she held up the teddy. "I thought Sangita might like this."

Sandie's face softened. "That's so thoughtful of you. I'm sure she'll love it—she doesn't have any toys or in fact any possessions of her own apart from the clothes she was wearing."

"I hope she likes it. Can I see her now?"

"Yes, come with me." Sandie opened the door and led her into the room.

It took a minute for Anahera's eyes to adjust to the gloom as the curtains were closed. The room had just one bed in it and lying on it was a painfully thin young girl. Her dark hair was long and straight with a part down the middle, and her dark eyes were large in her hollowed face. Instinct kicked in and Anahera had to restrain the urge to wrap the child up in a motherly hug. The inclination to protect felt raw and overwhelming, and she struggled to hold back the tide of her emotions.

"Sangita, this is Anahera. She is the police lady we told you about and she'd like to ask you some questions," Sandie said.

The other woman in the room spoke to Sangita in a language with sounds that were entirely foreign to Anahera's ear.

"Anahera, meet Binsa from the Consulate," Sandie said. "I'll wait for you outside."

"Nice to meet you. Here's my card." Anahera passed her a business card before sitting in the one spare chair.

"Likewise." Binsa reached in her purse and pulled out a card for Anahera. She was an attractive lady, tiny in stature with shoulder length dark hair that curled around her moon shaped face and eyes that lit up when she looked back at Sangita.

"Sangita, this is a present for you." Anahera passed the child the toy.

Binsa interpreted as the child took the toy and held it to her. Her eyes never left Anahera.

"Can I ask you some questions that might help other girls like you?"

She took out her notebook and a pen while Binsa interpreted.

Still Sangita stared at Anahera. After a long moment she nodded, the gesture barely perceptible, so much so it could've easily been missed.

"Please can you ask her if I can see the tattoo on her wrist?"

Binsa spoke and Sangita tentatively held out her wrist for Anahera to see. Sure enough, there on the inside of the right wrist was the same stylised red eye with similar markings to those on the two deceased girls.

"Please ask her where she got it."

The young girl shrank back into her pillow, staring at Anahera with wide eyes while remaining mute.

"Sangita, can you tell me how you got to the house where you were found?"

Binsa relayed the question.

A long silence followed.

Sangita spoke, hesitantly at first, her voice high like that belonging to a small child.

Binsa interpreted saying, "She says she was taken there by a man. He got her from the box where she had been living. There was a building falling over and she could see planes flying. The same man took her to the house where the woman with the colourful hair lived."

Anahera considered this for a moment before continuing her line of questioning. "Can you ask her what this man looked like?"

Anahera waited for the response.

Sangita continued to watch Anahera, her fingers feeling her new toy. Moments passed before she answered.

"She says he was mean."

"Nothing else? Was he Nepalese?"

The question was asked and the answer interpreted. "She says she doesn't know. He didn't speak her tongue."

"Were there other girls with her?" Anahera waited for the answer.

"She says there were seven of them living in a stuffy box. She doesn't know what happened to the others."

"What did she mean by a box?"

Binsa asked her the question and immediately the child looked frightened and seemed to clam up.

"I'm sorry, Anahera. She doesn't seem to want to answer that."

"Did she travel here on board a ship?"

Binsa asked, but Sangita just stared at the toy.

Anahera smiled at Sangita, trying to convey she wasn't going to hurt her. She changed tack. "Does she have a mum and dad at home waiting for her?"

Binsa spoke to Sangita before responding to Anahera. "Yes she does, in their village up in the highlands of Nepal."

"And does she have brothers and sisters?"

Again, it was translated and answered. "Three younger sisters and two younger brothers."

"Do her parents know where she is?"

Binsa asked and Sangita shook her head vehemently before saying something to Binsa who nodded in understanding.

"I take that to be a no?" Anahera asked Binsa.

"I'm afraid so. She said they sent her away to be married to a wealthy man. You must understand Anahera, in my country many people are very very poor. Her parents were possibly offered a bride price for her and if we are right in assuming the family are poor, they probably considered it to be good fortune, thinking she was marrying above their status. The so-called groom may have told them he was taking her to his mother's home. Unfortunately it is an all-too-common story in Nepal."

"But she's a mere child."

"Child brides are sadly a societal norm in my country. Nearly ten percent of girls are married by the age of fifteen. It's a consequence of dire poverty and a lack of education, especially in the remote villages where access is on foot across mountainous terrain."

"Do you mean she was bought?"

"Almost definitely. It is often the way of things."

At that moment Sandie entered. "I'm sorry Anahera, time's up. I don't want her stressed any more than she is."

"Understood." Anahera turned to Sangita. "Thank you. You're a brave girl and you may have helped other girls just like you."

Sangita held the toy out to Anahera as Binsa interpreted.

"Please tell her the toy is for her to keep as her own." Anahera stood up and added, "Thanks Binsa, I appreciate your help."

"Let me know if I can be of further assistance."

Anahera barely held back her tears as she followed Sandie out the door where she quickly thanked her and made her escape. At the top of the stairs she paused, her hand on the banister, as if the wind had suddenly left her. If only she could turn back the clock and return the children to their families, all three of them. Sangita's life was a living hell. Jane Doe One and Two had lost their lives prematurely, but perhaps they were finally at peace having been spared any further pain of living with the horrors they'd experienced. She took a moment to pull herself together before hurrying down the stairs, even more determined to see those responsible brought to justice.

As soon as she reached the bottom floor, she called Frank. "Any word from Brad?"

"Not as yet. How did you get on with the girl?"

"She's still extremely fragile and not talking much. I only had ten minutes. It appears she was taken with consent from her home in Nepal on the promise of marriage. But she didn't seem to want to talk about what happened between then and now, except she did say there were seven of them in a box. It seems like we might be right with human trafficking. Could a box be a container?"

"Could be—they could have been kept in one."

"It may have been how they were smuggled into the country, assuming she was brought here illegally. She didn't react when I asked her about being on a ship. She mentioned she was kept near a building that was falling over, so we may be looking for a demolition site near the airport. Once she's a bit stronger and more trusting, hopefully in a day or so, I'll have the chance to spend longer with her. She may be up to seeing some photos and identifying the girls and Chase Craddock."

"Meanwhile I'll have a word with Brad and try and get that search warrant moving. We need answers."

"I'm tempted to call it a day, that is unless Brad wants to see us tonight."

"You go, I'll ring you if you're needed."

*

Anahera stood in her kitchen staring at the top cupboard. This was the night Rangi had volleyball practice and Piri had a music lesson. Jim wasn't home from work yet, although he was due home anytime.

She was disturbed by her meeting with Sangita, incensed by how the girl had been betrayed. Greed was almost certainly the root cause. Whoever it was that duped the parents into thinking their daughter was off to marry into a wealthier family stood to profit from selling her. And the system only worked if there was a demand.

The guilt laid on her by Rangi over the porn incident was eating away at her. She was learning the links between teenage porn, paedophilia and underage prostitution were close. Although hating what she was about to do and knowing it breached the trust between teenage son and mother, she felt compelled to do it anyway.

The confiscated phone was in the cupboard where she'd left it. After waiting for it to boot, she entered the security pattern and was relieved to find it was still the original one from when they'd purchased the phone.

Google mail had nothing of interest. Same with Facebook. She checked his search history and found it had been cleaned out. The first item that came up on Instagram was a porn video involving a teenage girl who appeared not much older than the boat shed girl. It had been posted by one of his friends. She went through his history and found some similar videos. While none of them had been posted by him, he'd obviously looked at them.

She stood rigid, glaring at the screen. Her mouth became dry, her head throbbed.

At that moment Jim entered. "What are you doing?"

Realising her cheeks had become moist with tears, she wiped them away with the back of her hand. "I thought I should check Rangi's phone—I know Jim, you don't need to say it. But I'm glad I did because there's a load of hardcore porn on his Instagram account."

"Look I get it. Was he the source?"

"No, it's coming from just one of his friends from what I could see."

"Then I wouldn't panic, we can talk to him tonight."

She bit her lip.

"Are you okay?"

"I met with the girl found in the brothel today. She's such a sad case Jim. And it's the whole damn industry that supports that type of perversion that is at fault. I can't bear to think of Rangi doing his bit to create the demand."

Jim smothered her in one of his bear hugs and murmured into her ear, "We'll sort it. We can talk to him as soon as he gets home."

They worked together preparing dinner while they waited for Rangi. When he eventually got home, they asked him to join them in the lounge and when he saw their serious faces, he began to look worried. Anahera took the phone out of her pocket and laid it on the coffee table.

"I took the liberty of looking in your phone today."

"What! You snooped?"

"Yes, I snooped—but for your own good Rangi. I've seen some of the material that Stephen is posting in Instagram. And I shall be telling Tom Flinnagan."

"I didn't put any of it online."

"But you've been viewing it and that makes you guilty. I'm dealing with a case where girls are being taken from their homes under false pretences and shipped off to a distant country only to be sold as prostitutes. I'm talking young girls, Rangi. As young as nine years old, some may even be younger. And do you know why this is happening?" She was aware she'd raised her voice.

"No."

"Money. Greed. And all to supply a sick market. Rangi, there is a fine line between paedophilia, child pornography and underage prostitution. It's vile. And I don't want to look at my son and think he's part of the problem. The consequences for the girls are lifelong, it will likely affect their mental health, their future relationships, not to mention physical pain. These girls don't get a choice, Rangi, they are victims, pawns in someone else's game."

"Mum, I think you're over-reacting." He said it quietly.

"Do you? This is no joke!"

"Okay, let's take it down a notch," Jim said. "Rangi, your phone is already confiscated but when you get it back, I think there should be a ban on you having social media until we are confident you are using it responsibly. Deal?"

"I suppose so." Rangi looked at his feet.

Anahera got up and moved over to sit next to Rangi. "I'm sorry if I came over a bit strong, but this is a big issue. I want you to understand just what the consequences are for the victims here. I do not want my son part of the problem—do you hear me young man?"

"I'm sorry Mum."

"Okay, let's leave it there," Jim cut in. "How about you get your homework done before dinner. And don't forget you and I are going to spend some time together this weekend."

Rangi slunk off to his room and Anahera went into the kitchen to finish preparing dinner. She chopped an onion fiercely, barely containing her anger.

"Careful, you'll do yourself some damage." Jim came around and put his hands on her shoulders and began gently massaging them. "It's more about the case than Rangi, isn't it?"

She kept chopping. "I don't know."

"You're in danger of taking it too personally."

"I'm not in the mood, Jim."

He dropped his hands and moved to the fridge and pulled out the steak. "Shall I pop this on the barbecue?"

"Yeah. I'm sorry Jim, it's been a long day, and I just need some space to process."

"I hear you. Why don't you take a walk while I finish fixing dinner? You might feel better for it."

"Actually, I think I'll have a run. You sure you don't mind?"

Anahera got into her running gear and pounded the pavement for five kilometres. With each step she sweated out her anger. Anger that came from her annoyance that despite their progress they were still not close to solving why the girls drowned, why they were out at Rangitoto and who they were with. Anger deriving from the futility over Sangita and all the Sangitas of the world. Anger driven by her disappointment that Rangi had been exposed to pornography.

Arriving home bathed in sweat, she felt reenergised for the first time in what seemed like ages and with a renewed perspective, confident she could overcome these hurdles. She would not let those girls down.

16

Feeling the need for a kickstart, Frank stopped at the café down the street from Auckland Central to grab a coffee. A small queue had formed. He was second from the front when someone tapped him on the shoulder.

"Kia ora!" Anahera grinned at him. "Fancy seeing you here."

"You're in early—did you wet the bed?" He chuckled. "My shout, the usual?"

"Thanks. How about we drink it here before we go in? I'll get us a table."

Frank placed the order and joined her at a small table by the window. Speaking rapidly, she filled him in with more detail about her meeting with Sangita. Moisture welled up in her eyes betraying the depth of her emotions.

When their coffees arrived, she sat toying with the handle of her mug.

"Is there something else on your mind?" Frank asked.

She looked up. "I did something I'm not proud of, Frank. I snooped in Rangi's phone. I crossed a line and am afraid I've lost his trust."

"I'm sure you would've had just cause so don't sweat it. It won't do him any harm to be reminded that you're the parent and as such have every right to do what you feel is necessary, within reason of course."

"I found pornography posted by one of his mates on Instagram."

"Then I'd say you did the right thing. He is still a kid after all." Frank studied her as he sipped his coffee. "What did you do about it?"

"We're going to ban him from social media. He already has his phone confiscated for four weeks."

"Sounds reasonable to me. What does Jim think?"

"He was a bit surprised when he found me looking in the phone, but he supported me. He's the one who came up with the social media ban."

"Then I wouldn't worry about it. You did what a good cop would do, and you got a good outcome."

She watched the mug as she slowly turned it in a full circle, her face drawn into a frown. "I see porn as one step on the road to the kind of perverse behaviour we're seeing in this case. And I can't bear the thought my son is helping to create the demand."

"He's a smart kid. I can't imagine him going down that track. I'm sure he'll listen to reason."

She chewed her lip. "I hope you're right. Jim's confident it'll be okay."

"I'm sure I'm right." He finished his coffee. "Are you ready to face the music?"

"Uh huh." She drained her cup. "Let's go."

They walked down the block to their building and climbed the stairs to their floor, chatting easily like friends do.

Frank checked his emails and saw one had come in from the Harbour Master. He opened it to find a list of ships, but before he could digest the information Brad appeared at the door.

"Morning Frank, Anahera. Thought I'd drop by to let you know I've been in touch with the taskforce investigating human trafficking and we've scheduled a meeting at ten this morning in the small meeting room down the hall from my office to discuss the case. It's important you're both there."

Frank looked at Anahera and said, "We'll be there. Did the warrant come through?"

"We have the warrant, but there's a bigger picture at play here. That's what the meeting is about." Brad turned to Anahera. "How did it go yesterday with the girl?"

"She's beginning to respond. There's an interpreter with her and it appears she only speaks Nepali. I didn't get a lot out of her—the social worker overseeing her care was adamant I only had ten minutes and that I couldn't show her anything that might be confronting, such as the photos. But I'm quite certain we are dealing with child trafficking."

"Stay on it, Anahera. We'll need her testimony."

"I intend to."

"I'll see you both at ten then." Brad left the office.

"I've received the list of ships that visited the Port of Auckland just before the Rangitoto girls were found. I'm going to go through it and see if I can come up with a short list." Frank said, staring at his screen.

"I'll check in with Cara to see if she's had any success with finding the tattoo artist, although I'm beginning to question whether they were tattooed in this country."

"You could be right, although there's a chance that whoever received the girls here effectively branded them." Frank rubbed his chin thoughtfully. "Given the same design is on display in *Red Lights* it could mean something very significant to Chase Craddock. It may be his way of showing his ownership of the girls, if indeed he's the one running the racket."

"Or he too is a pawn in a bigger game and the racket is being run outside Aotearoa New Zealand. Chase Craddock may just be a customer. And whoever is running it may be the one tattooing the girls. There could be hundreds of them with these tattoos all over the planet." Anahera sighed. "I think we need to keep hunting for the artist. If they are here, then they could help put Craddock away."

"Fair point." Frank went back to staring at the list on his screen.

Fourteen ships had visited the port in the week leading up to the time Jane Doe Two had drowned. Given Nepal is a land-locked country, and they were looking for a transporter of Nepalese girls, it was a safe assumption that its port of origin would be India. Therefore, vessels from India had to be the highest priority.

Of the fourteen, three had voyages that originated in India. All carried general freight, and all had spent time at anchor while waiting to enter the port. He brought up the shipping schedules for each freighter.

The first was a *Star of India*, which had come to the Port of Auckland via Singapore. She had already left New Zealand waters and was currently sailing her return passage to India.

The second was *Kolkata 2* which had left her home port and voyaged to Auckland via Sydney. According to her schedule she was due to leave Port Chalmers in Otago to return to the Port of Auckland before making her return trip to Kolkata.

The third was *Bengal Challenger*, which had arrived direct from India. She had visited the Port of Napier after the Port of Auckland and was currently sailing to Perth.

Frank had his short list.

He looked across at Anahera who was typing.

"Any luck with the tattooists?" he asked.

"No. Cara's still working through them—however it's not looking good. How about you?"

"I have a short list of three vessels that originated in India. I'm assuming India given Nepal is landlocked."

Anahera looked thoughtful. "It sounds like a fair assumption, but if it is truly international then we may need to widen that net."

"Let's see what comes out of today's meeting."

*

Just before ten Frank and Anahera made their way to the meeting room where they found Brad talking to a striking woman and a man, neither of whom Frank had seen around. She was tall with a model's figure, auburn coloured hair with red highlights and wearing a fitting trouser suit complete with shirt and tie. He could only assume she was new to the area as she was the type that was once seen never forgotten. The man was also tall and looked more like a businessman than a policeman.

Brad beckoned Frank and Anahera over. "Meet Barbara Wright, who heads up the special crime unit investigating human trafficking."

"Please, call me Barbs." Behind her smile was a steely look that scrutinised first Frank and then Anahera. "I got that nickname because when I hook onto something I don't let go."

Frank smiled.

"And this is John Watts, my right-hand man," Barbs added.

At that point Tania walked in, dressed somewhat more casually than the rest in tight jeans and a loose jumper that matched her blue hair and glasses. "Sorry I'm late. Tania Jones, Puiwaitahi."

They all shook hands before sitting around the table; Barbs, John and Tania on one side with Brad, Anahera and Frank on the other.

Barbs took the lead. "I asked Brad to call this meeting so we can strategize how we best tackle the *Red Lights Adult Nightclub* case, since it crosses each of our areas of interest. We need to ensure none of us screw it up or get in the way of the other investigations." She scanned the faces opposite her with her piercing eyes. "I want to thank your team, Brad, for alerting us to this case. I have to say we were aware through intel from our offshore partners that there was a trafficking ring operating, but we hadn't been able to put a face to them. We're a relatively new unit, just established three months ago with the purpose of preventing it getting a foothold here. We are the New Zealand arm of an international collaboration with law enforcement teams in India, Nepal, Singapore, Australia and Canada."

Brad nodded. "I think we should start by briefing you on our case to date. Frank, would you like to update Barbs and John?"

"Sure." Frank opened his notebook and began with the discovery of Jane Doe One and went on to Jane Doe Two, noting the tattoos and abuse when summarising the Forensic report for each victim. He shared the results of the computer modelling and described Jerry Ramsley, explaining that they'd nothing they could pin on him. Then the public appeal that turned up the tip regarding the illegal brothel in New Lynn, which they'd passed on to Tania's unit, resulting in the raid and the discovery of Sangita. At that point he handed over to Anahera.

She told them what she'd learned about the significance of the tattoos and how they were still looking for the tattooist. Then how their liaison with Tania had led them to the *Red Lights Adult Nightclub* with the framed picture of the eye that was the subject of the tattoos, following up with a rundown of its ownership structure. She leaned forward to finish, saying, "When I spoke with Sangita, although she wasn't up for a full interview, she did say she was kept in a box with six other girls. We're now assuming two of these girls are likely to be the ones that drowned and that they all may have been brought into the country illegally in a container for the purposes of commercial exploitation."

"Tania, you might like to comment on what your specific interests are," Brad said.

"Puiwaitahi is a multi-agency centre set up to ensure agencies involved in specialist child abuse assessment and treatment, investigation and prosecution services, are all working closely together for the benefit of the abused children. My focus in the case is on Sangita, the child who has been subjected to horrific sexual abuse for commercial gain." She paused and looked from one to another. "My job is to see that those responsible for her exploitation and those who raped her are all held accountable. I have arrested two people to date. The first is a man who was caught in the act with her and who is now out on bail pending trial. The second is a woman who we believe was running the illegal brothel without a permit in a house in a residential area."

Brad cleared his throat. "My team have been focused on finding those responsible for the deaths of the two girls found out at Rangitoto Island. That means finding out who they are, how they got there and who was involved."

"I want to make it clear to everyone that our jurisdiction must take precedence and under no circumstances should any actions taken by the other teams get in the way of catching the traffickers." Barbs straightened upright in her chair and paused for effect. "That's the big picture here."

"My concern is that justice is done for crime committed locally. As I read it, yours is the international smuggling aspect of this affair." Brad's look was unwavering.

Frank could sense tension building in the room and although slightly amused by the unfolding turf war, he maintained his straight face.

"We now have the nightclub under surveillance." Barbs spoke with authority. "But we need to catch them red handed and I don't want them alerted to the fact we're onto them."

"We have a search warrant for the club that's been issued this morning. Our plan is to go in and get the evidence to tie the nightclub to the deceased. I'm hopeful it'll lead us to whoever had the girls out near Rangitoto." Brad's voice was firm.

A standoff ensued, filling the room with silence as the two senior officers stared at each other. The others shifted uncomfortably in their seats.

It was Brad that broke the silence. "Let's back off a bit. Are we sure we're looking at the New Zealand arm of a child trafficking ring with girls from Nepal being illegally brought into the country?"

Murmurs of agreement were accompanied by the nodding of heads around the table.

"Could we be wrong?" Brad raised an eyebrow and looked from Barbs to John to Tania to Anahera to Frank.

Frank spoke. "The tattoos tie all three girls to the nightclub, and we have the nightclub tied to the illegal brothel through Grant Tate. Then we have Sangita's comment about being kept in a box, and I think it's safe to assume that's a container, so I think the assumption is sound."

"Except that the container could have been used anywhere to imprison the girls." John spoke up for the first time. "It could've been located somewhere around Auckland and not on a ship."

"You're suggesting the girls were already in this country, and somehow ended up being exploited in this way?" Brad asked.

"I'm only saying it's possible—perhaps they'd been kidnapped," John replied. "I don't think we should rule anything out."

"Then how come nobody has come forward looking for them?" Anahera asked. "I've checked the missing person list and there have been no missing children notified that fit their description. That would suggest they were taken from their families or legal guardians with their consent, which sounds unlikely."

Tania cut in. "I agree it's improbable given Sangita doesn't appear to speak English and she did say her family are in Nepal."

Anahera added, "Nor do Immigration have them entering the country via legitimate channels."

"Okay." Brad paused. "Then I think we have to assume illegal entry with no family or legal guardians here."

Barbs sat back, dropping her shoulders. "And the most likely entry point is via a ship—we can easily rule out planes. That fits with the container."

"I would like to have another chat with Sangita as soon as she's up for it." Anahera glanced at Tania. "She must be able to tell us more about how she came to be here. And if she can recognise the identikits of the deceased then we can confirm they were together. She may also recognise the owner of the nightclub."

"I'll see what I can do." Tania smiled at Anahera. "We could interview her together."

"I've short listed the ships that came in from India around the time in question." Frank checked his notebook. "There were three, one of which is still in our waters and is due back in port here before leaving for India."

"They could have arrived earlier and been held ashore. Let's not limit the search to that time." Barbs' voice was sharp, leaving Frank in no doubt where the name Barbs came from. "If the girls jumped from the ship…"

"Or were pushed," Brad interjected.

"Granted." Barbs smiled thinly at Brad. "If they went into the water from a ship then the timing would be right. But if they were taken to Rangitoto aboard a private vessel, having been picked up in say Auckland, then they could've been in the country longer and been held captive somewhere."

"Good point," Brad conceded.

"We'll talk to our partners and get as much intel as we can on the shipping lines and the ships implicated," she said.

"How sure can we be that its port of origin is India?" Brad asked.

"Highly likely, given the rampant trade of Nepalese girls into India." Barbs paused. "Although it's possible they could have come via another port—we can't entirely rule that out."

"Are we agreed a vessel from India is the most likely and should be our first priority?"

"Yes. If the one that's returning to Auckland is the vessel, then it'll be loading cargo and unlikely to have more girls on it. I'd prefer to catch them red-handed. And I don't want the raid on the nightclub to tip the smugglers off," Barbs said emphatically. "I think we should continue the surveillance for now."

"But there may not be another shipment." Brad had the look of a boxer fighting his corner. "We should take the opportunity now to find whoever is responsible for the girls' deaths. And the key to that seems to be this nightclub."

"Sangita mentioned there were seven of them. To act now could save the remaining ones," Tania said quietly.

"Does anyone have any ideas regarding the whereabouts of the other girls? Brad asked.

Heads shook.

"Then I think it's clear we shouldn't delay the search of the nightclub," Brad concluded.

"Very well, let's reach a compromise. We can coordinate simultaneous searches of the vessel when in port and the nightclub." Barbs eyeballed Brad. "My team will take charge of each search and we can alert our partners overseas to the vessels and shipping lines in question. I'll organise the backup from the Armed Offender's Squad and a forensics team, given we're probably searching for evidence the girls were on the ship. I think it unlikely we'll find them on board on its return voyage. Out of interest Frank, what were the ports of call for the three ships?"

Frank referred to his notes. "*Star of India* visited Singapore. *Kolkata 2* came via Sydney, she's the one still here. *Bengal Challenger* is visiting Perth."

John was making notes.

"It's settled then. The raids will take place when the vessel is back in port. I'd like one of my team to be present at each one—Frank is from the Maritime unit and can assist at the port. Anahera can assist with the search of the nightclub." Brad looked satisfied. "We should be able to work together on this. After all, we are all playing for the same team."

"Agreed." Barbs smiled for the first time.

"In the meantime, I'd like to interview O'Connor again—I believe she's still in custody?" Anahera looked at Tania.

Tania nodded. "You'll need to be quick, she's due in court and is likely to be granted bail. What's on your mind?"

"If we confront her with the link to Grant Tate and the nightclub, we may be able to get her to talk about the other girls."

"We can agree to that." Barbs looked at Brad. "I think we are done. Our teams will need to work closely until we close this off. We appreciate your cooperation, Brad."

As the meeting drew to a close, several conversations broke out with a palpable easing of tension in the room. While enjoying a conversation with John where they each exchanged their background in the force, Frank surveyed the room. In the corner, Tania and Anahera were ensconced in a deep conversation. Standing at the front, Brad and Barbs appeared to be having a convivial discussion and at one point they seemed to share a joke when their laughter reverberated across the room.

They were definitely all playing for the same team.

17

Frank returned to the station with Anahera after grabbing a quick lunch in her favourite café just five minutes from their office. Having arranged to have Scarlett O'Connor brought back up for an interview that afternoon, it was with a sense of anticipation that Frank followed Anahera up the stairs to their office.

While waiting for the interview, Frank called Larry Cook, the Coromandel policeman who'd promised to do some digging on Jerry Ramsley.

"Frank, I was planning to call you."

"How did you get on?"

"Not too well. I asked around, but nobody knows much about Jerry. He's a loner like I thought. Keeps much to himself. No one seems to know anything about any females in his life. And no Asian link that I could uncover. Sorry I couldn't be of more assistance."

"And never any complaints about giving unwanted attention to minors?"

"Nothing that we've received. I think he's just an oddball with a chip on his shoulder."

"Okay, thanks Larry." Frank ended the call.

"No luck?" Anahera asked from her desk.

"Nothing that helps us. In fact we have nothing that would get us a search warrant. I'm thinking he might be a red herring."

"Let's think this through. He was the only one acting suspiciously in the bay, right?"

"Correct."

"But to place a body in an abandoned boat shed and then hang around the bay would take guts." Anahera furrowed her brow in thought.

"Or brazenness. Or stupidity."

"Or maybe it was a psychological thing, like being drawn to it, maybe even curious to see if it was found."

"I see where you're going with this. He could've been confident it wouldn't be linked to him," Frank said.

Anahera got up and began to pace the small room. "Let's put the possibility they jumped ship aside for a moment. We're looking for someone who had underage foreign girls, possibly non-English speakers, as escorts aboard a private vessel."

"Okay."

"If that's the case, what sort of profile would we be looking for?"

"Someone who can handle a boat."

Anahera went to the whiteboard, picked up a pen and began to write bullet points down.

"Male. Paedophiles or at least someone with perverted sexual preferences?"

"With or without a known record," she added.

"Presumably wealthy as the escorts that age wouldn't come cheap." Frank paused. "Someone likely to have begun their excursion in Auckland. I think with what we now know it's a safe assumption that the girls were picked up there."

"Good—keep going Frank."

"Either a boat owner or they could borrow or charter a boat."

"What sort of person would charter a boat with the express purpose of taking underage girl escorts out?" Anahera stopped writing and looked at Frank.

"Someone wealthy—boat charters generally don't come cheap."

"Do you agree it's starting to look like our Jerry Ramsley may not be the man? I don't associate him with the sort of money needed to hire those girls."

"And I can't see how he could've picked them up from Auckland, given we've a witness that saw him in Home Bay. His craft couldn't scoot in and out of the city when its top speed is only around five knots at a pinch." Frank sighed. "I concede he may have been a waste of our time."

"Never a waste Frank—you just never know with people." Anahera finished writing the list of bullet points before turning back to Frank. "I'm thinking that the type of punters visiting the New Lynn address probably fit the profile of the person responsible for the two drownings."

"A fair assumption."

"Let's see what we can get out of the O'Connor woman. What strategy do you want to use?"

"How about you take the lead—you're good at that."

Anahera chuckled. "You just like to be the good guy."

"Who doesn't?" He too chuckled. "Let's do this then. Ready for the ring?"

"I was born ready!"

*

Scarlett O'Connor was waiting in the interview room with Prue Thomas, her lawyer. Frank detected a nervous reaction as she looked up when he entered the room with Anahera. Dark circles surrounded her eyes, further highlighted by smudged mascara, bearing witness to the trauma of being held in custody. Someone had brought her a change of clothes as she was dressed in a red Nike tee shirt.

The two detectives took their seats opposite the prisoner and her lawyer. Anahera deliberately took her time placing her notebook, pen and phone on the table before looking up to address Scarlett.

"Scarlett O'Connor, may I call you Scarlett?" she began.

"I suppose, after all, you all know it's my name."

"We asked that you be brought up to answer a few more questions. I'll be recording this interview, do you understand?"

"Of course I do, I'm not stupid." The words were spoken in a quiet level voice lacking any of the bluster that you might expect with such a comment.

"Then we'll get underway." Anahera glanced at Frank who turned on the recording and stated the time.

"For the record, please can you give your full name and address."

Scarlett complied.

"I'm aware you've been read your Miranda rights, but I will repeat them for you now. You have the right to remain silent, you do not have to make a statement, anything you say may be recorded and given as evidence in court. You have the right to speak to a lawyer without delay and in private before deciding whether to answer any of our questions. Do you understand?"

Scarlett slowly nodded her mop of long and colourful ringlets that were matted to the point of becoming dreadlocks. "Course I understand."

"Scarlett, you are being held on the charge of commercial sexual exploitation of a person under 18 years of age and supplying her with cannabis and methamphetamine. Is that correct?"

Scarlett looked at Prue, who spoke on her behalf. "My client has been charged as such."

"Scarlett, when did you first meet Sangita?"

Scarlett looked confused and shot a look at her lawyer, before answering, "Who?"

Anahera responded in a calm and measured voice. "Sangita is the real name of the young girl that was found on the New Lynn property during the raid. I believe you called her Harmony."

A look of recognition showed in Scarlett's eyes before Prue jumped in, saying in a clipped voice, "My client doesn't need to answer that."

"Scarlett, where did you first see Sangita also known as Harmony?"

Scarlett looked down at her hands which writhed and twisted, taking on a life of their own. Long slender fingers covered in silver rings glided over the tips of each of her long and brightly painted nails. She peered over her glasses at Frank with what could only be interpreted as a seductive look.

"My client doesn't need to answer that question." Like a fox terrier, Prue's bark was sharp.

"Scarlett, we have two dead Nepalese girls, both of whom wear the scars of having been sexually abused. They and Sangita all bear the same tattoo on their wrists. We know they are linked. We know that you were running the illegal brothel where Sangita was found. And we know there are likely to be other girls. These children, because that is what they are, have been the victims of a serious offense and right now with all we know it appears that you are the one sitting in the middle of it. Right now, it looks to me that you could be an accessory to manslaughter on two counts." Anahera paused, giving time for her words to sink in. "If you help us with our enquiries, it may go better for you. While there's no guarantee, it seems to me the best you can hope for is that the judge will take that into account when sentencing."

"I want to talk to my lawyer, alone." Scarlett eyeballed Anahera.

"We'll wait outside."

After pausing the recording, Anahera and Frank left the room, shutting the door behind them.

Outside in the hallway, Anahera spoke in a low voice. "Do you think she knows anything that might help us?"

"I can't see it—she's feisty but frightened if you ask me."

"I get the feeling she's just a pawn. Remember how at the *Red Lights* nightclub Chase Craddock made a thing about not remembering former employees? I'd say she's one of his flunkies—and expendable at that and I bet she knows it."

"Hopefully common sense prevails, and she talks."

"Let's hope so."

They continued to speak in hushed voices until the door to the interview room opened and Prue called them in.

Anahera went through the motions of recommencing the interview.

Prue said, "My client wishes to assist you with your enquiries."

"Let's start again, shall we?" Anahera smiled at Scarlett.

Scarlett, picking at her nails, looked up and nodded her consent.

"Scarlett, are you the manager of the brothel in New Lynn where you were picked up?"

Scarlett narrowed her eyes briefly as she looked at Prue. The lawyer nodded reassuringly. "Yeah," Scarlett breathed it out and looked back down at her hands.

"And how long have you been operating the brothel?"

"I dunno, maybe three months, maybe more." Her voice was so quiet Anahera had to ask her to repeat it for the recording.

"Who do you work for, Scarlett?"

Scarlett hesitated and Anahera repeated the question.

"Grant Tate." It sounded subdued.

"In your time managing that brothel, how many underage girls were working for you?"

Immediately Prue pounced, saying, "I advise my client not to answer that."

"How long was Sangita, or Harmony as you knew her, working for you?"

"Not long, she was a newbie."

"Can you be more specific?"

"A week."

"Where did she come from?"

"I don't know."

"Who brought her to you?"

Scarlett turned to Prue before answering in a soft voice, "Grant Tate."

Frank tried to hide the satisfaction that surged through him threatening to explode into a smug grin. He looked at his partner and saw she remained poker faced.

"Where was she held before she came to you?"

"I honestly don't know."

"Where did you first meet Grant Tate?"

"At the *Red Light's* nightclub--he was a frequent visitor there."

"What's his association with *Red Lights Adult Nightclub*?"

"I don't know anything about his business." Her head had slumped forward again.

"Where did Sangita get the tattoo on her wrist?"

"How should I know?"

"What does it signify?"

She shrugged her shoulders.

Anahera paused and nodded to Frank, who on cue opened his notebook and took out a photograph of the Boat Shed girl taken at the scene by the police photographer. Placing it on the table for Scarlett to see, he asked, "Do you recognise this girl? For the record the photo is of Jane Doe One."

"Jane Doe? Really?" She smirked at Frank before studying the print, her face now expressionless. After a long moment, she looked up at him from under her long eyelashes and answered, "Nope."

Anahera stepped in, trying hard not to expose her growing frustration. "Are you sure? Take another look."

"I said no, didn't I?"

"What about this one? For the record, I'm showing a photo of Jane Doe Two." Frank tabled a photo of the bloated and grotesque figure.

Scarlett glimpsed the photo and quickly looked away, but not before he noted a slight glistening in her eyes. "Nope."

"I want you to think this through carefully. We have reason to believe these girls were with Sangita. Are you sure you didn't come across them?" Anahera asked.

Scarlett looked at Anahera. When she finally spoke, her voice carried some emotion. "Nope, I didn't see them."

A thought struck Frank, and he asked, "What was Sangita wearing when you first met her?"

Scarlett looked surprised. "Dirty old pyjamas, but I got rid of them and gave her some new clothes. I take care of my girls."

Anahera's phone vibrated with an incoming message. She glanced at Frank before calling for a break.

Outside, Anahera said, "I have good news. Cara has found the tattoo artist."

Frank let out a low whistle. "What do they know about the girls?"

"Cara didn't say. He's expecting us this afternoon."

"That's great news." He looked thoughtful. "And from what we've just heard it looks like we've got enough to nab Grant Tate."

"I hope so."

"I've the feeling we're about to crack this thing wide open." His grin was irrepressible. "Feels like we just won the lottery!"

She laughed. "How about you let Brad know while I get a photo of Grant Tate and Chase Craddock—it shouldn't be too hard to find them on the internet."

Anahera hurried back to her office. It didn't take long before the printer kicked into gear and produced a photo of each man. While there she decided to give Tania a quick call, knowing she'd be delighted Scarlett was talking.

Once back in the interview room, they resumed their places having agreed on the next line of questioning.

"Scarlett, let's confirm what you've told us already. You say you work for Grant Tate and that he brought Sangita to you for commercial exploitation and this was five days ago. Is that correct?" Anahera fixed her steady gaze on Scarlett.

Scarlett hung her head. "Yes."

"Do you recognise this man?" Anahera held up the print.

"Yes, it's Grant Tate."

Anahera passed her the second print. "Do you recognise this man?"

"He used to come into the *Red Lights* nightclub when I worked there. I think he was the owner."

"Is he involved in the New Lynn operation?"

"No, that's Grant."

"Is he involved in business with Grant?"

"No, I don't think so." She looked at Prue before adding, "Maybe, I really don't know."

"Okay. Let's move on to Sangita. You must have known Sangita was underage—did you?"

Prue quickly interjected. "I advise Scarlett not to answer that."

"But you say you never laid eyes on the girls in the photographs we showed you. Are you 100 percent certain about that?"

She looked up. "Yes."

"And you know nothing about the tattoo?"

"No."

"Are you quite sure? I should warn you that we've found the tattoo artist."

"Quite sure."

"What about the man found on the premises with Sangita? Was he a regular?"

"I'd prefer not to answer that."

"Help me to understand," Anahera sat forward, as if conspiring with Scarlett. "What sort of a man frequents your little brothel?"

"We provide a service that's hard to get and it comes at a high price. Most of the regulars are professionals or men with access to money. High rollers. Many are married and they like something kinky on the side." Scarlett smiled now, revealing a gap in her teeth. "You know the sort of thing. Sometimes we send girls out to their parties."

"What about the drugs? You were caught with cannabis and methamphetamine, and it was in Sangita's blood. Who supplied the drugs?"

She looked at Prue who once again stepped in with her standard response.

Anahera moved on to discussing the *Red Lights Adult Nightclub* but got no further. It seemed Scarlett had clammed up and was not prepared to identify Chase Craddock or anyone else associated with the club.

"Okay, that's enough for one day. I suggest we call an end to the interview." And she formally ended the proceedings.

Frank left the room with Anahera, and although Scarlett was off to her bail hearing where she'd likely be released until her pending trial, he was satisfied they had what they needed. Anahera had played her part well.

*

The street was lined with 1950s style state houses that were a mixture of those that had been lovingly restored and cared for by their new owners and others that were run down and badly in need of a paint. It was typical of a suburb that was transitioning from lower socio-economic housing to middle class driven largely by first home buyers in a buoyant housing market.

Frank parked the car outside a green weatherboard house surrounded by a 1.8 metre black stained wooden fence. Near the gate were two signs; one advertised the tattoo artist and the other warned of the dog within.

Frank reached through the small hole in the gate searching for the latch and was immediately alerted to the dog who slobbered generously over his hand. Thinking better of it, he pulled out his phone and dialled the number on the sign. A man answered, identifying himself as Chris, who agreed to meet them at the gate.

The call had only just ended when a whistle sounded beyond the gate and the dog barked and ran back to the house. Frank opened the gate and he and Anahera walked up the concrete driveway towards a middle-aged man holding onto the collar of a large German shepherd. The white tee-shirt he wore over jeans revealed arms completely covered in tattoos.

"What do you want?" Nodding towards the dog, he said, "Strauss here won't hurt you, just gets a little over-excited when we have visitors. He's more likely to lick you to death—that is unless I give him the signal."

Looking down at the dog, Frank asked, "Mind if we talk inside?" He flashed his ID.

Anahera cautiously patted Strauss before introducing herself and following Chris inside. Thankfully Strauss stayed outside. They entered a kitchen by way of a back door where he offered them a seat at a small wooden dining table that was strewn with magazines depicting tattoo art. The kitchen was tidy and clean, the floor was vinyl in the style of wooden planks. Anahera opened her notebook and sat poised with pen in hand.

Frank took the photos of the tattoos and passed them to Chris. "I understand these are your work?"

"Yeah, I remember them. Who wouldn't? That constable showed me these same photos and as I told her, you don't forget tattooing a young girl. Especially when they cry and make a fuss."

"We're looking for the adult who arranged the tattoos and who brought the girls to you." Frank retrieved the photos.

Chris scrutinised Frank, taking his time before answering, "Client confidentiality. I'm obligated to not discuss their personal business, after all I'm a professional. Privacy Act and all that."

"Then you'd be obstructing a police investigation." Anahera's voice was as smooth as silk.

Chris shifted his gaze to her and scowled. "You coppers are all the same."

Frank looked around at the freshly painted kitchen and took a punt. "You pay all your tax owed? The IRD might be interested in a backyard tattoo parlour."

Chris, his face now flushed, glared at Frank. "Now come on—that's a bit unfair."

"I'm going to ask you again. Who brought the girls to you?"

Looking a lot less cocky, Chris answered, "It was a man—I remember now, he paid cash."

"Can you recall his name?"

"Yeah. It was Ajay, but I didn't get a last name."

"Can you describe him for us?"

"Indian, well dressed and with no obvious tattoos. Wore a heavy gold chain around his neck."

"Are you sure about this?" Anahera asked, her face puzzled.

"Of course."

"Any other distinguishing features?" Frank asked.

He rubbed a hand over his heavily gelled hair. "Not that I can remember."

"Would you be able to identify him from a photo or a line up?"

"Maybe, or maybe not."

"How many girls have you tattooed with this design?"

"Just the three. And I earned every cent with those ones—screamed like I was murdering them!"

Anahera asked, "Three girls? Not seven?"

"Like I said, three of them. Could have been his kids, I don't ask questions." He eyed Frank. "Anyway, why do you want to know?"

"It's a homicide enquiry."

"Not the one that's been in the news? The girls out at Rangitoto?"

"Yes, I'm afraid so. We're trying to track down their guardians."

"Nah, I can't help you with that."

"Where did the design of the eye come from?" Anahera asked.

"The client brought it with him and asked me to copy it. There were actually three separate ones with different symbols in each."

"Did he say what they mean?"

"Not my business." He hesitated. "He didn't talk much at all—just the way I like it."

"What was his relationship like with the girls?"

"How would I know? Those kids were frightened of the needle and yelped like puppies at the least bit of pain. I can tell you this—I won't be in a hurry to tattoo any other kids. Not worth the grief." He paused as if taking time to remember. "Come to think of it, they didn't say much—in fact they spoke more gibberish than English. At least he paid well."

"Is there anything else you can tell us that might help to track him down? Did he give you his phone number? Or did you see his car?"

"Nah, that's it. It was a casual job. I never saw what they came in ... you would've noticed my high fence."

"How did he pay?"

"It'd be with cash, I'm pretty sure."

Frank passed him a business card. "If you think of anything else, anything at all, please give me a call."

"I won't. And don't you go letting people know I talked—I don't want it affecting my business."

With that they made their way out the back door and down the path to the gate while Strauss followed only a breath behind.

18

Anahera's alarm went off and she struggled to open her eyes as she reached out to punch the snooze button on the little electronic clock. After a restless night she had to fight the desire to snuggle back under the covers and fall back into the deep sleep that she'd finally succumbed to.

Jim reached out and pulled her into his arms. "Don't you need to get up?"

"Yeah, I suppose so. I feel like I've only just fallen asleep." As she kissed him her passion stirred. Then she sighed and disentangled herself. "But I'd better get going. We're finally making some good progress on the case and we've got a meeting to update Brad first thing. Now an international taskforce is involved, he wants to stay even closer."

Once showered, dressed and breakfasted, she left Jim to see the boys off to school and drove into the city. Just as she was parking, her phone bleeped.

"Anahera? This is Binsa Dahal, the interpreter."

"Binsa, what can I do for you?"

"I've been thinking a lot about Sangita and thought it might be helpful if I meet with you and tell you my own story. It may help join the dots and give you an understanding of some of the big issues we Nepali people face."

"I appreciate the thought. Can we include Tania, given she's dealing with Sangita's case?"

"Yes, of course. I was meaning to call her as well."

They arranged to meet at the hospital café later that morning.

Frank was already in their office waiting when she arrived. Together they went up to Brad's office where they found him at his desk engrossed in a pile of paperwork with a coffee in hand. They knocked on the open door and entered.

"Great, you're here." Brad looked up. "How did it go yesterday?"

"It went well." Anahera said with conviction, opening her notebook. "We re-interviewed Scarlett and this time she agreed to help. She admitted working for Grant Tate and identified him from a photo. But she didn't seem to know anything about Chase Craddock being involved in the New Lynn property."

Frank added, "We're fairly certain Scarlett's not the one orchestrating all of this. She doesn't appear to know anything about the other girls or how the girls were acquired."

"We think she's just a player in the overall game. I'm guessing she's been kept in the dark and just does her little bit so she can't spill the beans." Anahera tucked her hair behind her ear. "Incidentally, we hear she's now out on bail."

"Not to worry, sounds like you got what you needed. Hopefully you'll get the chance to interview both Tate and Craddock after the raid. Then we might finally get the answers we need."

"That is if we can get them talking." Anahera consulted her notes. "We also found the tattooist."

"That's great news!" Brad beamed.

"He says he tattooed three girls, and claims it was an Indian man by the name of Ajay who brought them in—he didn't know anything else about him. No last name or contact details. Paid cash." Anahera looked up at Brad. "We need to find this guy—how many Ajay's can there be in a city the size of Auckland? Sangita said initially there were seven girls so whatever happened to the other four remains a mystery. Perhaps we'll get lucky with the raid on the *Kolkata* when it's back in port."

"Let's hope so—between that and the raid on the nightclub things should become clearer."

"Not only the answers relating to the girls but also what the links are between this Ajay, Chase Craddock, Grant Tate and Scarlett O'Connor," Frank said. "I'm confident the net's closing at last and it's only a matter of time before we find the person who knows something about how and why the girls died."

"I hope you're right. We need to feed the media some good news. It's time we closed the file."

Anahera smiled at her boss. "We're on to it."

"Good work you two. I expect some more good news soon!"

The meeting ended and they left Brad to his paper war.

*

The hospital café was on the ground floor. The room was bustling with most of the tables taken. The noise level was constant and reverberated off the polished concrete floor and bare walls. There were doctors with stethoscopes around their necks, nurses in their uniforms, administrators with clipboards, patients—some in their hospital gowns and others more aptly covered up with dressing gowns, and then there were those who may have been day patients or visitors. Chairs had been dragged to enlarge the circles of patrons chatting around the small tables, creating a maze that obstructed the way to the counter. Cabinets displayed a range of delectables and on the wall behind the counter were blackboards that advertised the menu. Staff buzzed about the tables with trays of food and drinks.

Towards the back of the room Anahera spied Binsa sitting at a table with Tania, and she zigzagged her way between the tables and chairs to join them.

Once the greetings were over and they'd ordered their drinks, they sat huddled around the small table so as to hear each other over the noise.

"I asked you both to meet with me because I thought that by sharing my own story it might help you to better understand Sangita and the two girls who tragically died." Binsa's big brown eyes looked at them uncertainly. "I haven't shared it with many people in this country because it's personal. And it's painful."

Anahera said, "Then we're honoured that you're willing to share it with us."

"Yes, it is an honour. Please go on, Binsa," Tania added.

"My story begins when I was born. My mother died that day, giving birth to me. I never met my father or his family, no one has ever told me about them. My grandmother took me in, that is my mother's mum, and she raised me on the outskirts of Kathmandu. She was a Christian woman, which was unusual at that time in our society as it is a Hindu country and back then the regime was actively persecuting the few Christians for their faith. Christian churches were kept small and had to operate underground, so to speak. Most were house churches that met in someone's home. In the early nineties you could have counted the Christians in the hundreds—today, although it is still not encouraged by the regime, there are many more and the numbers continue to grow."

She waited while their coffees were delivered.

"My grandmother was a good woman and loved me very much. Those early days were good." She looked away. "My grandmother became sick with tuberculosis when I was eight years old and was dying when my uncle started to take an interest in me. He promised her that he would take care of me if she died." Her voice cracked as she spoke.

"Just take your time, Binsa," Tania said, her voice soft.

Binsa's eyes brimmed with tears. "My grandmother passed away that year. And my uncle began to negotiate a price for me with a stranger. I found out this man purchased girls and sold them on to a brothel cartel in Mumbai."

"Oh Binsa, you were only eight!" Anahera sounded indignant.

"Yes, I was eight years old. But as it turned out, I was one of the lucky ones." She took a tissue out of her purse and dabbed her eyes. "A kind lady from my grandmother's church learned what my uncle was going to do. They begged him to not sell me but instead to allow them to care for me. He refused. He only thought of the money he could make by selling me to this brothel. My uncle was a bad man with a gambling problem. And he liked to drink, so the lady and her husband waited until my uncle was drinking and when he got drunk, they stole me away from him."

Anahera was both horrified and fascinated by the story. "Really? What happened?"

"They had relatives living in Darjeeling in India who were unable to have their own children and when they heard about me, they offered to adopt me. The nice couple took me there where I was brought up by this other family as their own daughter. It was a happy childhood, and they educated me through private schools and later I was able to attend university. As you can see, my life turned out very well, in the end." She paused to sip her tea. "But I am telling you this story for a reason. In my country it is not uncommon for girls to be taken, often under false pretences, to India where brothels pay a premium for young Nepali girls. The youngest I know of was only six when she was taken."

"That is terrible!" Tania's eyes were wide.

"Nepali girls are highly sought after because in India they are deemed to be very beautiful. Each year, around 12,000 Nepali girls are sold into sexual slavery by their families and forced to work in Indian brothels. It's an epidemic."

"Can't something be done about it?"

"There are many charities trying to rescue these girls but with limited success—the problem is just so great. Some are working to educate villagers about the risks and scams that some families fall for. Like I told you the first time we met, it is not uncommon for a man to come and pretend he wants to marry the girl, pay the bride price, only to sell the girl on to a brothel."

"What about the government?"

"Ha! In my view they are not doing enough. This problem has been a scourge on our nation for many years." Her voice had taken on a bitter note. "To their credit the government has increased their efforts to enact new legislation and to convict these criminals, but the progress is slow, and I question how much impact it is really having on the trade of girls."

"I'm so sorry." Anahera spoke softly, her concern genuine.

"When I graduated university, I was offered a job with an NGO who was running programmes to educate young girls from the villages in Nepal and teach them skills to make them self-sufficient and less likely to fall victim to trafficking. The idea being they in turn would return to their villages and the awareness would spread." She paused to finish her drink. "In those days I was more of an activist and was determined to do something to make a difference. But I needed to experience it—to feel it so it wasn't just academic. Before starting my new job, I decided to visit Mumbai to see the brothels for myself."

Captivated, Anahera couldn't take her eyes off the slight Nepalese woman whose stature seemed to grow. "How much do you think the experience with your uncle led you down this path?"

"I have no doubt that it was my motivation. In a funny way, my uncle did me a favour and it turned into a positive for me." Her eyes glistened. "But I came so close to being one of those children—there was probably only hours between becoming a victim and being saved and given the tools to fight the practice."

She was silent for a while, as if contemplating her next words. Anahera and Tania waited.

"Of those 12,000 girls who are trafficked from Nepal to India each year, we have no idea how many return or die in sexual servitude. But there are many girls, and many brothels. I remember walking down one road that was lined with these establishments. They were three storeys high. I went into one, you couldn't begin to imagine the terrible living conditions. And the filth was disgusting. I was taken up the stairs. On the top level were the youngest girls. They were the most valuable attracting the highest prices. Prized possessions. There were guards stationed there to stop them escaping." Her voice broke and her tears flowed freely, only to be contained by the fresh tissue she pulled out from her bag. "I'm sorry, I just need a moment."

Anahera's eyes filled with tears as she watched Binsa struggle to contain her sobs. Across the table she was aware of Tania dabbing her own eyes with a tissue.

After a short while Binsa continued. "I wasn't allowed near those girls. Their so-called minders refused to allow me to talk to them. But they were just children, some were quite young. I was told they are at peak value when they are still virgins. Then I visited the middle floor and there the girls were teenagers and young women. Many had been there a long time already and were considered used. I could talk to these girls."

She looked past them with a faraway look in her eyes. "It was sweltering in that place, and the smell of sewerage and body odours was overpowering. The girls' faces were heavily made up and their clothes revealing. Each small room was bare but for a small single bed and filthy sheets. They told me that when they first arrived, they were drugged and when they woke up their hair had been cut. I think this was all part of the control. They were told they were to work at pleasing men—and the girls learned from each other what was expected of them. One girl said she could see as many as 30 to 35 men in a day—sometimes many more. If they refused to do what the men wanted, they would get beaten or worse, burned with a cigarette. They showed me their scars. Can you imagine that?"

She stopped to dry her tears and blow her nose.

"On the bottom level were those who were older and therefore less desirable. The prices they fetched were the least in the establishment. They lived and worked in squalor, the likes of which I have never seen anywhere else. It was heart-breaking."

"So why don't they run away?"

Binsa looked at Anahera, her doe-like eyes now fierce. "Because they are watched all the time. They are afraid. They have nothing, no money—they're paid nothing. They have no way of surviving on their own. And because they don't know how to take care of themselves or how to get home. They are trapped."

"Why so many from Nepal? And why not Indians given the brothels are in India?" Tania asked.

Binsa smiled. "Good questions. Nepal is such a poor country. Many villages are in remote parts of the country that are difficult to travel to with poor or non-existent roads due to our mountainous terrain. It makes these villages easy targets for the traffickers who will often prey on girls who are uneducated and come from lower castes. Perhaps the most important reason is Nepalese women tend to be prized for their fairer skins." She sighed. "At one stage it was rumoured that if you have sex with a young girl you recover from HIV. Many have apparently believed this lie and it has added to the impetus that has seen the industry thrive. According to researchers at the Harvard School of Public Health, 60 percent of young Nepalese sex slaves in Mumbai are infected with HIV."

"How can a girl survive that sort of life and go on to live what we'd consider a normal life?" Anahera strained to keep the emotion out of her voice.

"Not easily. They suffer psychological, emotional and physical damage. They miss out on an education. Their cultural 'norm' doesn't fit society's 'norm'. Some try to return home and find themselves shunned for being prostitutes. Shunned by their families. Shunned by those who profited when selling them to the traffickers. Treated like they are the ones who are disgraced and consequently they are the ones who keep on paying when it was never their fault. They need to be taught life skills to be given a chance at a normal life. Things like dressmaking, hairdressing, beautician work, and crafts. This is where some of the charities who are working with girls rescued in the red-light districts can make a difference."

"Wow, I really had no idea." Tania shook her head.

"Many people either don't hear about it or they choose to ignore it." She paused to wipe a stray tear. "So you see, I was one of the lucky ones. I came so close to becoming another statistic, one of the 12,000. Thankfully God was looking out for me and provided my new family. Sangita wasn't so lucky."

"So why did you leave the NGO?"

"I met my husband and when he got the posting to New Zealand, I took the interpreter's job and here I am." She looked at her watch. "Goodness, is that the time? I must be getting back to Sangita."

"How's she doing—really doing?" Anahera asked.

"She seems numb. Paralysed with fear and very confused. It's going to take a long time to rehabilitate her." Her eyes welled up again. "I look at her and see what I could have been. I give thanks every day for the good people who rescued me."

She stood up. "I hope you understand a little more about what you are dealing with."

Tania was first to stand and hug her, thanking her for sharing her story. Anahera followed suit. They watched in silence as the petite lady with the brave heart made her way through the congested tables and out into the corridor, before they sat back down.

"Far out, what a story!" Tania said.

"I feel more determined than ever to bring the ringleaders to account." Anahera fiddled with her wedding band. "And it leaves me appreciating my own life. Remind me never to complain again!"

"I know what you mean. We might get a glimpse of what some children have to deal with through our work, but we don't really know the half of it. It makes me angry to think so many are getting away with it."

"Not only that, those responsible are becoming extremely prosperous in the process—at the expense of their innocent victims. And that really bugs me."

They discussed Binsa's story until their indignation waned and they were ready to get back to work. Still mulling over what she'd heard, Anahera navigated the busy streets back to the station.

Once back in the office she shared the story with Frank and watched as his indignation turned to anger. They fell silent while they each digested the horrors associated with the trafficking of young girls.

After some time, Frank broke the silence. "While you've been out, I've been searching for information on this Ajay character. But I've drawn a blank. All I can think is somehow he must be related to the *Red Lights* nightclub."

"The raid on the nightclub might turn something up. It's our best lead."

The workday finished with a briefing of all those who would be involved in the teams carrying out the simultaneous raids of *Kolkata 2* and the nightclub. A sense of excited anticipation grew among those present, affecting Anahera's earlier mood, and she went home satisfied that justice would soon be done.

19

It was early in the morning when Anahera met the others down the street from *Red Lights Adult Nightclub*. The reddish glow emitted by the lights in the open stairway was apparent from where she stood. It was the witching hour, the hour before it closed. She glanced about nervously. Patrons were beginning to leave, weaving their way out the door and onto the footpath. Most were in couples or small groups. They appeared generally dishevelled after a long night of booze and whatever else they'd loaded into their systems.

Barbs' team had insisted on this timing. The club had been under surveillance for the past few days, providing the intel that the owner and manager were in the habit of being present until closing time.

Anahera was wearing her sabre vest over her police jacket, as were the rest of the team. With the rise in the use of firearms amongst the criminal fraternity, they no longer took any chances. John Watts, his face pulled taut in the light of the streetlamps, stood silently beside her. Close by were four members of the Armed Offender's Squad or AOS as they were known, and four policemen and a policewoman, their faces in shadow as they quietly waited for the green light.

Tania was unexpectedly late, which was strange when the raid meant as much to her as it did to Anahera. She tried calling her, but the call went to voice mail. Something important must have come up for her to miss the raid.

John carried the search warrant and was charged with coordinating the operation. The AOS would go in first and secure the building. Once they received the 'all-clear' signal John would lead the remaining cops in to round up the staff and patrons. Only then would the search of the premises begin. Their orders were to identify all present, but to then release the clientele, keeping only the owner, management and staff for questioning, with the discretion to hold anyone else who they deemed to be of interest to the case. One of the team had expertise in electronics and her brief was to find and take into evidence all electronic records—computers, backups, security camera footage, mobile phones, and anything else that might contain evidence.

Footsteps sounded on the pavement as one of the patrons approached the small gathering of police. Anahera felt the familiar feeling of apprehension as the adrenalin surged through her veins. She held her breath. Thinking the man too intoxicated to notice the force of police standing at the corner, Anahera exhaled quietly. But it soon became apparent that he wasn't as intoxicated as they'd first thought when he pulled out his mobile phone and tapped the screen.

"GO!" John commanded.

One word was enough.

The AOS led the way. They rushed up the stairs, pushing aside a punter they encountered who reeled against the wall. Behind them, John waited in the stairwell with the rest of the team, giving the assault team time to ensure the property was now safe. Anahera shifted her weight from one foot to the other as she waited for the affirmative from the leading AOS officer that it was safe to enter. She felt the warm trickle of perspiration and could hear her own heart thumping. It was nearly time.

*

It was dawn when Frank checked his watch for the umpteenth time. *Kolkata 2* had arrived during the night and lay at anchor just to the west of Rakino Island. The pilot had been despatched to bring her into port. Colleagues from the Maritime Police Unit, members of the special crime unit on human trafficking who were running the operation, some constables brought in to assist with the search, specialists in forensic services, and members of the Armed Offender's Squad, had all gathered in the Port of Auckland office. They wore their tactical vests over standard police issue uniforms, although the Maritime Unit could be differentiated by their blue overalls, and the AOS wore their black kit complete with helmets, goggles and guns.

The police had rendezvoused just before dawn to prepare themselves for the arrival of *Kolkata 2* in port where they were set to provide a surprise welcoming party. It had been debated at length whether to board her at anchor or wait until she docked. The decision to board her in port was largely based on logistics. It had meant that the nightclub raid would occur a little ahead of the *Kolkata 2* but in the end they'd agreed the risk was small.

Those present were now quietly chatting in four groups. Barbs Wright, who outranked the rest of the contingent, stood in a small huddle with four young constables, three men and a woman, whom Frank had seen around but did not know. They spoke in subdued tones. The younger ones watched Barbs with wide eyes suggesting they were somewhat in awe of the assertive woman who towered over them. Beside them but in their own huddle was the forensics team, including a police photographer, scene of crime officer and fingerprint officer.

The six members of the highly trained AOS stood together, speaking quietly. Their stance had a hint of swagger and they carried firearms much like a woman carries a handbag, which Frank hoped would be an accessory only and not be fired.

Frank and the Maritime Police component stood apart, where Frank had just finished briefing his unit on the case to date. He was thankful Dick, Stephen and Jammie had been rostered on.

A sense of nervous anticipation emanated from those present. After all the planning and waiting, the moment had finally come. The younger members of the group, who rarely got to board a ship, were as eager as young pups on leads, Jammie included. This was the sort of policing that many of them had signed up for.

A murmur went around the room as the burgundy hull of *Kolkata 2* came into view around Devonport Heads. Flanked by the pilot boat, it steamed its way towards the port while leaving a trail of dark smoke in the early morning sky. It was laden with few containers, having distributed the bulk of its load in Sydney, Auckland on its inward journey, and Port Chalmers. It was scheduled to load cargo at the Port of Auckland before leaving New Zealand waters bound for Kolkata in India.

Of course this ship was only one of three probable vessels that Frank had identified, but his instinct was that it was a likely candidate.

The question regarding the whereabouts of the other four girls was top of mind for Frank. There was a small chance they were still on the ship, and he hoped they'd get lucky. If they'd been on board, and given the ship's schedule, it was more likely they had already been off-loaded in either Sydney or Port Chalmers, or even Auckland. In the very least, he hoped to find evidence they had been there so they could nail the culprits. Hearing Anahera relate the interpreter's story had filled him with a deep disgust that hadn't lessened overnight, making him all the more determined that this raid would be a success.

As the vessel neared the wharf, shrill caw-caws of seagulls accompanied the whine of the motors, the birds providing an escort for the ship as they swooped and glided in the air currents made by her movement.

The police men and women waited patiently. They couldn't be more conspicuous to the port workers and stevedores if they all had green skin and Frank hoped none of the shore-based workers would tip off the crew of *Kolkata 2*. The idea was to not give the captain or any of the sailors aboard the opportunity to forewarn any accomplices on shore. Equally, Frank hoped that the ship's crew had not been forewarned by those subjected to the nightclub raid, potentially giving them time to destroy or hide any evidence on board.

The ship came alongside, parallel to the dock with its row of cranes that wouldn't look out of place in the movie *War of the Worlds*. Its hull dwarfed the workers on the quayside below. Weighted heaving lines, that were attached to the vessel's heavy mooring lines, were thrown over the gunwhale to the dock workers. The mooring lines then dropped from the ship, the eyes of which were looped over the large steel bollards on the wharf using forklifts.

Those in the Port of Auckland office waited, their sense of anticipation palpable.

Once the ship was moored, Barbs spoke with the pilot who requested the gangway be lowered. She then gave the command to board. A constable was stationed at the bottom of the steps and the AOS boarded first with the plan being to secure the bridge and the living quarters.

As soon as they heard it was clear, Barbs led Frank and the remaining troops onto the ship. The Maritime team accompanied her up six flights of steps to the bridge, their footsteps echoing in the steel chamber. An old rugby injury that never ceased to pinch whenever he climbed steps caused Frank to grit his teeth in pain.

The bridge was the control centre of the ship, with numerous instruments and communications equipment as well as a large chart table. A bank of windows across the front and sides provided a view of the array of colourful containers on the deck below. Port and starboard doors gave access to the external bridge wings.

Frank had just acknowledged the pilot who stood at ease beside one of the AOS team members, when an Indian man approached him. The man wore a pristine white buttoned-up shirt under a well-fitted navy-blue blazer with brass buttons and navy-blue trousers with a sharp crease. He asked Frank, "What is the meaning of this?"

Before Frank could speak, Barbs said, "I'm Barbara Wright, the senior police officer, and you are?"

"My name is Joseph Sharma and I am Master of this vessel." He glared at Barbs. "What right do you have to board my ship?"

"I have a warrant to search this vessel." Barbs held out the piece of paper.

Master Sharma took it and read it, then passed it to one of the two ship's officers who had been watching the interaction.

"We are conducting a search for illegal contraband and we expect your complete cooperation."

"I was not told about this." Sharma sounded indignant. "How long will it take? We are on a tight schedule."

"I can't say, but your cooperation will speed things up." Barbs looked around the bridge. "How many staff on board?"

"My First Mate and Second Officer are here on the bridge." He pointed at the two men. "The Third Officer is supervising below, and the Chief Engineer and his First Engineer are in the engine room, as is the Electrical Officer. We also have 14 crewmen."

Barbs said, "We'll split up. One of your officers may like to escort each of our teams."

"What exactly are you looking for? I can tell you my ship is clean. No drugs or contraband. You're wasting your time, and mine." Sharma was sounding more assertive.

"I hope you're right for your sake," Barbs shot back. "Now can I please see your cargo plan?"

Frank bent over the screen with Barbs to study the plan. It identified the containers and showed their location in each hold in a three-dimensional stacking arrangement of bays, rows and tiers. The holds were topped with hatch covers with more containers stacked above the deck. All were 40-foot containers. As expected, nothing in the plan alluded to a container carrying human cargo. Nor did anything look odd or out of place.

Barbs divided her people into three teams. Frank was given the task of searching the living quarters and chose to take Jammie and Hamish, one of the constables, with him leaving the remaining Maritime Unit members to the other two teams. The First Mate came over and introduced himself to Frank as Mohan Prasad and attached himself to Frank's search party.

Knowing it unlikely a container holding the girls was still on board led Frank to believe the private quarters would be the most likely place to find any evidence and he was quietly pleased to have drawn that straw. Whoever was responsible wouldn't want any evidence to be found by the Pilot or through a chance Customs' inspection.

The plan was to make a thorough search of the cabins and if they found anything that might tie the girls to the ship, they were to alert Barbs who would send in the forensic services team.

The tower beneath the bridge contained the living quarters, which were not dissimilar to a budget hotel. It soon became obvious the shipping line didn't place high priority on the comfort of the crew during their long passages at sea.

Based on the assumption that nothing happens aboard ship without the captain knowing, Frank decided to begin with the Master's cabin. Located on C deck, it was spacious and light. Large windows provided views forward and down the centre line of the ship, over the containers to what would normally be the ocean beyond. Under the windows was a storage cabinet that ran the full width of the room. A door opened into a private utilitarian ensuite that resembled an oversized aeroplane toilet with a shower at the end. The cabin was ship-shape with the double bed neatly made and all surfaces were clear. The room also contained a desk, wardrobe, sofa and chairs, and a large screen mounted on the wall.

Either side of the desk were two drawers and a filing drawer. Frank and Jammie took one side each while Hamish worked his way through the clothing and personal effects in the cabinetry and wardrobe. They didn't talk any more than was necessary, conscious of the First Mate scrutinising their every move. It took time to work through the papers in the desk and after a thorough search they came up empty.

They moved down a level to the officers' cabins. The First Mate and Chief Engineer had the most spacious cabins on that level although significantly smaller than that of the Master's. The junior officers had their own cabins but with a lot less room for personal effects. The engineers' cabins were to port and the officers' were to starboard. All contained windows that made them light and airy. But here too they found nothing to suggest the ship had been involved in the trafficking. As they left the First Mate's own room, Frank sensed the man relax—not necessarily because of guilt but more likely whatever the frame was he was no longer in it.

Another level down were the crew's cabins. The furnishings were spartan. Each cabin contained bunks, two to a room with drawers that slid out from under each bed. Above the mattresses and stuck to the wall were arrays of photographs and posters of minimally clad women. Two small desks were fixed to the wall, each with a chair, the size of which might be found in a kid's bedroom—these were the only other furniture. With no attached washroom, they shared a communal one located down the corridor. The three policemen looked in every drawer, every nook, every cranny, but found nothing to suggest the girls had been on board.

As they moved on to the officers' mess and lounge rooms, Frank was beginning to get that sinking feeling that perhaps the search was futile. By the time they'd completed their search of the remaining rooms which included the ship's office, officers' laundry, galley, crew's mess room and smoking room, crew's laundry, communal washrooms, and gym, he was sure that either they had the wrong ship, or it had been cleaned of any evidence. It was lunchtime when the First Mate led them through the maze of containers to find Barbs and her team.

She was standing with the Master beside a blue 40-foot container with her notebook in hand. As Frank approached, she stroked her hand across her short auburn hair, her face strained. "How did you go, Frank?"

"All clear."

"Likewise, nothing so far." She shook her head. "I think the team would appreciate a break for lunch. The members of the AOS have gone, they pulled out as soon as it was established there was no real risk to the searchers. I suggest we take lunch in two shifts."

"What are you thinking? Take something at the port office?" Frank asked.

"I'll get our galley to cater for your team—it'll be no trouble," Sharma offered with a rare smile.

"You sure?" Barbs asked, before adding, "That would be really good of you."

"Not a problem. I'll go and arrange it." He was all charm.

"Frank, could you or one of your team see to it with Master Sharma?" Barbs gave Frank a look that said *I don't trust him.*

It was agreed Jammie would go and he followed Sharma back towards the bridge tower.

The rest of the day went slowly, with the searchers losing their enthusiasm as it became clear they weren't going to find anything. Weary and dejected, Frank disembarked behind Barbs, having completed their search. With no evidence found, he only hoped Anahera's day had been more productive. Looking up, he saw Sharma standing at the rail with a smug expression plastered across his face.

Back in his car, Frank called Brad to give him the update, concluding they either had the wrong ship or the ship had been cleaned of all evidence. Although they couldn't entirely rule out *Kolkata* 2, it did increase the odds that the traffickers had used either *Star of India* or *Bengal Challenger,* both of which were different shipping lines. The search hadn't helped find the remaining four girls and that was his first concern. However, as he'd pointed out to Brad, *Star of India* was already on its way back to its home port where it would load a fresh lot of containers bound for Auckland, and Barbs had already alerted their Indian counterparts of the possibility it would be loading young girls.

Stopping the trade at the source would make the operation a huge success.

It had been a frustrating day, and he longed to get home and treat himself to a cold beer.

20

Anahera was on John's heels as they ascended the stairs to the nightclub. The music was still pumping, and it seemed to echo in her pulse. Behind her she could hear the footsteps of the others.

John opened the door into the nightclub. The bouncers were no longer at their posts, no doubt distracted by the four AOS members who now stood in a square formation in the large room.

The music stopped mid song. Pole dancers slid down their poles. Bar tenders stopped serving. Confusion showed on the faces of the clientele. The room became quiet as every eye locked onto the group of police men and women who were emerging from the stairwell.

Four men in suits sat at the same booth near the stage where Frank and Anahera had spoken to Chase Craddock on their last visit. She recognised Craddock and touched John's sleeve, pointing to the booth.

John nodded, then cleared his throat. In a loud voice he said, "Listen up. I have with me a search warrant. How long this takes will depend on the amount of cooperation we get. To make it easy on us all, I want everyone to group together in the middle of the room. NOW!"

The police fanned out and herded the stragglers into the centre of the room to form the group, much like sheepdogs move sheep.

The AOS continued to stand guard.

Quiet words of complaint came as the group amassed in the middle, which grew in decibels until it became a rumble of dissent.

"Quiet!" John called. "This shouldn't take long, and most of you will soon be free to go home. My colleague and I will take your names and advise who can go and who we require to stay. Chase Craddock, let's start with you."

Anahera recognised the smooth looking man with the gold bling who now moved towards them as the same man she and Frank had met. He wore thick dark rimmed glasses in keeping with his short black hair that was combed into a perfect wave, and a neat black moustache. Under his suit jacket he wore a partially unbuttoned black shirt with a Cuban collar revealing tufts of black chest hair and a heavy gold chain.

"Chase Craddock?" John asked.

The man nodded. "I hope you know what you're doing—my lawyer's going to be all over this."

John handed him a copy of the warrant. "We believe you are involved in the exploitation of underage girls for the purpose of commercial gain, and we will be searching your premises."

Chase read it and scowled. "You're making a mistake, a very big mistake."

"That's for us to determine."

"You'll ruin my business."

Ignoring him, John said, "We're going to need you to stay. Please can you wait over there?" He pointed to a small cluster of tables beside the stage.

Shaking his head while muttering under his breath, Craddock went to the area indicated and perched on a table.

A maverick looking man in a suit complete with bowtie and a handkerchief in his breast pocket stepped towards them, and said, "I'm Rick Talcon, legal counsel for Chase Craddock, and I demand to wait with my client." Without waiting for permission, he joined Craddock, and the two men conversed quietly.

Anahera and John, flanked by constables, sat at another table. One by one those present were brought over to them. They took their names and contact details. Having checked them against their proof of ID, customers were free to leave. Chase Craddock's cronies and all the staff including the dancers were asked to stay. It was difficult for Anahera to hide her satisfaction when one of them was identified as Grant Tate. But none of them were identified as Ajay.

Once the clientele had left and only the smaller group remained, they began the task of interviewing each staff member, leaving the owner, manager and directors to last. Meanwhile, the other police present began a painstaking search of the premises.

The dancers, bar staff and bouncers were all free to go once it was ascertained they would not be able to assist with the enquiries into the illegal immigration of young Nepalese girls and the underage prostitution racket. Anahera had catalogued their details should they be needed for further questioning. Only four men remained—all of whom had been sitting at the booth when they'd arrived.

Before they had a chance to interview them, one of the constables came and whispered in Anahera's ear, "I think you should come and see this."

She followed him past the booth where Chase liked to sit with his pals and out through a side door that she hadn't noticed, perhaps because the door was covered with the same noise dampening fabric as the walls. It opened into another room, only slightly smaller than the main nightclub. The interior was red and black with diffuse lighting. Although devoid of punters, it contained a bank of pokie-machines, a blackjack table, and in the centre was a card table with six chairs. A cashier's booth was behind a screen to one side and a bar was on the other. Another door opened into what she assumed was Craddock's office.

Being behind a closed door with no signage gave the impression the casino was unavailable to the general public and therefore private or for those who were lucky enough, or in most cases unlucky, to be extended invitations. It made sense of the company structure that Anahera had pieced together. And it was a well-known vehicle for laundering money.

She turned to Bill, the constable who'd alerted her to the room. "Would you conduct a search of the office? It's important nothing is missed. Take Stella with you, she's a whizz with electronics."

Despite his obvious weariness as a result of the early start, he answered, "It would be my pleasure. And don't worry, if there's evidence Stella and I will find it."

"Great, thanks. And best get some photos before you start."

She watched him remove his phone from its pocket before returning to John.

The man about to be questioned was Brian Headley, the manager. Confident and good-looking in a rugged masculine sort of way and dressed in a suit with an open neck white shirt, he could've been a movie star. He was the same man who'd answered Craddock when asked if they knew Scarlett during Anahera's earlier visit. It was explained to him that at this point he wasn't being arrested but that they'd like him to come down to the station to help them with their enquiries. To cover themselves they explained his rights when being questioned and he was asked to wait apart from Craddock.

Anahera recognised Grant Tate from the photo she'd found on the internet. He was short, thickset, and his eyes seemed to be too close together making him look like he wore a permanent frown. He confirmed he was a director of the nightclub's operating company and that he'd acquired the lease of the New Lynn property. He too was read his rights and was asked to wait so that he could help them with their enquiries back at the station.

The only person left was Rick Talcon. In a loud voice, he informed John and Anahera that he would be accompanying his clients down to the station. His thick silvery-grey hair left Anahera imagining the stress of being a lawyer for the likes of Chase Craddock would prematurely age even those with the thickest of skins.

Drawn over to the bar, Anahera picked up the picture of the stylised red eye in the gold frame and studied it. The size was roughly six by eight inches. The eye was created in enamelwork giving it a brilliantly coloured effect. The frame looked like it was gold plated—an expensive memento and not a cheap rendition of the eye symbol. The symbol must mean something very special to someone. Turning it over she was disappointed to find no clue on its back. She placed it in an evidence bag.

With the electronic equipment, files and other evidence now in police hands for further examination, Anahera and John propelled the four men down to the waiting squad cars to be transported across town to Auckland Central. The sun was already up and the traffic heavy with rush hour in full swing, giving Anahera a much-needed break.

The satisfaction of having the ringleaders in custody and her confidence they would soon apprehend those responsible for the deaths were overshadowed by her fatigue. And now the hard yards were only just beginning with the interviews back at the station. With Tania a no-show, the job would take longer, and she hoped there was a good reason why she hadn't turned up. She called and left yet another message on her phone.

*

Brad met them as they arrived at HQ and asked them to provide a briefing over coffee in his office once the guests were sorted.

Headley, Tate and Craddock were put in separate interview rooms, with Rick Talcon insisting on being with Craddock. Refreshments were offered giving Anahera and John some respite. They trudged up the stairs to Brad's office where a coffee pot and mugs were waiting.

During the briefing with Brad, Anahera had to stifle several yawns. But as the caffeine started to take effect she was reenergised and ready to do battle. They agreed their strategy for the interviews. Craddock would need to be interviewed simultaneously with Headley and then Tate, meaning Rick Talcon couldn't be present at all three since they feared he had more skin in the game than just legal work. John would conduct the interview with Chase Craddock, and in Tania's absence Anahera would have to do both Brian Headley and Grant Tate.

As yet there was no word from the team down at the port.

Anahera entered the interview room where Brian Headley was waiting. She reminded him of his rights and because Rick Talcon was unavailable to represent him, they had to wait for an alternative lawyer to arrive. Anahera took this time in her office to relax, allowing her to fully recharge.

Shane Jeffries, a junior partner in the same law firm as Rick Talcon, arrived and announced he was the acting legal counsel for Headley. Anahera commenced the interview. It soon became clear that Headley was a lightweight, employed to run the night club and the casino but that was where his involvement seemed to end.

The one piece of information he offered was to confirm the casino operated for a select clientele only, whose names were in a database on the hard drive from the office. He believed Grant Tate worked for Chase Craddock. Little else could be gleaned from him—nothing about the tattoos or Sangita or the New Lynn property, nor the drowned girls, nor about the racket bringing illegal immigrants into the country as underage sex workers. And he claimed he didn't know any Ajay. He was free to go home—and they knew where to find him if they needed anything further.

Anahera moved on to the interview room where Grant Tate was waiting with his legal counsel, Dee Roberts, another of the partners in Rick's law firm. She began by charging him with running the illegal brothel in New Lynn, and for commercial sexual exploitation of a person under 18 years of age.

After formally beginning the interview, she asked, "Mr Tate, what is your association with *Red Lights Adult Nightclub?*"

"I am a director of the operating company." He smirked at her. "Being a director isn't a crime."

"Does Scarlett O'Connor work for you?"

Appearing a little less sure of himself, Tate looked at Dee Roberts and said nothing.

"We've already heard from Scarlett, so shall I ask you again? Does Scarlett O'Connor work for you?"

He looked at his legal counsel and laughed.

Infuriated and somewhat puzzled at his response, Anahera asked again, "Does Scarlett O'Connor work for you?"

"All I'm saying is that woman is a law unto herself."

"Look, we know Scarlett O'Connor was running the joint. Now I'll ask again, was she working for you?"

"I'm not saying anything."

"How did you meet Scarlett?"

"I refuse to answer your questions. I know my rights."

"You may be interested to hear we've already interviewed Scarlett, and she confirmed she works for you."

"Is that so?" he looked at his lawyer who nodded. "Alright then—if she says she works for me, she must work for me."

"Did you recruit her to run the New Lynn establishment?"

He looked uncertainly at Dee. "Look, I'm not saying a damn thing."

Ignoring him, Anahera moved on. "Was the lease for the New Lynn brothel taken out under the operating company you are director of?"

"I'm saying nothing."

"Fine, but remember we have access to the company records." Anahera was starting to feel frazzled, the temporary effects of the caffeine high already wearing thin. "Now was the lease for the New Lynn brothel under the operating company you are director of?" Anahera persisted.

He hesitated and shuffled in his seat. "Yes."

"How did you come across Sangita or Harmony as she was known?"

He looked at his lawyer. "I'm not going to incriminate myself. I won't answer that."

"You don't need to answer anything you don't want to," Dee reassured him.

"How do you know Ajay?"

A look of surprise crossed his face. "I'm not saying anything."

"Are you a business associate of Ajay's?"

He sat tight lipped.

Anahera asked, "Does the picture of the tattoo behind the bar belong to you?"

"That? Hardly my taste in art—it's hideous!"

"Who does it belong to?"

His eyes widened momentarily as he shifted his gaze. "I don't know."

Anahera put two photos on the table. "Two Nepalese girls drowned out at Rangitoto Island. Do you know these girls? We know they are linked to Sangita."

He made a point of not looking at the photos. "No."

His contempt wasn't lost on her, compounding the effect of her early start and fuelling her frustration. "Were you involved in the trafficking of these girls?"

"No, absolutely not."

"Did you hire them out to a punter?"

"No!" He spat the words out.

"How did you acquire these girls?"

"I'm not answering anymore of your questions. I reject your insinuations, and we are done here." He looked at Dee, who placed a hand on his shoulder as if to calm him.

Infuriated, Anahera called for a break and after ending the recording, left the room.

In the corridor, Brad was hovering. "How's the interview going?"

She said, "Grant Tate is guilty on Sangita's account, that's a tick in the box—I've charged him for his involvement with the illegal brothel. But we're not getting anywhere with him regarding the Rangitoto drownings or the trafficking. I think it's best to wait and see what the analysis of the computer from *Red Lights* reveals. It will be a lot easier with some evidence to dangle in front of him."

"Whatever you think is best. Trust your instinct Anahera, it rarely lets you down." Brad's smile was earnest. "You look tired. Why don't you take a break? He can stew while he waits."

"I could do with a caffeine break, but first I'll organise for him to be taken down and processed. I need to check in with the techie working on the club's hard drive." She pushed her hair back from her face. "Any news from the port?"

"Not yet. I'm going to see how John is getting on with Chase Craddock."

After organising for the booking sergeant to see to Tate, Anahera returned to her office.

She stretched out in her chair and tapped the familiar number into her phone. "Stella? Anahera here. Have you found anything of interest?"

"Kia ora! A few things. I've found accounts for the club and separate accounts for the casino—does that surprise you?"

"No, I expected that. I wouldn't be surprised if the casino is used for money laundering and the club accounts are kept clean. What else?"

"There's a database of names and their contact details—and there're some fairly public figures among them. Any ideas?"

"It could be those are the high rollers that make up the elite group invited into the casino." She thought for a moment. "Or they could be special clients given exclusive access to underage girls. Can you send a copy of the list through to me?"

"No problem."

Anahera asked, "One thing, is there an Ajay on that list?"

The line went quiet for a few seconds while Stella searched. "Actually there is. Ajay Singh. And there's a phone number."

"That's very good news!" Anahera exclaimed.

The sound of tapping on the keyboard came through clearly and they waited.

"I'm just looking at the accounts and there's a fairly substantial invoice from Singh Imports Limited..." More tapping. "Which is owned by Ajay Singh. The invoice doesn't specify what it was for, just says general goods. I'll send it through to you now."

Following the call, Anahera sat back in her chair and couldn't help but grin. The trap was closing—if only it was a gin trap. She smiled ruefully, thinking about how she'd like to punish them.

"Any more news?" Brad asked.

Startled, having not been aware he'd come in, she recovered her composure quickly. "Kia ora Brad. Ae, some good news. We've connected the nightclub to Ajay who, according to the tattooist, brought all three girls in for their tattoos. So I'm hoping we have enough to book Chase Craddock and find Ajay Singh."

"More good news." He looked pleased.

Anahera rubbed her tired eyes. "How's John going with Craddock?"

"He's still not answering anything—his lawyer's instructing him not to."

"This will help. Oh and by the way, there's a database of names which we think could be the select clientele who receive invitations to the casino. It includes some high-profile names."

"You'll need to tread lightly then. Don't contact any of them without first clearing it with me. I don't want this thing blowing out of proportion."

"I hear you."

"It's excellent progress." He looked genuinely pleased.

"Do you think we have enough to arrest Chase Craddock? He's the sole shareholder of the parent company that runs the *Red Lights* nightclub operating company, which holds the lease for the New Lynn brothel where Sangita was being forced to work. The manager of the club said he believed Grant Tate worked for Chase Craddock. Then there's the connection to Ajay Singh who took the girls for their tattoos and the nightclub had a picture of the tattoo in a frame. I'm guessing Craddock is more than a brothel owner supplying underage girls. He could well be the mastermind."

"I'm sure we can make the charge stick." Brad ran his hand over his blond hair. "For now, we can book him with the same as Tate."

"We're on the home straight."

Brad smiled. "Not quite there yet. Oh and before I forget, I came to tell you I heard from Frank. They're still searching the ship but as yet nothing. Don't forget to pass the information about Ajay Singh to John—he'll be relieved to have something he can use to push Chase Craddock a bit harder. In fact, why don't you join him in the interview?"

"That would be my pleasure—I'd like nothing more than to see his face when he's charged."

Brad turned and walked back down the corridor.

Anahera went down to join John. She knocked on the door and opened it.

John turned to look at her and she said, "A minute?"

She waited outside the room.

John emerged, shutting the door behind him. "What's up?"

"We have some good news." Anahera proceeded to brief him on all she'd found out including the link to Ajay Singh, emphasising its significance to the case. "Brad thought I might assist you in the interview."

"I think that's a good idea. I'm not getting anywhere. And the lawyer is a pain. Every question is being met by silence."

"Well, maybe this information might change the slope of the deck on his sinking ship."

John looked exhausted but managed to chuckle at her analogy. "I don't want the ship to sink before we find the culprits behind the people smuggling."

"Nor with the children on board. Perhaps not such a good analogy." She giggled. "Seriously though, Brad agreed we have enough to book Craddock with ownership of the illegal brothel in New Lynn, and for commercial sexual exploitation of a person under 18 years of age."

"Great. How about you conduct the questions for a bit? A change in tempo could be useful."

"Happy to oblige. But you should make the arrest, after all you've been leading the charge all morning."

He held the door open for her and they entered the room.

Craddock watched Anahera enter through his thick black rimmed glasses. "Ah, the cop with the nice tush."

Anahera ignored the comment and placed her notebook on the table, calming herself as John restarted the interview.

Believing it best to get straight to the point, Anahera asked, "What is your relationship with Ajay Singh?"

A flicker of surprise crossed Chase's face.

Rick said, "I advise my client not to answer."

Anahera didn't take her eyes off Craddock. She said, "We've got the information from your computer, and we know you have had dealings with him. Now I will ask you again and I suggest you think very carefully about your answer—it may go better for you if you cooperate with us." She paused for her words to sink in. "What is your relationship with Ajay Singh?"

He looked at his lawyer who shook his head, and said, "I don't have to answer."

"Okay. Perhaps this might jog your memory." Anahera checked her notebook and read out the details of the invoice, ending with, "And his name is on the list of your special customers. We know you know him."

"I know lots of people."

Changing tack, she asked, "Where did Sangita come from?"

"Who?"

"Sangita, the underage Nepalese girl you had locked up in the New Lynn brothel, otherwise known as Harmony."

He maintained a poker face, saying nothing.

Taking a punt, she asked, "Did Ajay Singh supply Sangita?"

Although maintaining his silence, his bluster seemed to evaporate, his body slumping a mere fraction, further convincing Anahera she was on the money.

"Did you have two other Nepalese girls in your custody besides Sangita?"

More silence.

"Who took them out to Rangitoto Island?"

His refusal to talk was infuriating when she was sure he had the answers.

"Does the picture of the eye in the gold frame that sits behind the bar belong to you?"

A long silent pause.

"We know that the New Lynn brothel came under the nightclub's operating company, which you own. Grant Tate has been arrested."

To this, Chase raised an eyebrow.

"We know Grant Tate works for you. We know you own the parent company of the operating company where he is listed as director, the company that runs *Red Lights Adult Nightclub*. Furthermore, we believe Scarlett O'Connor, the woman who ran the brothel, works for Grant Tate. And an eleven-year-old girl was being drugged and kept in a locked room in your brothel and forced to work as a prostitute. The child had a tattoo on her wrist, the same graphic as the eye in the frame in your bar. The tattooist can identify Ajay Singh as the person who brought all three girls in for tattoos." She bored her eyes into him, willing him to speak. "What do you have to say for yourself?"

Silence.

Anahera looked at John. It was time. John made the arrest.

21

Frank tossed and turned. Sleep had come only in snatches all night. He tapped the face on his watch, waking it up so it glowed in the dark. 3:17. Margie lay quietly next to him, her breathing slow and regular.

Something was plaguing him. Something about the interview with Scarlett O'Connor. Something she'd said. Something missed. Like waking from a dream and trying to remember it but it was just out of reach, he couldn't quite catch it.

His mind wandered with random thoughts. He pictured young girls in a sealed 40-foot shipping container. How long until the air ran out? That was the longest time they could have survived being shut inside. If they'd been accommodated in the living quarters in the tower once underway, the entire crew would know about it from the captain down. Unless they travelled hidden in a hold or an open container.

What was the price for shipping them? Was it shared amongst the crew? Were they paid hush money?

His mind returned to Scarlett O'Connor. Then it came to him.

Taking care not to wake Margie, he snuck out of bed and dressed in his work clothes before sneaking out the door. The drive to work was quick with next to no traffic on the streets.

Once inside their small office he turned the lights on and settled into his chair. After a mega-sized yawn and stretch of his tired limbs, he picked up his notebook and began to flick through the pages. There, scrawled in his untidy handwriting, was the clue he'd overlooked. Scarlett O'Connor had said high rollers frequented the brothel. High rollers.

These girls did not come cheap—not something a man like Jerry Ramsley could afford. Ramsley had a chip on his shoulder and disliked authority, but he had been a red herring and that's why Frank hadn't been able to make the pieces fit together.

There had been another boat in Islington Bay the day the boat shed girl was found. A 70-foot party launch named *Neptune*. She was the boat they should have scrutinised more closely. He'd assumed it was someone's work party because there were mostly men on board. But what if it was another type of party, one that hired escorts for entertainment? And not just women escorts but young girls?

He booted his computer. While he waited, still berating himself for having become so fixated on Ramsley that he'd overlooked the party boat, he went to fix himself his first coffee for the day.

Back at the desk, with caffeine firing his neurons, he searched the database for the owner of *Neptune*. And there he was. Louie Fabio. Working quickly now, he put the name into the police database and drew a blank. No previous charges.

"You're in early." Anahera breezed into the room. "The sun's not yet over the yardarm. Did Margie kick you out?"

He chuckled. "I could say the same for you."

"How did it go down at the port yesterday?" she asked, turning on her computer.

"We didn't find any incriminating evidence on board." He suddenly grinned. "But I think I know how the girls came to be out at Rangitoto Island."

"You do?"

His eyes had drifted back to his screen.

"Well, are you going to fill me in or keep me in suspense?" She stood with her hands on her hips.

"Okay, okay. It came to me in the small hours when I couldn't sleep. Something Scarlett O'Connor said about high rollers. There was a party boat in the bay that day we found the boat shed girl's body. I'd made a note of it—a large launch called *Neptune*. It didn't strike me as strange at the time. I did note that the party was well underway with lots of drinking. The thing is, they were mostly men on board, so I assumed it was some sort of work party. You know, any excuse to take the work colleagues out and show off your flash boat."

"A pseudo strategic planning day?"

"That's right, an excuse for a day off."

"But they'd be fools to stay in the bay if they'd disposed of a body in a boat shed there."

"We might think so, but some guys act like they're bullet proof."

"Above the law, you mean."

"Exactly."

"Have you got a name?"

"Just found the owner online. One Louie Fabio."

"What do we know about him?"

"Nothing as yet." He leaned back in his chair. "Anyway, tell me about your day."

She related all that they'd found at the nightclub, the evidence in the computer, the arrests of Craddock and Tate, and how she believed the Ajay who took the girls for their tattoos was Ajay Singh of Singh Imports Limited. Finishing, she said, "So we have nabbed those behind the illegal brothel, and we've made the connection between one Ajay Singh and Chase Craddock. I'm looking forward to bringing in Ajay Singh."

"Good work. The net is closing, but we still don't have the ship that transported the girls here. My gut tells me we shouldn't be ruling out the *Kolkata 2*. It was almost too clean. If they did have the container on board, it's likely they would have had to remove the girls and hold them elsewhere on the ship because those containers are sealed, meaning there would be limited oxygen." He sighed.

"Or perhaps the container was modified with breather holes."

"That's possible."

"So where is it now?" she asked.

"Good question. Somewhere in Auckland I suppose—some storage place. If it was offloaded in Auckland, the ship has had plenty of time to remove any evidence while sailing down to Otago and back up. But according to Sangita's account, we still have four missing girls."

Her dimple deepened as she sucked in her cheeks. "There could be another brothel operating with underage girls somewhere in the city. Like the New Lynn establishment."

"Maybe. But wouldn't the risk of discovery be greater if operating two establishments?"

"You're assuming it would be the same operator—there could be another Chase Craddock. Where did the *Kolkata 2* come from?"

"Kolkata via Sydney," he answered.

"What if those girls never came to Auckland? What if they were offloaded in Sydney?"

"Good point and one I hadn't considered. I might run this past Barbs and suggest she talks to her Sydney counterpart." Pausing to consider this, he added, "And the Singaporeans, should the carrier turn out to have been *Star of India*."

"While you do that, I'll see what I can dig up on Louie Fabio."

Frank made the call to Barbs, who agreed it was worth following up with both the Sydney and Singaporean arms of the network.

"Take a look at this," Anahera said, looking at her computer screen.

A Facebook account in the name of Louie Fabio was on the screen. His cover photo was a picture of *Neptune*.

"Was this the boat?" she asked.

"Yes, as far as I can remember it. What else have you dredged up?"

"He's married and lives in a mansion on the North Shore. Runs a property development business and is currently negotiating with the council to get the zoning changed on a golf course he owns. There's a lot of media attention and it seems he's upset a lot of folks in the process. He's also been banned from being a director because of some sort of mismanagement he was involved in."

"Sounds like a nice chap."

"I'll see what else I can find." She turned and looked at Frank. "I've an idea."

It only took a few keystrokes before she said, "Yes!"

"Yes what?"

"Remember I told you we found a database of names on the computer from the nightclub?"

He nodded.

"Louie Fabio is on the list."

Frank let out a whistle. "A client?"

"Maybe. I thought they might be the select ones who were players at the casino. But perhaps they also are clients of the illegal brothel. That could be how payments are made... through the casino so they can't be traced."

"Is the name of the punter who was caught with Sangita on the list?"

"Just a minute, I'll check." She looked up the name and checked it against the database. "Yes, he's there."

"I think it's time we paid this Louie Fabio a visit." Struck by an idea, he said, "Before we do that, I'll give the two who found the body in the boat shed a call. Maybe *Neptune* featured in one of their photos."

Finding their numbers in his notebook, he placed the first call to Jeff Watts who apologised and said he'd purposely chosen an angle that gave a clear shot of the boat shed without the distraction of any boats in the background. Next Frank called Rochelle Ioane.

"Yes?" She sounded like he might've woken her up.

"Rochelle? Detective Frank Smythe here. I met you that day on Rangitoto Island."

"Hi Frank." She sounded puzzled.

"I'm wondering if you can help us. Did you happen to take any photos of boats in Islington Bay that day?"

"Not specifically. Just a minute." The line went quiet. "There are some boats, but they're just in the background of one of my shots. I'm afraid it probably isn't much use to you. Do you want me to send it?"

"Yes, thanks. It might be of help."

"Have you found the culprits yet?" Her voice was low and husky.

"We're close—that's all I can say at this stage." Frank gave her his email address and finished the call.

Within moments a new email was flagged on his computer screen. He opened it and found the photo attached. It was of the wharf with boats in the background. Zooming in, he could see *Neptune* with some figures on the deck but too small to make out the faces.

"Come and look at this."

Anahera came over and peered at his screen. "Mmm, that's interesting. I'll bet one of the techies could get us a clearer image of the faces. How about you forward it to me so I can get Stella to have a go."

Frank had just forwarded the email when his phone chirped.

"Frank, Brad here. I've just come off a call with Barbs. She's planning to visit Singh Imports Limited this afternoon to round up Ajay Singh, and I want you and Anahera involved."

"We definitely want to be in on that one."

"Great. I'll leave it to you to make contact."

"By the way, we think we might be on to the person who could be responsible for the drowning victims."

"You do? That's great news. Do I assume it's not Jerry Ramsley?"

"I'm afraid he may have been a red herring. On the day the first body was found, there was a party boat in the bay with mostly men on board, and the owner happens to be on the list of names found in the nightclub's computer. He's a wealthy property developer, goes by the name Louie Fabio. We're just preparing to head out there now."

"What do you want to do then, Frank?"

"We'll provide the back up for Barbs and John if they can wait. In fact I'd be disappointed to miss it—I want to see Singh's face when he learns we're onto him."

"I'll let her know." The line went dead.

They gathered their things and left the office. Frank tossed the keys to Anahera. "Must be your turn to drive."

*

Morning rush hour was still causing traffic delays on the arterial routes when Anahera pulled up beside the kerb across the road from the residential property belonging to Louie Fabio. High security gates were flanked on either side by a stone plinth on which a beautifully carved lion stood guard. A high stone fence with spikes set on the top provided a deterrent to any unwelcome visitors. Through the gates the driveway intersected a lush lawn which was being doused with water from inground sprinklers. The mansion was pretentiously large, its two storeys spread wide. Reminiscent of ancient Roman opulence, it was clad in stone and built in a Mediterranean style. A grandiose entrance under a portico was held up by large pillars that rose to the full height of the building.

At the gates Anahera pushed the button on the intercom. A voice asked, "Who is it?"

"Detective Anahera Raupara and Detective Frank Smythe here. Please open the gate."

As soon as the gates began to open, they walked into the beautifully manicured garden that had a perimeter of exotic trees encompassing neat flower beds. A fenced Astroturf tennis court was on the far side of the property.

Anahera rang the buzzer. After flashing their IDs, a petite woman opened the over-sized door and asked them to wait inside while she fetched Mr Fabio. It was a grand entranceway that made Anahera feel small and insignificant. Her eyes followed the symmetrical staircases that curved up to the floor above. It was the most ornate and opulent home she'd ever seen.

Rapid footsteps approached on the Italian tiled floor. A short, middle-aged man who was stylishly dressed in an open-necked silk shirt over designer chinos and leather boat shoes approached and extended his hand. "Louie Fabio. How can I help?"

They each shook his hand and introduced themselves, backing it up with their ID cards.

"Mr Fabio, we just have some routine questions regarding your boat, *Neptune*." Anahera said.

"Ah, my pride and joy. Do come through." He led them to an informal lounge with windows overlooking a patio with a lap pool surrounded by strategically placed urns, each with a large and luxuriant palm. "Take a seat."

Anahera chose one of the comfortable leather chairs. Once seated she studied Fabio. His mannerisms signalled a cockiness she despised, the sort one associates with someone who thinks they are a cut above everyone else and as such, above the law.

"Drinks?" Fabio asked.

"No thanks," Frank replied. "We just have some questions for you."

"Fire away."

It was clear he hadn't been forewarned.

"You may remember I spoke with you in Islington Bay about a body in the boat shed. At the time you said you hadn't seen anything of interest."

"Of course I remember. Why the visit now?"

"There have been some developments that we'd like to speak to you about, so we'd appreciate it if you would accompany us down to the station."

"That's really not very convenient." Fabio began to fidget with the thick gold rings on his fingers. "Do I need my lawyer?"

"That's up to you. You're not under arrest, nor being detained, just helping with our enquiries. But I should caution you that you have the right to remain silent. You do not have to make any statement. Anything you say will be recorded and may be given in evidence in court. You have the right to speak with a lawyer without delay and in private before deciding whether to answer any questions." Frank paused to look at his surroundings. "And if you need it, we have a list of lawyers you may speak to for free."

Congeniality now forgotten, Fabio said, "I'll come down to the station, and I'd like my lawyer present."

Seeing his composure dissolve confirmed they were on the right track, and intensified the feelings of dislike Anahera felt for him when she thought about what he might have been involved in.

They stood up and followed him to the door before escorting him back to the station.

*

Back at headquarters, Dee Roberts arrived in the reception area just as Frank and Anahera were bringing in their guest Louie Fabio. Upon introducing herself as Fabio's lawyer, Frank had to hide his surprise given she'd also represented Grant Tate—obviously a very busy woman. She and Fabio were shown into an interview room to wait.

Meanwhile Anahera went to organise a search warrant for *Neptune* while Frank organised their refreshments, believing it would be best to start on a good footing. As soon as Anahera returned, they began the interview, with her taking the lead once more.

Once she'd formally begun the interview, she asked, "Mr Fabio, may I call you Louie?"

"Yes, of course. That is my name." He seemed to have regained his self-assurance.

"And are you the owner of *Neptune*?"

"Yes, I am. She's a lovely craft."

"Where do you keep her?"

"Westhaven Marina."

"Louie, I'm going to show you two photos, and I want you to think hard about whether you've seen these girls before."

She placed the first photo of the boat shed corpse in front of him and carefully watched his face. It remained unmoved. "Do you recognise her?"

"No."

"What about this one?" She put the photo of the bloated Jane Doe Two down.

He grimaced and looked away. "No."

"Have you ever been to the *Red Lights Adult Nightclub*?"

"No."

"Louie, I'm going to ask you that question again, because you may want to reconsider your answer. You see we have carried out a raid on the nightclub and have found your name in a computer. Have you ever been to the *Red Lights Adult Nightclub*?"

"Yes, I remember it now."

He had lied and Frank almost gloated knowing they had him—they just needed the evidence.

Anahera asked, "Have you been in the casino at the nightclub."

"Yes."

"And what about the New Lynn brothel?"

He glanced at his lawyer.

Dee said, "I advise my client not to answer."

"Have we finished? I'm ready to go home—I have better things to do with my time than be party to this ridiculous inquisition. I told you at the time, I didn't see anything in the bay that day. We were just enjoying ourselves on my lovely *Neptune*."

Undeterred, Anahera asked, "Who was on board with you?"

Frank repressed a smile as he watched his partner go on the attack.

"Just good friends. They are private people and won't want me to give their names."

"Why not?"

"My friends are married men and they may not want their wives to find out—it was a party after all." He looked at Frank with a conspiratory smile and said, "It's a man's thing."

Frank shifted uncomfortably in his seat at the inference all men were alike.

Anahera asked, "What exactly do you mean?"

"I organised for a couple of ladies to entertain us on board. That's why." He winked at Frank. "Now can I go?"

"Were they underage?"

"Look, I have nothing to hide. I'm free to visit a nightclub if I wish. And I can party with my friends however I like." He glared at Anahera.

"At any time during that particular cruise did you have two underage Nepalese girls on board?"

He thumped his hands on the table. "This is enough!"

"Did they go into the water and drown—perhaps it was accidental? Perhaps you saved one only to die later and you disposed of her body in a boat shed?"

"This is absurd!"

"You are badgering my client. I'm warning you if you don't desist I'll make a complaint to the Independent Police Conduct Authority," Dee Roberts said. "If you're not going to charge my client then this interview is over."

She was certainly feisty, and Frank wondered what she had to prove. His attention turned to his phone as it buzzed with an incoming message. He looked at the phone before turning to Anahera. "A minute outside?"

She suspended the interview and followed him out.

In the corridor, he said, "The search warrant for the *Neptune* has been granted. I suggest we stop the interview until after the search. Do you agree?"

"Makes sense. I'll put money on him being guilty." She shook her head. "I'm not getting far in there—I suspect my dislike for him might be getting in the way. I thought if I push him, he might crack. He's all bluster."

"You're doing okay. I can take over anytime you want me to." He made a call to Forensics to request a technician accompany them on the search.

When they re-entered the room, Dee was speaking quietly to Louie.

Frank said, "We have a warrant to search your launch."

Louie suddenly looked rattled, before quickly collecting himself. "This is an outrageous invasion of my privacy!"

Anahera ignored him. "You can either give us the access codes and keys or come with us and open her up."

"Absolutely I will come—and so will my lawyer."

Anahera formally ended the interview.

*

Neptune was indeed a beautiful vessel. Her hull gleamed black and shiny, her cabin white and immaculate. Polished brass fittings gleamed in the sunlight. The deck was teak, its caulking unblemished. Fabio was quiet now, no longer full of self-importance. He punched a code into the security pad and opened the door into a massive saloon lined in stained teak, with white leather upholstery and colourful cushions scattered about. A sparkling galley complete with oven and fridge was on the starboard side.

Forward of the saloon, steps led down into a large state room with a king size bed and ensuite. Frank noted a lock had been added to the door, not on the state room side of the door, but the other side which could only be to lock someone inside. He photographed it with his phone.

Aft of the saloon were double cabins, each with their own ensuite and lockable doors.

Back in the cockpit, Frank climbed up some steps to another door that opened into the helm station with a varnished wood wheel, all manner of electronic equipment including radar and sonar, and a navigation station.

The boat had been cleaned and Frank only hoped that the cleaners hadn't been too efficient. He instructed Louie Fabio to wait outside while he, Anahera, and the Forensics technician, Delia Lee, made a thorough search of the boat for any trace of the girls.

They got into disposable overalls, peeled on gloves and set to work.

It was a laborious task. They painstakingly worked their way through the layers of bedding and every inch of surface area. Time marched on. They stayed the course.

Just when the search was beginning to look futile, Delia called from the state room, "I think I have something."

Frank left the port quarter berth and went to see. Anahera was already in the state room when he got there.

Holding tweezers in a gloved hand, Delia held up a small piece of ripped fabric that was no bigger than a few threads. "If you ask me, this looks very much like the pyjama material on the Jane Does."

"Bag it. Let's keep going," Frank said, before returning to the cabin he was searching.

By the end of the search, they had bagged two straight black hairs which had been found down the edge of the state room bed as well as the piece of cloth.

Now they would have to wait on the analysis. The cloth could be checked for a match back at the Forensics' lab. However the hair would need to be sent away to ESR for DNA testing and that could take a week. In the meantime, Louie Fabio was free to go.

22

Anahera was back at her desk when she made a call.

"Stella? Anahera here. How's it going with the computer information? Have you found anything that could implicate the nightclub and casino in the trafficking and prostitution racket?"

"No. I'd say whoever kept the books knew what they were doing and were careful not to leave a trail."

"Anything on Louie Fabio? We believe he hired some escorts including the two young Nepalese girls whose bodies we found."

"Only his name on the list I sent you. I have managed to get a reasonable image of the faces of two men on the deck of the *Neptune*. I'll send them to you. I ran a face matching program and got a definite hit for one of them. His name's Adrian Forsythe—I'll send through his details."

"Great. What about Ajay Singh?"

"Just the invoice and again, his name on the list. No emails. It appears to have been wiped clean of anything that might implicate them in underhand dealings. I suspect the cash going through the casino held a lot of the answers you're after. It's a pity money can't talk!"

"Anything about the purchase of the girls?"

"Nothing obvious."

"There was an eye symbol used as a tattoo for the girls, and it was found framed in the club. You might want to do a search on that."

"Thanks, I'll try that. I'll let you know if I find anything else of interest."

As an afterthought, she added, "Oh, and see what you can find on Scarlett O'Connor. I want to know where she was born, where she grew up, where she went to school, jobs, travel, everything about her."

She'd just hung up when her phone chirped.

"Kia ora, Anahera speaking."

"Anahera, it's Sandie. Sangita is responding better and I'm happy for you to interview her. Just you though, she's still very fragile."

"I can come now if that's okay."

"Great. See you in a bit."

Anahera hurriedly google-searched Singh Imports Limited and bingo—there in the *About Us* page was a photo of Ajay Singh, which she printed. After placing it in a folder with copies of the other pictures she'd need for her interview, she wolfed down a belated sandwich and drink before rushing over to the hospital. En route, she stopped to purchase some sweet treats for Sangita, hoping they'd be allowed.

*

The ward bustled with staff and visitors when she arrived. Sandie was waiting for her outside Sangita's private room. Looking decidedly relaxed and motherly in a pretty floral top and jeans, it seemed the perfect image for a social worker helping traumatised children.

Surprised that Tania wasn't there too, she asked, "Where's Tania?"

"I'm not sure. I left a message on her phone and expected her to be here by now."

"That's strange. She must be sick; she didn't turn up to something yesterday as well."

"She must be poorly, I would've expected her to let me know. Not to worry, let's go on in and see Sangita—she's been spending a lot of time sleeping, but she's awake now. Although her condition's still delicate, you'll see a difference in her—it reminds you how resilient children can be."

She opened the door and led Anahera into the room which was light and airy from the daylight that streamed in through the open curtains. Sangita was sitting up in bed and still holding the toy Anahera had given her.

Binsa was sitting beside the bed and stood up to greet Anahera.

"How do you want to do this?" Sandie asked, flashing her pearly whites. "We could commandeer the small lounge we used last time, but I think it may be best for Sangita if we stay in the familiar setting of her room. It seems there'll be just the four of us."

"Here's fine by me." Anahera nodded in agreement, before offering the bag of treats to Sangita and gesturing to show they were for her. "For you Sangita."

Binsa spoke to Sangita who peered into the paper bag. Her eyes lit up and she chose a green aeroplane lolly and popped it into her mouth.

Sandie disappeared out the door and moments later came back in dragging a chair.

"I've explained to Sangita why you are going to ask her questions, and she says she is willing to help you." Binsa looked concerned. "But please be mindful she is still in a precarious emotional state."

"Remember we can stop at any time she wants to, and if the questions are too hard then I'll call for a break and let her have a rest," Sandie added.

"Is there any objection to me recording our chat on my phone?" Anahera asked.

"No, that should be okay." Sandie smiled agreeably.

Anahera opened her notebook and balanced it on her knee as she considered how to go about the interview. She didn't want to frighten Sangita and have the plug pulled early before she could get any incriminating evidence.

"Okay. How about we start at the beginning—that might be a good way to warm up in preparation for the hard questions." She smiled engagingly at Sangita. "Tell us about your home in Nepal."

Binsa interpreted the question and Sangita answered in a faltering child's voice. When she'd finished, Binsa answered in English. "She lived with her mum and dad, her father's parents, three sisters, a brother, and a baby brother, in a small village in the mountains. She likes to play with Soneeya and Palisha, her friends who also live in the village. The only access to the village is on foot and it is a very long walk."

"How far from the nearest road?"

Binsa consulted her and said, "She doesn't know, only that it took two days to walk out. The tracks are difficult to walk and there are a lot of places that are hard to cross because they haven't been fixed since the big earthquake."

"Ask her to tell us what her life was like in the village."

Binsa touched Sangita's hand as she put the question to her. The child looked directly at Binsa and spoke, gaining confidence as she did so. There was an interchange between them for some minutes before Binsa answered. "She says her dad works hard breaking rocks for tracks and new roads. Sometimes he is away for days, even weeks. Her mum cares for the children and cooks and cleans. She also weaves dokos, or traditional baskets, from dried bamboo. She said her sister and the baby were very sick before she left—from what she described it could be tuberculosis which is rampant in the rural areas. There is no school in the village, so Sangita and her siblings haven't received any formal education. Being the eldest, she had to help her mum with the chores and looking after the other children. Often when they had nothing left to barter for food, the family would go hungry. They have no electricity, and it is very cold in the winter months when it snows."

"Why did she leave her family and the village?"

Binsa translated. "She says that a man came to the village. A very wealthy man. He saw her and liked her and asked her family if he could marry her. Because she was the eldest and he had the bride price, her father accepted. They were so happy that good karma had fallen on their family. It was a huge honour. Many of the people in the village were pleased for her family. They told her she was very lucky and that she should be a good wife and do everything her husband told her to do. He paid her dowry price and took her away to live with his family."

"Where did he take her?"

Again, the question was repeated and answered in the foreign tongue before Binsa said, "They walked for two days and came to a road where he had a car parked—it was her first experience of a car. For the next three or four days, she's not sure exactly, they drove through towns and countryside. It appears he hired overnight rooms where she was made to sleep on the floor beside his bed. She thinks she must've done something wrong, because they never got to his mother's house."

Binsa spoke to Sangita again, who started to answer. And as she did, tears welled up and what began as a whimper became a sob and the tears a river. Binsa put her arms around the child and held her as Anahera felt her own heart break.

The brave young girl began to converse with Binsa and after what seemed to be a long time, Binsa relayed more of her story. "She says they were in a large town that was very busy with loud noises and bad smells and people everywhere. She doesn't know where it was. She was given to another man and told to be good and do whatever he told her to do without question. I'm guessing it could have been Kolkata as that is roughly three day's drive from Kathmandu. And it is likely she was sold to this new man. She would have fetched a very good price as she says the man who was to marry her didn't touch her, so she would've been a virgin."

"The man took her to a place where other girls like her were living. It was a large building in a busy street with rickshaws and tooting and shouting all day and night. She was obviously disorientated and fearful, having no idea where she was or what she was meant to do. They kept her shut in a room for the first few days and didn't feed her but gave her some medicine that made her very sleepy—I assume she was drugged. Her story becomes vague at that point but from what she said this must have been when the sexual abuse began and I'm guessing the place was a brothel." Binsa's voice betrayed her emotion, and she stopped to wipe away the tears that were rolling down her cheeks.

Sangita, not understanding a word that was being translated, was playing with the teddy and periodically popping a lolly into her mouth.

"Then one day another man came and rounded up some of the girls and took them in a truck to a place where they were locked in a metal box, which must have been a container. She hadn't known the other girls but there were seven of them in all. The box was loaded onto a ship. Most of the time they were inside in the dark. It was hot, smelly and scary. They had to go to the toilet in a bucket. Apparently the container was situated above deck, because two men would visit them to give them a bowl of food and let them out in the fresh air to empty their slops and wash before shutting them back inside the container. The men were mean to them, often slapping and hurting them. It was here that she caught her first sight of the ocean. I can't say if she was being sexually abused on the ship, she is reluctant to talk about that. The girls were often sick when shut in the container, making it unbearable. One of the girls died in that container, and the men took her body away." Binsa took out a tissue and blew her nose. "Would it be okay if we take a short break?"

"Yes, of course," Anahera agreed, wiping away a stray tear from her cheek with the back of her hand.

"Binsa, why don't you go out? You too Anahera. I can stay with Sangita." Sandie looked at her watch. "We could resume in fifteen minutes."

Anahera, following Binsa out to the corridor, struggled to keep her emotions in check. "The cruelty that poor child has suffered is unimaginable."

"Yes, life can be very unfair. If you'll excuse me, I think I'll take a short walk." Binsa, who was visibly shaken, wandered off down the corridor towards the exit.

Relieved to have some time out, Anahera went to the family lounge and helped herself to the coffee. As she sat quietly, the details she'd just heard rolled around her head like a reel of film on a repeat circuit.

Back in Sangita's room, they recommenced the interview.

"Is it okay with Sangita if we continue?" Sandie asked Binsa.

Binsa asked Sangita, who looked wide-eyed and fearful, but nodded her consent."

All eyes looked expectantly at Anahera.

"Please ask her how many days aboard ship," she asked.

Binsa asked and she answered, "She says it was a long time but doesn't know how many days, like a long and very bad dream. There was a lot of sickness in the container, especially as it was hot and stuffy. They had to stand tall to be near the fresh air, I'm assuming she means fresh air was coming in near the top of the container."

"Is she sure there were seven girls?"

After a short discussion, Binsa answered, "She says they started with seven, but then three of the girls were taken away and she never saw them again." Binsa shook her head. "I'm sorry, she's very confused and I really don't know what she means by this. I suspect they were being kept drugged."

"Were there just the three of them that left the ship together?" Anahera was desperate to understand.

Binsa interpreted and Sangita nodded. "Yes."

"How did they leave the ship without being spotted by the port authorities?"

Binsa conversed with Sangita before interpreting for the Kiwis. "Her answer is quite vague, but it seems they were locked inside the container when it must have been unloaded. She mentioned some sort of swinging motion. The next time it was opened they were on land among several other containers. I'm guessing it was a storage place somewhere."

"And what happened next?" Anahera asked gently.

More conversing in Nepali, before Binsa said, "An Indian man with a fancy hair style came and brought them food. Then he took the three of them to a house where they were kept confined for a day, but she is unable to say where. The others were taken from the room by a European man, but she was left with the woman with colourful hair and some older girls."

"Was that the house where we found her?"

Binsa asked the questions, and responded, "Yes."

"Does she recognise any of these men?" She laid out photos of Chase Craddock, Grant Tate, Brian Headley, and for good measure, Rick Talcon.

Sangita took her time looking at the photos, her eyes seemed to lock onto one image in particular, before slowly reaching out to point at the image of Grant Tate.

Sangita spoke to Binsa, who said, "This is the European man who came and took the other two girls away from the brothel. She doesn't recognise the others."

Anahera collected up the photos. "Does she know what happened to the other two girls?"

Binsa asked Sangita and translated it back for Anahera, "Apparently not."

"Does she remember their names?"

Binsa didn't need to translate the answer. "Geeta and Feba."

Anahera looked at Sandie and said firmly, "I'd like to show her identikit photos of the deceased girls"

Sandie nodded.

Anahera took out the two sketches she'd had made of the girls representing what they would have looked like in life. They'd been developed out of concern that the Forensics' photos would be too disturbing, and she had no wish to traumatise her further.

"Does Sangita recognise these girls?" She watched Sangita's face for a reaction as she laid them on the bed beside her.

Binsa asked her and she nodded excitedly, stabbing her finger at them. "Feba! Geeta!"

"Can she confirm that it was this man who took Geeta and Feba away?" Anahera asked, placing the photo of Grant Tate next to the images of the girls.

Binsa translated and slowly Sangita reached out towards the photos. Her hand hovered over the photo of Grant Tate for a moment before her slim fingers jabbed at his face, accompanied by a childlike whimper.

Next Anahera laid the print of Ajay Singh on the bed. "Does she recognise this man?"

Binsa had no need to interpret. Sangita became very animated and pointed at her tattoo while rapidly speaking in her own tongue.

"It seems he took her to get her tattoo before leaving her with the woman with the colourful hair."

Anahera looked at Sandie. "We will need her to come into the station to see if she can identify both Singh and Tate in a police lineup. Do you think she'd be up for it?"

"Possibly. Depends how soon, but she's becoming stronger all the time."

"Can you ask her where she got her tattoo?"

Binsa complied.

Anahera found herself holding her breath.

"She doesn't know where. The Indian man in the picture took her and the other two girls to a man in another house to get it. She says there was a scary dog there."

"Does she know what the tattoo means?"

Binsa asked and answered, "No. She just says it hurt."

Sangita tugged on Binsa's arm while saying something.

Binsa said, "She is asking to see Geeta and Feba."

Anahera retrieved the pictures and shook her head before answering in a whisper, "They're deceased."

Sangita understood the meaning behind the words. Tears came quickly as she was reduced to loud and persistent sobbing. Binsa moved to comfort her and Sandie, looking angry for the first time, ushered Anahera out of the room.

Outside the room, having closed the door behind them, Sandie said, "That's enough for one day. I didn't want you to upset her like that. It was too hard on her."

"I'm sorry, I didn't mean for her to find out today." It was a genuine apology. "It was a brave thing for her to open up and tell us her story."

Sandie relented. "It was. But now she needs to rest. I'll be in touch."

"What's going to happen to her?"

"I have a foster family lined up who'll take her in until such time as we know what's next for her." With that Sandie turned and went back into the room.

*

Frank was in their office when Anahera arrived back from the hospital. After briefing him on her interview with Sangita, he told her that they now had a list of names of the party goers on board *Neptune* at the time when Feba and Geeta drowned. These names had been extracted from Fabio's phone. Tomorrow they'd pay the first of them a visit.

But first they had one very important mission. Although the intense emotions and long hours were starting to catch up on her, Anahera could feel the familiar adrenalin beginning to surge through her veins.

23

The motorway south was clogged with traffic making the journey frustratingly slow, which wasn't unusual in the city regardless of the time of day. They turned into an industrial area near the airport and navigated their way to the address of the Singh Imports Limited warehouse. Barbs and John emerged from an unmarked car that was parked outside as Anahera pulled in behind it.

After a quick strategy briefing from Barbs, they walked down the alleyway to the warehouse building behind. All four wore their tactical vests. Anahera could feel her excitement build as if reaching a climax, like a child on Christmas Eve, reminding her there's no better feeling on the job than the one you get when you're about to solve a case.

The warehouse was a large building behind an industrial complex of units. A forklift laden with boxes exited the warehouse and placed them on the tray of a waiting truck. Behind the warehouse were half a dozen 40-foot containers sitting in a row.

Barbs led them in through the open door where the forklift had just passed. There were bays of pallets stacked three high and several pallets deep on the far side of the space. On their left was a small internal office, which had a window with a sign to show it was the reception. Next to it were stairs to a level above. The man who was sitting in the office using a computer looked up when they stood at the window. "Can I help you?"

Barbs flashed her badge. "Can you direct us to Ajay Singh?"

The man gestured. "Up the stairs."

The wooden stairwell was narrow and gloomy with light coming from a naked bulb. They opened the door at the top to find a small reception area and unmanned reception desk. Along the hallway that opened off the reception were three offices. Inside the first office, an Indian man in his mid-thirties sat at the desk, fully engrossed in whatever was on one of the computer screens in front of him.

"Ajay Singh?" Barbs asked.

The man looked up. He was well groomed; clean shaven with thick black hair styled into a faux hawk. His white cotton shirt was open necked under a smart grey jacket. "Who wants to know?"

"I'm Inspector Barbara Wright, head of the special crime unit investigating human trafficking. With me are detectives John Watts, Anahera Raupara and Frank Smythe."

A look of surprise crossed his face. "Sounds important."

"It is." Barbs stood towering over the man sitting at the desk, her face stern. "We have reason to believe you are involved in the illegal immigration and trafficking of underage Nepalese girls."

"That's outrageous. What is it with you Kiwis? You have no problems with Indian immigrants bringing their money into this country, but once here you like to pick on us." He fiddled with his hands, turning the ring on his finger.

Anahera bristled at his outburst.

Barbs countered smoothly. "Mr Singh, I think you'll find the system is fair and it dishes out justice regardless of ethnicity to reflect the crime committed."

"I'm going to call my lawyer. You'll be hearing about this." He picked up his phone.

"Mr Singh, although you haven't been charged with anything, I'm still obliged to tell you that you have the right to remain silent. You do not have to make any statement. Anything you say will be recorded and may be given in evidence in court. You have the right to speak with a lawyer without delay and in private before deciding whether to answer any questions. And if you need it, we have a list of lawyers you may speak to for free. Now we would like you to accompany us to the police station to answer a few questions to help us with our enquiries."

"I'm calling my lawyer now."

Singh was making the call when a familiar-sounding voice called from further down the hallway. "Ajay, what's going on?"

He dropped the receiver back into its cradle.

Steps sounded on the wooden floor. "I thought I told you to ..."

The woman that appeared froze in the doorway.

Stunned, Anahera stared, her mouth open.

Frank said, "Scarlett O'Connor? What are you doing here?"

Barbs looked at Frank. "Scarlett O'Connor?" she repeated.

Scarlett looked startled. Her wild and colourful hair and bright makeup were now immaculate, and she was dressed in skintight jeans, a smart shirt and high heels. She looked at Singh and seemed to compose herself. "What's going on?"

He was silent.

Barbs answered, "I think perhaps you need to tell us what you're doing here."

"I'm not saying a word without my lawyer present."

"Then you'd better accompany us to the station," Barbs shot back. "We're also taking Mr Singh in to answer some questions."

Glaring through her glasses, she snarled, "I'm not bloody well going anywhere—you've got nothing on me. Zip."

Frank slipped quietly out of the office.

"What's your involvement in Singh Imports Limited?" Barbs' eyes bored into Scarlett O'Connor.

O'Connor and Singh exchanged knowing looks.

"You might as well answer—we'll be talking to each of the staff."

"Like hell I will. Not without my lawyer present. And nor will Ajay." She shot him a warning look.

Frank came back into the room carrying a photograph of O'Connor and Singh looking like tourists and standing arm-in-arm outside a temple. "Seems you two know each other fairly well—I think you have some explaining to do."

They escorted the two of them down the steps to the stares of staff in the warehouse.

"Mind if I take a look around?" Frank asked.

Singh looked at him with contempt. "Do I get a choice?"

"Of course. But we will be coming back with a search warrant."

Singh looked at O'Connor and shrugged.

Scarlett said, "You're wasting your time—you won't find anything."

As Frank and Anahera wandered out to the containers at the rear of the yard, Anahera said, "Scarlett O'Connor has played us, and I've been completely taken in by her. I reckon she gave us Tate to take our focus away from her."

"Yeah, I'd trust her as much as I would a pet crocodile!"

"I feel foolish. I honestly took her to be a pawn in somebody else's game. Never for a moment did I expect her to be associated with Singh."

"I know what you mean."

The containers were far enough apart for them to squeeze between them. They circled each one searching the external walls for vents.

And there it was. One of the containers that sat in the middle of the row had been tampered with. A 50-millimetre hole had been drilled high up on the side wall.

"Barbs, John, over here!" Frank called.

When the others joined them at the front of the container, Barbs instructed Ajay Singh to open the container. Reluctant at first, he complied. As it began to open, a shuffling sound came from within.

Anahera held her breath. The tension was palpable as she stood by. Watching. Hoping.

A soft sound came from within. Definitely human.

Anahera prayed they had just found the missing girls.

And no one moved.

Frank snapped to and hurried to assist. He flung the door back and pulled the torch from his belt in a single movement. The beam from the torch shone on a figure slowly rising to her feet at the rear of the container, her hand shielding her eyes from the light.

"Tania?" Anahera gasped beside him.

"Thank God!" Tania's voice was feeble.

Anahera ran to her, taking her into her arms as she sank back down onto the floor.

"Are you alright? What are you doing here?"

"I'm a bit dizzy." Tania struggled to get up again. "What day is it?"

"Wednesday."

"Help me out of here, will you?"

Frank was already calling for an ambulance when Tania, with Anahera's support, walked past him and out into the light. Her hair was matted with dried blood, her face pale and her movements weak. Anahera helped her sit down on the edge of a pallet near the entrance to the warehouse. The forklift had stopped working and a handful of staff were standing around watching the drama unfold.

"How on earth did you get to be in the container?" Frank asked, crouched on his haunches beside the pallet.

"After our chat with Sangita at the hospital, I thought about what she said about where she'd been taken. She mentioned hearing planes, so I assumed the container must have been near the airport. Then I remembered seeing a building with unusual architecture—the outside shell was clad in a sloping design, which could account for the one she described as falling over. I drove out here on my way home to see if I could see a yard with containers close to the sloping building." She forced a grin. "I know, it was stupid to come without backup. I thought I'd just do an initial recce and... well I just didn't bother to radio it in."

"It's okay, you're safe now." Anahera spoke with soothing tones. "Take your time and tell us what happened."

"When I saw this place with the containers stored at the back, I decided to investigate. I remember coming down the alleyway and walking over to the row of containers. Something must have hit me, because that's the last I remember." She touched the back of her head and winced. "I woke up with a sore head, feeling dizzy and groggy—I think I may have been drugged. I figured out I must have been in the same container as the girls, because I could see a little light coming in through ventilation holes." She looked from Anahera to Frank. "I sure am glad to see you two."

"We'll make the bastard that did this to you pay. You've my absolute assurance on that score," Frank said through clenched teeth.

Anahera sat holding Tania, seething at the thought of a fellow officer being taken out.

Frank advanced towards Singh. Anahera could sense his aggression and was just about to warn him against doing anything stupid, when Frank stopped short and growled, "How dare you assault a policewoman!"

Singh backed away, clearly afraid. "I thought she was from the media."

"Shut up you fool!" O'Connor barked at him. "You keep your mouth shut!"

Ajay looked crestfallen. "I warned you against keeping her here.

Scarlett's eyes flashed as she glared at him.

"And we should've disposed of the container." His words were rapid, his voice high. "You never listen."

"Don't say anymore!" she hissed at him. "You're going to incriminate us all!"

Amazed at this interchange, Anahera began to sense Singh might be the weaker link.

Barbs charged them both with kidnapping and assault of an officer and John cuffed them. Then Barbs came over to talk quietly with Tania while John stood guard over Singh and O'Connor.

With matters now in hand, Anahera and Frank left to inspect the inside of the container, looking for evidence the girls had been there. A small amount of sunlight came through two holes, one in each side wall at the top, showing the 50-millimetre hole seen on the outside did indeed provide a source of ventilation. But it was empty. Nothing to suggest the container had been home to seven young girls.

After a brief discussion with Barbs, it was agreed they would take the prisoners in while Frank and Anahera waited with Tania for both the ambulance and the Forensics team to arrive, ensuring none of the staff touched any of the evidence. Once Forensics had completed their examination, the container would be taken and kept in secure police storage.

After a short time they heard the siren of the ambulance drawing near and moments later it pulled up in front of the warehouse. Tania was helped into the back before being checked over. The doors closed and it raced away.

It was after Barbs and John had left with Singh and O'Connor that two Forensics' technicians arrived carrying their bag of tools. They changed into their disposable jumpsuits complete with overshoes, bonnets and gloves, and began the painstaking task of examining the interior of the container for fingerprints, hair, or any other clue that would prove the girls had been inside. Once the container transporter arrived on site, it was time for Frank and Anahera to leave.

24

While Frank drove back to the station, Anahera sat checking her emails in the passenger seat. Among them was one from Stella with a dossier on Scarlett O'Connor, which she forwarded to Barbs. Scarlett was the daughter of a wealthy spice exporter and had spent her formative years in India before coming back to finish her schooling in New Zealand. The pieces of the jigsaw were beginning to fall into place.

Once back, they immediately went to find Barbs and John to get an update on their progress with Ajay Singh and Scarlett O'Connor. As luck would have it they found them outside the interview room where Ajay Singh was sitting with his lawyer.

"How's it going in there. Has he admitted to anything yet?" she asked.

"No, he's a closed book," Barbs said. "He denies everything, including being responsible for locking up Tania."

"What's your impression of him?" Anahera's curiosity was getting the better of her.

"He comes across as a clever businessman. Very hard to read him." Barbs shook her head. "But I don't think he's got it in him to be the mastermind."

"What about the relationship between him and O'Connor?"

"Nothing." She sighed.

"How about the interview with Scarlett O'Connor? Anything?"

"We've left her in the remand cell for now. We figure she's a tough nut and Singh seems more likely to crack, so he's our first target. As I was telling John, we need a change in tactics. How about you two go in and question him about the two girls that drowned. Show him the photos—maybe the man can find some compassion."

"I'd be happy to oblige." After listening to Sangita, Anahera was chomping at the bit to get into the ring with him, boxing gloves off. She wanted this guy to go down for a long time and she wanted to be the one to do it.

"Then let's go in now and see if we get any reaction," Frank said. "I want to see the kind of person who deals in trafficked girls squirm."

"We'll watch through the glass," Barbs said. "Good luck in there—I hope you get further than we have."

With her adrenalin pumping, Anahera raced back to the office to arm herself with the folder of photos.

Inside the room, Ajay Singh sat at the table, his hands playing with the ring he wore and looking less sure of himself than when they first saw him. Next to him sat a young Indian woman smartly dressed in a pastel blue shirt with a frill at the high neckline under a junior navy suit jacket.

Anahera and Frank introduced themselves and formally restarted the interview.

"We have been looking into the drownings of two young Nepalese girls. Do you recognise this girl?"

Anahera laid down the photo of the boat shed girl.

"No, I've never seen her before."

"What about this one?" She put down the photo of the bloated face of Jane Doe Two.

He unclasped his hands. "No!"

Her eyes locked onto a gold signet ring on his left hand. The ring had the symbol of an eye engraved into it. The same stylised eye as the one on the tattoos. She glanced at Frank and could see he'd also seen it. Flicking through her folder, she found the photo of the boat shed girl's tattoo.

Placing the photo on the table next to the photos of the corpses, she asked, "Do you recognise this tattoo?"

He looked at his lawyer, and she said, "I advise you that you need not answer that."

Ignoring her, Anahera turned to Frank. "It's quite an unusual design—wouldn't you say Frank?"

Frank looked a trifle bemused at the line she was taking. "I've not seen anything like it, and we see a lot of tatts coming through the station."

"That's what I thought." She turned back to Singh. "Would you agree it is the same stylised symbol as on your signet ring?"

Singh looked decidedly uncomfortable. "No comment."

"And the same stylised symbol as that in the frame in the *Red Lights Adult Nightclub*?"

"No comment."

"What's your relationship with Scarlett O'Connor?"

He looked her squarely in the eye. "That's none of your business."

"Is she your partner?"

Singh's dark eyes were defiant as they bore into her.

"Are you her lover?"

He remained tight-lipped.

Beneath her professional demeanour, Anahera's anger flared with each refusal. He was guilty, no question, and so was O'Connor. Those girls deserved justice, and the weight of that responsibility rested heavily on her shoulders.

Frank stepped in. "You know we will find out the answers in due course, so I suggest you start cooperating."

Singh stared at the wall.

"Look, we have enough evidence linking you to the dead girls and the illegal brothel—so much so it won't be difficult to convince a court you're guilty as hell. You're staring down the barrel of considerable time inside."

A pregnant pause filled the room. Eventually Singh's head began to bobble side to side. Slowly he turned to look at Frank.

Frank tried again, his tone bordering on sounding congenial. "Who is Scarlett to you?"

"She's my partner." It was barely a whisper.

"How long have you been together?"

"Five years." His head wobbled as he spoke.

"How does a businessman like yourself partner with a brothel madam?"

"No! She's really not like that—you've got the wrong idea. She cares deeply for the girls—that's why she personally runs the brothel. I tried to get her to give it up, she didn't need to do it herself, but they're her girls. She always says no one looks after them the way she does."

Frank looked at Anahera, his brows raised. She caught the pass.

"Really?" Anahera asked, incredulous at his naivety. "Is that how we have had two dead girls out near Rangitoto? And one repeatedly raped while in her loving care? She failed those girls!"

Singh's shoulders had slumped, his head drooped.

Anahera looked at Frank. "I think we are done here."

Suspending the proceeding, they walked out closing the door behind them.

Barbs and John came out, looking like they'd just won the lottery. She said, "I'm embarrassed to say I'd missed the significance of his ring."

"Easy to do, but the tattoos have been central to our case so we're a lot more familiar with them," Frank said.

"We have enough to book him. It might do him some good to sweat it out in remand for a while." Barbs checked her watch. "We can take it from here. Thanks Team."

25

Anahera arrived home exhausted after what had turned out to be a pivotal but long and tiring day. Short of energy for any form of exercise, she'd collapsed onto the couch with a cold beer and a packet of chippies. Dinner could wait. In fact take-aways would have to do as she couldn't be bothered cooking—something that would please her boys.

As usual, her men folk were out. Rangi had volleyball practice, Piri was at band practice and Jim was due home from work at any time. She couldn't wait to tell him they were on the home straight with the case.

She breathed out a long sigh of relief. This case had really played with her, but she was elated they'd come through. Within the next day or two the last of the arrests should be made. They'd see justice was done for those poor young girls. She munched on some crisps before taking a deep and satisfying guzzle of her drink.

The back door opened.

"Hey Mum," Rangi said as he entered the room. "What're we eating tonight?"

"I'm thinking take-aways."

"Cool. Can we have pizza?"

"We'll see what the consensus is." She looked at her adolescent son. "How was your day?"

"Ka pai all good." He sat down on the arm of the couch. "I had a long chat with Mr Harris."

"Oh?"

"Yeah, I've been thinking, a lot. I told him I want to focus on my volleyball and try for one of those scholarships."

"What did he say?"

"He said it won't be easy, and I'll have to keep my record clean. But he's happy to keep coaching me towards that goal."

"That's great news. Your dad will be thrilled too."

"There's something else." He paused and looked down.

Anahera steeled herself.

"I'm really sorry, Mum. About the porn. I was being a dick and didn't think about the girls being... well you know... real girls. I get it. I get why you're upset with me."

"Oh Rangi, I'm so glad to hear this."

"Okay Mum. I'm going to go practise my serves." And he hightailed it out of the room.

Anahera sat motionless for some time. Proud of her son and relieved at his attitude. The take-aways were going to be a celebratory dinner and she couldn't wait for Jim to come home.

*

Next morning, Frank and Anahera visited the first of the men on the list of alleged party goers aboard *Neptune*. Adrian Forsythe was an architect in a large company on Queen Street. His office was on the seventh floor.

Unable to suppress his growing excitement, Frank knew it would only take one of these men to fold for the whole pack of cards to come tumbling down. His feet shuffled impatiently as the lift ascended floor by floor, stopping at the second, fourth and fifth to let people in and out.

The receptionist took one look at their IDs and put a call through to Mr Forsythe requesting him to come to reception. He was short in stature and seemed to Frank to be socially awkward. Dressed in standard corporate garb, open neck shirt with black pants and black shoes, he looked harmless enough. Frank was sure his coworkers would have no idea of the sort of evil the man had been involved in. When his visitors identified themselves as police officers and produced a warrant for his arrest, Forsythe looked about anxiously as the colour drained from his face.

They escorted him to his office and collected his laptop before transporting him to the station for questioning. While they waited for his lawyer to arrive, Stella took a look at his computer and discovered folders of pornography involving young girls on his hard drive.

Frank's phone vibrated with an incoming call. After hanging up, he said to Anahera, "I just took a call from Delia in Forensics."

"And?"

"The fibres from the boat match those in the pyjamas, with a high degree of certainty based on the tests they can do in the lab here. The results are preliminary at this stage, as they'll need to send the samples to ESR for a more detailed analysis to get conclusive results, but it's enough to make the arrest. We can do that as soon as we finish the interview."

"That's great news. I can't wait to see him humbled." She relaxed her shoulders and sighed deeply. Someone was going to pay for what happened to those poor girls.

Once Forsythe's lawyer, Ali Catto, arrived, they formally began the interview with Frank taking the lead and reading him his rights. He then explained they were investigating the case of two drownings out near Rangitoto Island, that fibres had been found in *Neptune's* stateroom that matched the fibres on one of the girl's clothing, and Louie Fabio had been arrested. Forsythe's stature seemed to shrink even more as he kept glancing nervously at his lawyer.

"Mr Forsythe, can I call you Adrian?" Frank asked amicably.

He looked at his lawyer who nodded, "Yes."

"Before we start, I want you to know we've found the pornography on your hard drive in evidence."

Forsythe looked panic stricken.

"Adrian, can you confirm you were on board *Neptune* on the days in question? Before you answer this question, you should know data from Louie Fabio's phone is in evidence as well as a photograph of *Neptune* taken on the day in question."

Adrian hung his head and spoke in a soft voice. "I was."

"Please can you speak up for the recording."

"Yes."

Frank placed a photo on the table. "Is this you?"

"Yes." He hung his head again.

"Where did you leave from?"

"Westhaven Marina."

Frank put the photos of the deceased in front of Adrian. "Do you recognise these girls?"

He shifted about in his seat.

Ali Catto said, "I advise you not to answer this line of questioning."

Adrian looked at her and back at Frank. "I don't think so."

"Adrian, if you help us with our enquiries, it may go better for you. Not that I can promise anything, but the judge may take it into consideration when sentencing. This is a murder inquiry, not a game." Frank's voice was stern.

"But you haven't charged me with anything." It was almost a whine, like that of a spoilt child.

"I'm giving you the chance to tell your side of the story." Frank paused for effect. "A man like you might not enjoy life inside Mount Eden prison."

Forsythe pointed to the boat shed girl. "Maybe that one. But I'm not sure of the other one—it doesn't look human."

Anahera put the identikit sketches out that she'd used with Sangita. "What about these?"

After a long pause, and in a tone of resignation, he said, "Yes, they were on board. But it wasn't my idea—they were already there. Louie said they were for entertainment."

"Were these men on board?" Frank showed him a list of names.

His lawyer put up her hand. "Adrian, you don't need to provide that information."

Ignoring her, he said, "Yes, I think they were. When we came onto the boat there were two other women as well."

"Who were they?"

"Louie said they were hostesses. Escorts really. They called themselves Bonnie and Sapphire." He looked at Frank as if drawing him into a conspiracy. "There was a lot of drinking and sex—Louie's well known for his parties."

"Why were the young girls on board?"

"We didn't know about them until we left the marina—Louie said he had a surprise for us, a gift from him to us." Adrian started to cry. "I didn't want to hurt them. None of us wanted them dead. They were beautiful, and so innocent."

"Did you witness them being abused?"

He whimpered. "Y-y-yes."

"By whom?"

He was silent for a long moment.

"Who abused them?"

"Everyone," he blurted.

"How did they drown?"

"They were in the cockpit, and we were all just having a bit of fun. Honestly, that was all. Everybody was a bit high by that time. Then one of the girls jumped over the side, followed by the other one." He became agitated. "Stupid girls! By the time we realised what was happening and turned around to find them, they were gone. We tried to save them. One of them must have sunk, there was just no trace of her. But we found the other one and rescued her. She was limp when we pulled her out of the water, so one of the men tried to resuscitate her. You see we really did try. She came to and we thought she'd survive, but then she died. You have to understand we were scared. Louie came up with the idea of dumping her body in the abandoned boat shed. He didn't think she'd be found for weeks. We carried on partying in that bay—all night. Then we crashed and only just surfaced before the police came around asking questions."

"Why did you stay in the bay?"

"I don't know. Now it seems foolish, but at the time we were high as kites. It was dark and I don't think anyone was in a fit state to take us back to the marina safely. We weren't thinking straight."

"But when we saw you, you were partying."

"When you're with Louie, that's what you do. I woke in the saloon with the music cranking and one of the girls poured me a drink."

Frank had heard enough. "Adrian Forsythe, I am charging you with accessory to manslaughter and with the rape of a minor. Other charges may follow."

"No. No. NO! I've helped you. I've given you the information you wanted. You can't do this!" It was a pitiful wail.

"I remind you that you have the right to remain silent, you do not have to make a statement, anything you say may be recorded and given as evidence in court. You have the right to speak to a lawyer without delay and in private before deciding whether to answer any of our questions. Do you understand?"

Forsythe looked to Ali for help, before answering, "Y-y-yes." It was little more than a whisper.

Forsythe was taken away to be processed. Over the course of the next day, Louis Fabio and all six guests from on board *Neptune* were interviewed and charged accordingly.

26

Frank and Anahera had just finished the last of the interviews with the party goers when Brad's assistant called them to a meeting in the conference room with Brad, Pam Downer the Police Prosecutor, Barbs and John. Frank's senior officer Andy was invited as a courtesy. Tania was noticeably absent, having taken a few days off after her ordeal, and a young woman introduced herself as Rachel Kibblewhite from Puiwaitahi, explaining she was standing in for her.

The vibe in the meeting room was relaxed with a congenial buzz of conversation in stark contrast to the somewhat frayed politics that had surfaced in their first meeting. Looking around the room at those present heightened Frank's pride in his uniform. Together they'd achieved the desired outcome and those responsible should soon be getting what they deserved. Grinning as he took his seat, he felt as if he'd passed his academy exams all over again—something he always felt when successfully closing out a case.

Brad called the meeting to order. "Kia ora and welcome everyone. There's been a significant amount of progress on the case over the last 24 hours and I think we need to debrief and discuss any loose ends. As you all know, there's been a major development with the assault and abduction of Detective Tania Jones. She's recovering well and should be back on deck soon."

Barbs, looking relaxed, picked up the narrative. "Singh and O'Connor have been charged on that account but are both denying their role in it. We've interviewed the staff and are led to believe Singh's security man was also involved—we've yet to charge him. The rest appear to know nothing about it. Unfortunately the Forensic Team were unable to find evidence that it was the same container used for the girls—it'd been swept clean. But we are strongly of the view it was, given it had been modified with breathing vents."

"And I am pleased to report that Frank and Anahera have now arrested all those involved in the abuse and deaths of the two Jane Does," Brad added.

"Feba and Geeta," Anahera corrected him, not hiding the emotion in her voice. "Let's give them the dignity of their names."

"Sorry." Brad turned to Anahera looking sheepish.

Applause broke out accompanied by a number of exclamations, to which Frank murmured, "Thank you." Beside him Anahera was smiling modestly, equally embarrassed by the praise.

"That is good news!" Barbs said. "How did they come to be out at Rangitoto Island?"

"It seems one of the clients of *Red Lights* nightclub, Louie Fabio, hired the girls, that is Feba and Geeta." Frank glanced at Anahera before continuing. "For a party on his boat with some of his friends. According to Sangita, Tate delivered them. Fibres found on the boat match those of their clothing, although we do need to wait for more detailed analysis. But it was enough to make the arrest. We also found two hairs in the stateroom in his boat, and they too have been sent away. He's been arrested on charges of sexual violation of a child under 12 and a young person under 16, as well as procurement of commercial sexual services of a person under the age of 18 and accessory to manslaughter on two counts. As yet he's not talking, however we've got testimony from the other men that were present on his boat and there's no question of their guilt. They too have been charged. And all of their names were on a register found in the nightclub computer along with Singh's."

"Interestingly, his state room where we found the fibres and hairs had a lock on the outside of the door," Anahera added, causing a low level of chatter to break out.

"Let's move to how the three girls came to be in the country." Brad looked across at his colleague. "Barbs?"

"Thanks Brad." Barbs surveyed the faces watching her. "We now know they came in a container aboard a ship. Having drawn a blank with the raid on *Kolkata 2*, it doesn't mean they hadn't been on board, but at this stage we can't rule out any of the three ships identified by Frank. I'm working with my contacts offshore to follow the movements of those ships. We also know that originally seven were put in the container. One died during the voyage and three others left early. It's not clear exactly when or where—it's possible it was in Auckland but more likely they left prior to its arrival here, possibly in Sydney or Singapore. I've already talked to our Australian and Singaporean counterparts who are investigating at their ends but as yet there's no trace of them. It's a bit like the proverbial needle in a haystack."

"So have we got enough to make the charges stick for the trafficking of the three that we know came into Auckland?" Brad asked.

"We have Sangita's testimony—she's able to identify Singh as the one who first took custody of her, fed her and had her tattooed before delivering her to the brothel that was raided by Puiwaitahi," Anahera said. "I showed her identikit pictures of Feba and Geeta who she confirmed were in the container with her, and she identified Grant Tate via a photo as the one who took them away, presumably to deliver them to their last fateful appointment."

Barbs stepped in. "We've charged Singh with people trafficking under section 98D and he's currently in custody, potentially looking at 20 years imprisonment for that alone."

"That's justice!" Anahera nodded enthusiastically.

Barbs continued. "But he hasn't yet confessed to the trafficking even though he's implicated with enough damning evidence that he should get the guilty verdict. What with the signet ring he wears having the same stylised image of the eye etched into it, his name in the register of alleged high rollers at the nightclub, a substantial invoice from his import company made out to the nightclub, and of course the testimony from Sangita, it's going to be hard to deny."

Pam looked up from her note taking. "All circumstantial. The invoice is made out for general goods as I understand it and we don't know it was a transaction for girls. To be sure it will stick we need some hard evidence that can't be disputed. How sure are we that Sangita will identify him and be able to testify against him?"

Rachel cleared her throat and glanced nervously around the room. "It's early days and she's still very traumatised although starting to make good progress. While I can't guarantee it, I think there's a reasonable chance."

Frank added, "We also have the tattooist who can identify him, although I have to admit he wasn't overly cooperative."

"Good," Barbs said. "We're still hoping Singh will confess—I see him as quite weak, unlike O'Connor who's as tough as old boots. The other weak link is Tate, and we could work some more on him. He obviously knew about Singh's involvement."

"What about O'Connor?" Brad asked.

"She's our real problem. We're sure she was involved in the trafficking and believe she was the kingpin, but she's not saying a word. And nor is Singh regarding her involvement, in fact I suspect he will try and protect her. We haven't found a scrap of evidence to pin on her. We only have her on the lesser charges of running the illegal brothel and the drugs. We think she's been extremely devious, setting the racket up while maintaining an arms-length involvement." She sighed deeply while shaking her head. "We've nothing concrete with which to charge her on the trafficking offense."

"Why are you so sure she's running the NZ arm?" Pam asked.

"It was in the way she spoke to Singh and how she reacted when we apprehended them. Personally, I have no doubt about it."

Pam sat forward on her seat, pen poised on her notebook. "Who would know of her role as the mastermind?"

"Singh, obviously—he's her partner in a personal capacity. We could press Tate, but I'm not sure he was even aware she was the mastermind." Barbs nodded at Anahera. "We suspect she gave Singh the gold signet ring he wears with the same stylised eye as the tattoos, but we can't be sure."

Frank sat back, releasing the tension in his shoulders while shaking his head. Scarlett O'Connor was the brains behind it all—of that he too was sure, and it'd come as a surprise. Rarely did he get it wrong like he had with this Madam. That she might get away with it was infuriating, and once again he was reminded how easy it is to underestimate the cunning of criminals.

"But what I don't get is why O'Connor was running the brothel in New Lynn when she was the mastermind and could obviously afford to be living in a mansion. Why risk getting her hands dirty?" Brad asked searching each of the faces around the table.

"I wondered that myself." Anahera smiled. "According to Singh she had some false idea of being the girls' guardian. I prefer to think she likes being a Madam and it served as a front—and it nearly worked. If we hadn't found her at Singh's business, she might have got away with the trafficking."

"She still might," Barbs reminded them. "And even though she may have masterminded the New Zealand end, she was just one link in an international trafficking ring. And a link can be replaced easily enough."

"But why the tattoos?" Rachel asked.

Barbs answered, "I'd say it was about ownership and power. Making her mark. I'm guessing the eye symbol itself means something special to her—after all, we know she was brought up in India. We also think she might have given Singh the signet ring and that's why he wears it. The picture in the frame may well have been gifted to Chase Craddock to commemorate their business partnership. But it's a lot of guesswork."

"And the hieroglyphics? Are we any further with understanding their significance?" Frank asked, keen to solve this part of the puzzle.

"We think you and Anahera were right about their meaning. They were a form of branding or identification for each girl. Not a lot different to slavers in years gone by."

"Do we know the exact nature of the relationship between Singh and O'Connor and *Red Lights?*" asked Brad.

"Craddock owns Cee Cee NZ which in turn owns the nightclub assets under one company and the operations under another where Tate is named as a director. The casino was a third company in the group, and we believe its purpose was to launder the money from the illegal brothel. We believe the nightclub was a client of Singh Imports as shown by the invoice. The New Lynn brothel was run under the nightclub operating arm with Tate taking out the lease. O'Connor ran it probably because she couldn't let it go. They were her girls and that's probably why she had them tattooed."

"Sangita identified Grant Tate but not Craddock, Headley or Talcon. Before O'Connor turned up at Singh's business, we'd charged Tate and O'Connor with commercial sexual exploitation of a person under the age of 18." Anahera's gaze swept around the faces watching her.

"So back to Chase Craddock and the nightclub." Brad looked at the others expectantly.

"Again the evidence is all circumstantial. The fact that Tate was a director and took out the lease on the brothel isn't enough. We need more hard evidence linking the nightclub to the girls," Pam said. "Without it, I can't guarantee the charges will stick."

"Unfortunately, the computers were fairly clean—they knew what they were doing," Anahera answered.

"Surely there must be something. Those girls wouldn't have come cheap—each one would be worth their weight in diamonds." Brad shook his head. "If the computers are clean there must be a paper trail of transactions linking these girls to the nightclub. Are you sure you searched every possible hiding place? What about a safe?"

John replied, "We made a thorough search, including the safe. Nothing."

"We'll bring Tate back in for questioning. I'm sure he'll talk eventually." Barbs looked confident.

"The biggest issue seems to be pinning the trafficking on Scarlett O'Connor." Brad's voice trailed off.

The room fell silent.

Frank had a thought. "Can we take a short recess? I have an idea."

Even before Brad got a chance to respond, Frank was standing up.

27

O'Connor paced her remand cell. Anger burned through her veins. Someone had dobbed Ajay in and as a result she was now on thin ice.

She'd been doing some emails when voices had come from Ajay's office next door. Brassed off that he was wasting time chatting with the staff, something he did a lot to her annoyance seeing he was supposedly the boss, she'd gone to give him a bollocking. And that's when she'd seen the cops. What a stupid idiot—she could've lain low.

This was a now a big problem. Assuming they were onto Ajay, then it wouldn't look good for her especially as she'd already been charged. Being so sure that she'd sucked them into thinking she was just an ignorant fool looking after her girls, she thought she'd got away with only a minor charge of managing the brothel—and she could play the victim for that. Thought she'd been clever too, setting poor old Grant Tate up to take the fall. And he would—she didn't doubt that because he knew the future of the network was at stake. And he'd do whatever Chase told him. Yes, they needed her. She was the one with the contacts—she'd been careful about that. She was the one with the golden goose.

Why hadn't they come for her already? Had they locked her up and purposely left her to stew? Well, she wouldn't fall for that. Maybe they'd picked Ajay as the weaker one and were interviewing him first to see if he'd break. The trouble was she wasn't confident he'd keep his mouth shut.

He'd been a fool to take out that woman cop. Keeping her on site was a mistake, but she was only drugged in the container while they argued over what to do with her. Her solution was to hand the cop over to Chase for one of his thugs to deal to her. Too late now.

Growing up in India as the only child of a wealthy businessman, she'd seen things. Although subjected to his endless abuse, at the same time he'd treated her like a high-born princess, a maharaja's daughter—a maharani. He'd taught her everything in life was a transaction. You give something to get something. He'd provided the best education a girl could want, teaching her to wheel and deal and get what she wanted.

Her mother was absent for a lot of the time, finding her comfort in booze and men, but she didn't hold it against her. After all you have to do whatever it takes to survive. Her mother was disappointed in her father, or was it the other way round? Whichever way, the marriage was a sham and she'd sworn never to end up like them.

Damn! Her nail polish had chipped, and she'd only just had them done. She banged on the door. Hard. "Hey! Get me a drink!" There was no response.

The eye symbol was her father's business logo and represented all the wealth he'd gained and the cunning she'd learnt in return for being his little princess. She'd dreamed of owning her own empire.

Her mind drifted back to when she left school to be a dancer, gravitating to pole dancing and prostitution where she'd earned good money. That was where she met Chase Craddock, after a stint dancing at his nightclub. She'd floated the idea to open the brothel and launder the money through his casino, and unsurprisingly Chase had leapt at it. Being such a damned good business proposition, it'd made him a packet.

When Ajay followed her from India, she'd helped him set up his import business in Auckland, using the lessons from her father. It was her idea to import girls and she knew just where to get the contacts she needed in India. Convincing Chase to become a customer had been easy.

And she'd needed him to front so that she could stay at arm's length from the trafficking side.

The girls were her own little princesses, the beginning of her new business venture. The tatts showed they belonged to her, part of the family she was building. She understood them like nobody else did. That's why she'd risked staying involved with the brothel—to look after them. It wasn't the money—after all she had plenty. It was the girls. She felt strangely responsible for them. Maternal even. She almost laughed at the thought of it.

But the girls were more than that. They were valuable assets and she needed to ensure a return on her investment. They'd arrived in a sorry state, but she'd taken extra care to present them well to the client. After all her reputation was on the line. She'd dressed them in fine oriental silk and took pains to make them up to add to their exotic allure.

It was all going to plan, so much so that she'd already been working on expanding the business. Bugger those girls dying. It'd brought it to the notice of the cops and was going to ruin everything. How they'd found Ajay was bloody concerning when she'd been so careful to cover their tracks. Someone must've leaked. Now she'd have to think fast about how she was going to get out of this one.

*

Frank hurried out to the evidence room. After finding what he was looking for, he used a pair of office scissors to quickly examine it before logging it out and hurrying back up the stairs to rejoin the others.

"Well?" Brad asked, looking at Frank.

Frank began slowly. "I realised we'd only seen one side of the eye's picture frame, and not the inside. It struck me that the eye is key to this whole thing. Assuming O'Connor masterminded it all and gifted Singh his ring and had the girls tattooed, then the symbol must mean something very special to her." He couldn't suppress his grin as he held up the framed picture of the stylised red eye. "I've just removed the back and… well I suggest you see for yourself." He passed the frame to Brad.

"Well, knock me down!" Brad grinned broadly.

"What?" Barbs asked.

"There's an inscription etched into the back of the enamelwork that reads '*To my darling Scarlett. From Dad.*' It appears this was a personal item belonging to Scarlett."

Simultaneous chatter broke out around the table.

Brad cleared his throat. "Good work, Frank."

Frank, though pleased with himself, found it hard not to beam like a schoolboy who'd just gotten a good report. Believing it was now only a matter of time before justice would be done for Feba and Geeta, he found he couldn't suppress his grin any longer.

Pam spoke up, "That may be enough in that it shows the stylised eye image is personal to Scarlett and indirectly links her to the girls through the tattoos and to the nightclub. I admit it's flimsy at best but may be enough to get a confession."

"We can work with that." Barbs spoke with confidence. "Now all that remains is to find the ship."

"And to tie up a few loose ends. I think we can congratulate ourselves on a job well done. I want you to focus on squaring away the last of the evidence and then it's up to Pam and her legal team to make the charges stick." Brad leaned back in his chair. "Excellent teamwork everybody."

"Thanks to your police work, these guys will almost certainly be incarcerated for a long time," Pam added.

"And they'll find the other inmates won't take kindly to them," John said. "Their lives are about to get a whole lot tougher."

"At least the trafficking ring is broken," Anahera said with conviction.

"These operations are like an octopus." Barbs leaned forward as she addressed the group. "Every time you cut off a tentacle a new one takes its place. These criminal rackets are impossible to stop. Now they've tried to establish themselves here, it's likely they'll keep trying. We are on their radar and will have to be more vigilant in future. Trafficking is extremely well organised internationally—it's a plague."

"All the same, we stopped them this time," Brad countered. "I plan to make a press release this afternoon, once the last of the charges have been laid."

Barbs raised her eyebrow.

Brad added, "Barbs, how about we make a joint statement?"

"Of course."

Andy, who had been silently observing throughout, said, "Good, so I'll expect to see Frank back tomorrow."

"It'll be good to be back." Frank could almost feel the call of *Deodar III* and he relished the idea that he'd be back in the Maritime Unit in the morning. Then he spoke out over the melee. "Who's for a celebratory drink after work? How about joining me at Smugglers' Bar? Around five? I think we've earned it."

Frank's invitation was met with enthusiasm.

28

Anahera stood outside a neat weatherboard bungalow in a leafy suburb where Sangita now lived with her foster parents. A large magnolia tree was in the front corner and a concrete path lined with standard roses in full bloom led up to the front door. Beneath the roses were clumps of flowering perennials. The pale green house gleamed brightly in the late afternoon sunshine. She followed Sandie to the front door where she rang the doorbell.

The woman who greeted them was in her mid-thirties, dressed in a floral top over jeans. She had an open face with a generous smile and dark hair that curled softly behind her ears and around her face, exposing large wooden drop earrings.

Once the introductions were made, Irene, the foster mum, invited them in. The interior was fresh, light and spacious, and may have recently been renovated. They followed Irene into a lounge where they sat in oversize leather recliner chairs while she went off to make them refreshments. A piano sat in the corner. The cream walls were littered with family photos and a stylised wooden cross. Windows overlooked the front garden on one wall, and French doors opened out to a patio on the adjacent wall, with pretty floral curtains providing a homely feel.

Irene came back in with a tray. "I wanted to thank you, Detective Raupara, for all you did for Sangita."

"Please, call me Anahera. And it wasn't me. I was only part of a team, and really it's Tania you should be thanking." Anahera smiled at Irene. "How's Sangita doing?"

"Really well. Kids are so resilient, and so quick to learn. Her grasp of English is coming along very rapidly now, it seems her vocab is expanding every day." Irene passed a cup of coffee to Anahera. "We love having her here with us. She's such a delight. I just wish she could stay, but in time she will go back to her own country."

"Can she not stay here in Aotearoa?" Anahera looked at Sandie.

"I'm afraid not. We are trying to trace her family through the Nepalese authorities."

"Is she going to school here?" Anahera asked.

"Yes, of course. But it's hard for her as she's so far behind her peers, only just learning to read and write. She was very shy at first, but now she seems to have made a friend and by all accounts is enjoying being with other children." Irene sat facing Anahera. "She's made huge progress in the last few weeks since she's been with us. Initially she was so withdrawn, and I really did wonder if she would ever recover. I was so worried about her future. But to look at her now, there's just no comparison to that frightened child that arrived on our doorstep. Our daughter Jasmine is just two years older, and they've become firm friends. She related well to Jazz right from day one. I noticed even before she would look us in the eye, she followed Jazz's every move."

"That's wonderful news."

"My husband and I are firm believers in the power of love and grace. We try to live by it and teach our family the same. It is only through love and grace that Sangita stands a chance. And she is responding well."

"I can see she is one of the lucky ones." Anahera looked through the window to the magnolia tree. "The other girls that came over in the container with her weren't so lucky."

"No, I wish we could've saved them too." A tear came to Irene's eye. "That a fellow human could inflict that sort of abuse on defenceless children is despicable. I struggle to understand it myself."

"I know what you mean. I see some of the worst of humanity every day in my job and it's hard not to get blinkered into thinking it's more widespread than it really is."

Irene's face brightened. "Would you like to see Sangita?"

"Yes, please."

She went to the door into the hallway and called to her. A young girl came into the room carrying the little teddy bear with the friendly face. Her eyes were large and brown, her hair was neatly parted in the centre and tied back into a ponytail. She had filled out, no longer emaciated. She smiled shyly at Anahera.

"Sangita, do you remember me?"

"Yes, you are the police lady." She held up her teddy.

"I hear you are going to school."

"Yes, I like school." Sangita went over and sat on the arm of Irene's chair.

"That's wonderful."

A middle-aged male entered the room dressed casually in an open shirt and jeans. His face was clean shaven and tanned, his smile easy and his green eyes looked full of life

"Good to see you again, Sandie. And you must be the detective." He held out a hand to shake Anahera's. "I'm Peter, Irene's husband."

As they all chatted, Anahera studied the interactions between Sangita and her foster parents. She concluded the girl was genuinely happy, and trusting. Safe. And loved.

Later as she was driving home, she marvelled at the resilience of children. To be exploited, to experience some of the worst that life could throw at you, things no child should even know about, and yet still be able to find happiness. Although Sangita was still recovering, and she might never fully recover, never be able to forget, there was hope.

And if Sangita could find hope, there was hope for us all. Awed by the power of that hope, Anahera drove home to her own family.

Epilogue

Kolkata 2 steamed into the Hauraki Gulf bound for the Port of Auckland. Her burgundy hull sat low in the water under the heavy load of the towers of colourful containers on her deck above.

It had been six months since Frank and Anahera had worked on the case of the two Nepalese girls who'd been trafficked into the country and drowned near Rangitoto. They'd never found the other three girls and it was believed they'd left the ship in Sydney but the authorities there had not been able to trace them. While arrests had been made in Auckland, the perpetrators hadn't yet been tried and convicted.

After the case had been solved, Frank had returned to his job in the Maritime Police Unit and Anahera continued in her role as detective for CIB working mostly on missing person cases.

Barbs remained head of the special crime unit investigating human trafficking as part of an international collaboration to try and stamp it out.

A tip off had been received via the unit's Indian counterpart that a container of young girls may be heading to Auckland on board the *Kolkata 2*. It was thought that the traffickers had gone to ground after the arrest of Scarlett O'Connor and Ajay Singh and now sufficient time had passed that they were once again working to re-establish the trade.

Gathered in the Port of Auckland office were members of the Armed Offender's Squad, Maritime Police Unit, the Special Crime Unit, Forensic Services and Customs. Binsa Dahal, the Nepalese interpreter, was also present. The mood was intense as adrenaline surged through everyone present. Nobody spoke. All eyes were on the ship being piloted towards the port, as if all were connected in one body and poised like a lion ready to pounce.

Frank thought about the last time they'd boarded the *Kolkata 2* and the disappointment when they'd failed to find any evidence the girls had been on board. Since then, the *Star of India* had returned to Auckland and a search of that vessel under the guise of a routine inspection had also borne no evidence of people smuggling.

This time was different. They'd received a tip off and they knew exactly what they were looking for. If girls were on board, they'd be held in a container that'd been modified with ventilation.

The contingent of police and customs watched from their vantage point as the ship docked. They waited until the gangplank was alongside and secured in place.

"Okay everyone. It's time." Barbs spoke loudly with authority. "AOS, you're on."

The six AOS members moved out and stormed up the gangway onto the ship. Nervous tension filled the room. At last the radio crackled and the all clear was received.

"We're on. Frank, I want you with me." She looked at the customs officials. "You may like to join us—we'll head straight for the bridge to find the captain. John, take the rest and start with the containers above the deck."

A swarm of men and women all dressed in police and customs uniforms and wearing tactical vests boarded the ship.

Once they were on board they split up and Frank experienced a déjà vu moment as he followed Barbs up the flights of steel steps to the bridge.

The Master, Joseph Sharma, stood flanked by his First Mate and Second Officer. His face was flushed with anger. "What is the meaning of this?"

"I have a warrant to search your vessel." Barbs passed him the paperwork.

"How dare you come storming onto my ship. This is the second time we've been subjected to this harassment. You found nothing last time and you'll find nothing this time. You're wasting your time and ours—we have containers to unload and a schedule to keep."

Fred Giles, the Senior Customs Officer, stepped forward. "Master Sharma, we have reason to believe that you have illegal contraband on board. Nothing will leave this ship until we have made a thorough search."

A look passed between Sharma and his First Mate, which Frank interpreted to be one of foreboding.

With no apparent threat shipboard, the AOS pulled out. Barbs and Fred Giles remained on the bridge with the captain and his officers while Frank and the other customs officers went to join the search.

The searchers had been divided into groups and each group was allocated a bay to search.

It wasn't long before he heard Stephen's voice through his radio. "I think I might have found the container. Bay 3 row 2."

Frank hurried down the rows of containers that towered above him to the location provided.

Stephen was standing with his ear to the container. "I think I heard something."

Frank put his ear up against the side. There it was. A faint tap, tap, tap.

The container was locked. On closer inspection they could see a 50-millimetre hole in the top corner of the steel box. It had to be a breather hole.

The Second Officer was brought down and instructed to open it up.

Inside and cowering in the corner was a huddle of young girls. Their wide eyes showed their fear as they became accustomed to the light that penetrated their darkness.

Binsa and one of the policewomen entered the container and crouched down beside them. Binsa spoke quietly and attempted to reassure the girls, before calling, "There are eight Nepali girls here."

Once the girls were calm, Binsa led them out of the container. They appeared to be under 16 years of age. All were thin and their hair, skin and clothes were filthy. They passed the group of police with their heads low, shuffling their feet, with some of the girls sobbing uncontrollably.

They held hands as they were taken off the ship and into waiting ambulances.

The captain and officers were arrested on charges of trafficking and taken away to be interviewed and processed by Barbs' team.

The consignment paperwork provided the information on the importer and a man by the name of Sanjay Patel was arrested and taken in for questioning.

It was a wrap.

Author's note

The statistics for trafficking in Nepal are horrific. India Today claims 50 women from Nepal are trafficked every day. Many good people are working hard to stem this flow and International Needs is one of these organisations.

In 2009 I visited Kathmandu where I met young ladies who were just completing the Lydia programme established by International Needs Nepal. This programme helps educate and upskill young women from around the country in an attempt to reduce the trafficking of Nepalese girls across the border into India and to help lift them out of poverty. Subsequently I hosted their director who had witnessed firsthand the fate that awaited many of these young women. I was also fortunate to have the opportunity to visit a girls' home in India for at risk girls, many of whom have now gone on to higher education. These experiences provided the inspiration behind *The Boat Shed* and informed both Sangita's and Binsa's stories.

If you have been moved by what you have read and would like to donate to support the work of International Needs Nepal, you can donate through one of their partner organisations in your own country:

International Needs NZ   https://innz.org.nz
International Needs USA   https://internationalneeds.us
International Needs Canada   https://internationalneeds.ca
International Needs UK   https://ineeds.org.uk
International Needs Australia   https://ina.org.au

Glossary

ae	Māori term used when agreeing or saying "yes"
aft	The rear or back end of a marine vessel
Aotearoa	The Māori name for New Zealand
bollard	A short thick post to which a ship's mooring line may be secured
ebb tide	Outgoing tide
EPIRB	Emergency Position-Indicating Radio Beacon
E.T.A.	Estimated time of arrival
E.T.D.	Estimated time of departure
flood tide	Incoming tide
gunwhale	Upper edge or planking of the side of a boat
ka pai	Good
kia ora	Māori greeting wishing good health
knot	Unit of speed equivalent to 1 nautical mile per hour
pōhutukawa	Type of tree native to New Zealand
port	Left side of a vessel when facing forward
RHIB	Rigid-hulled inflatable boat
starboard	Right side of a vessel when facing forward
stern	The rearmost part of a marine vessel
tacking	Changing course by turning a boat's head into and through the wind
tender	A dinghy or small boat used to ferry people and supplies to and from a larger vessel
tikanga	Māori customs and traditional values
transom	Flat surface forming the stern of a boat
whānau	Māori word for family or extended family

Reviews

Dear Reader

Thank you for reading *The Boat Shed*, the second book in the series featuring Detectives Frank Smythe and Anahera Raupara. If you enjoyed this book and have not already read *The Jibe*, you may be interested in reading it next.

As an author I rely on my readers spreading the word about my books. If you enjoyed *The Boat Shed*, I would appreciate you taking the time to post a rating and a brief review on your favourite digital platform.

If you would like to follow me to keep up to date with my books, you can find me as follows:
Website: https://hatheropbooks.wordpress.com
Instagram: robyn_who_writes
Facebook: robyn.cotton.5

Thank you,

Robyn Cotton

About the author

Robyn Cotton grew up in South Taranaki and studied at Massey University, before embarking on her "O.E." to the UK. Settling back in NZ, she enjoyed a career in the dairy industry before becoming a management consultant and director. Inspired by her own experiences, she explored her interest in creative writing and launched her first novel *A Skylark Flies*. She followed up with her second book *Mary & Me*, also based on personal experience. Her third book *The Jibe* is her first mystery story and features detectives Frank Smythe and Anahera Raupara, who also appear in *The Boat Shed*.

She now enjoys life on the Hibiscus Coast with her husband, where they indulge their love of sailing while exploring the beautiful Hauraki Gulf.

Robyn is a Christian living with Parkinson's disease and likes nothing more than spending quality time with family and friends. Her other interests include photography, travel, various sports and exploring Aotearoa New Zealand's natural environment.

The Jibe

By Robyn Cotton

Ella Hampton makes a mayday call from Aurora on the Hauraki Gulf saying her husband has been lost overboard during a jibe manoeuvre. A body identified as Dean Hampton washes up with a gash to the head and other injuries. The coroner rules it an accident.

Amy Fagin, Dean's sister, while dealing with her recent diagnosis of young-onset Parkinson's disease, suspects something is amiss. Determined to find the truth about her brother's fate, she convinces Frank Smythe, of the Maritime Police Unit, to investigate the case further. Frank partners with Anahera Raupara to determine what really happened aboard Aurora.

Mary & Me

Two women with Parkinson's disease two hundred years apart

By Robyn Cotton

Mary lives with Parkinson's disease in the early nineteenth century. Rose has it in the twenty-first century. Separated by two hundred years their experiences are vastly different, reflecting the change in attitudes and understanding.

Rose's story is inspired by the author's own experience of living with Parkinson's. It is deeply personal and honest and will take you on an emotional rollercoaster, from the shock of diagnosis to hope and resilience.

This journey illustrates the importance of responding positively to a life with a debilitating disease.

Mary & Me provides a novel approach to unpacking Parkinson's and the mix of emotions that may accompany it.

A Skylark Flies

By Robyn Cotton

Rose, a young Kiwi, is on a working holiday in the United Kingdom to discover her roots. When in Scotland, she is subjected to a brutal assault by a local man, Tommy. Their lives will never be the same again. While Rose fights to recover from her emotional trauma, Tommy, a victim of a lifetime of abuse, struggles with guilt. The choices they make will ultimately determine whether they live life as victims or rise above it.

Inspired by true events, A Skylark Flies is a poignant story of forgiveness. It gives the reader a window into the souls of two very different characters whose stories converge at critical points. The assailant has power over the victim, induced by fear—and the victim has power to release him from his guilt and shame.